THE FINE ART OF HOLDING YOUR BREATH

CHARITY TAHMASEB

Collins Mark Books

Copyright

Land of the Free (Haircuts) first published in *Proud to Be: Writing by American Warriors*, Volume 2 (Partners in the Military-Service Literature), edited by Susan Swartwout, November 2013

Breakfast in the Desert first published in Every Day Poets, January 2014

The Boys' Club, first published in *Proud to Be: Writing by American Warriors*, Volume 3 (Partners in the Military-Service Literature Series) edited by Susan Swartwout, November 2014

For my mother, who taught me about bravery.

In memory of my father, who taught me about integrity.

Prologue

MARCH 2003

I DON'T REMEMBER what woke me the night the second Iraq war started. The volume on the television barely reached the threshold of the den. How I heard it in my room is anyone's guess. But something—a vibration in the air, maybe—woke me and led me to Dad.

He stood in the middle of the room like a man on sentry, a silent vigil for the nearly silent battle on the screen. Explosions lit the angles of his face, the stripe in his plaid pajama bottoms, the yellow Ranger emblem on his T-shirt.

I don't know how long I stood there. My feet ached, and I was vaguely aware we'd slipped from late night into early morning. I needed to go back to bed, to sleep—a pop quiz in algebra was inevitable.

But leaving him alone? With nothing but the flashing light and endless brown expanse on the television? With nothing I really recognized in his face?

I knew so little about his time in the First Gulf War, except that he came home and my mom didn't. We never talked about the war. We never talked about my mom. I don't remember ever asking how she died, but I could hear Grandma Adele's words, her voice a soft, sad echo in my head.

It was a Humvee accident.

For years, the phrase remained a mystery, a secret only Dad and Grandma Adele knew. I pieced together what I could. Location: Kuwait. Date: Sometime in March, Year: 1991. I never dared ask for more. Seeing my dad now, I understood why I never did.

A line of tanks and Humvees rolled across the screen. Dad had the heat cranked. I felt weighed down by it, my lips dry, my skin hot.

"I should be there," he said.

I jumped, startled by the sound of his voice, startled that he wasn't speaking to me, that he didn't even know I was there.

He blinked several times, swiped his fingers across his eyes, and left a damp trail across his cheek. I'm not sure I understood what the Army had meant to Dad, how big a piece of him it was. But in watching him now, it was like there was a piece of him missing. I'd always known things weren't quite right, especially during March, but I didn't know how ... fragile Dad was—how wanting something so badly could stretch your soul so thin it threatened to snap.

"Dad?" I said at last.

Nothing. Wherever he was, my voice couldn't reach him.

"Daddy?"

He jerked. All I could see were the angles and planes of his face, lit by explosions. He didn't say a word.

"Can we watch cartoons?"

"Sure, princess." He blinked a few more times, as if he was coming back from somewhere far away. Then he shook his head, like he was shaking water—or possibly sand—from his ears. "Sure."

It'd been a while since I'd called him Daddy. But then, it'd been a while since we'd watched endless cartoons together. Cartoons, *Mystery Science Theater 3000*, *Hercules*, and my favorite, *Xena*. Back then, I was MacKenna, Warrior Princess. If I'd learned anything over the years, it was this: Warrior princesses didn't cry.

Dad aimed the remote and the Road Runner filled the screen where a tank had been. Oddly, things looked almost the same—harsh sun, endless desert, occasional explosions.

I remember thinking to myself that if Dad couldn't go then someday I would. I'd pick up where he left off. Sons did that all the time. Why couldn't daughters? On the screen, the Road Runner zipped by. Then the coyote was falling, falling, falling.

I don't remember if he ever hit bottom.

Chapter 1

MARCH 2007

THEE SECONDS after I pulled the front door closed, I heard the sound of helicopters in the den. They weren't real helicopters, of course. But it meant Dad was home early, on a Friday. It meant he'd listened to that particular playlist, with that particular song, at least once. It meant he was in one of *those* moods.

Billy Joel was singing about Vietnam. I'd peeked at the playlist once, and *Goodnight Saigon* was seven minutes worth of song. Back when I was dumb enough to ask Dad questions about it, he'd say, "It reminds me that some guys had it a lot worse." But that was all he ever said.

It was early March, which meant things weren't normal in the Meyers household. For us, March wasn't in like a lion, out like a lamb. Even on days when the sky was clear, March meant low-hanging clouds. If there were an obvious path through the whole mess of this month, I was sure to miss it. It was like crossing a minefield.

It hadn't always been like this. When I was in grade school, when Dad got sad (how I thought of it back then), I'd dash for my electric pink CD player with the built-in radio. My fingers would fumble on the dial until I landed on the all-80s-all-the-time station.

A blast of heavy metal or—even better—techno pop could clear the clouds from Dad's eyes.

"I can't believe you like these old songs, princess." The crinkles deepened around his eyes when he added, "They make me feel old."

But he'd pull me into the center of the room, and then, we'd dance. And Dad could dance—not in a flailing-chicken-make-it-stop kind of way either. If I wished hard and held my breath, the station would play one of the magic songs, one that would make Dad pause and say, "This was one of your mom's favorites..."

When he trailed off, I'd pull him back with, "Dance, Daddy! They want us to dance!"

"I still can't believe you like this old music," he'd say.

I loved that music. And in those moments, he never looked younger.

But that was before the second Iraq War. Something about it—and not Afghanistan—changed him. After that, his black moods went deeper, lasted longer, and the stormy March clouds threatened to stay until June.

Today, I went for a calculated move, letting my backpack slip off my shoulder. The textbooks thudded against the floor, but he had the volume cranked. The bass, and helicopters, vibrated the soles of my feet. When the music softened at the end, and before Billy Joel morphed into Billie Joe Armstrong—not that I had anything against Green Day—I pulled open the door and slammed it.

The music cut off, and a flash of warmth washed across my face. If silence could be guilty, then this was it. Still, that was better than hitting the end of the playlist and U2's *All I Want Is You*. I knew what that song could do to Dad's mood. There was never a time I was young enough or dumb enough to ask him about it.

I crept through the kitchen and poked my head into the den. Dad was sitting up, one leg sprawled along the length of the couch.

The remote for the stereo was still in his hand. On the TV, Iraq, or maybe Afghanistan, the view brown, dismal, and heartbreaking.

"Hey, princess," he said. "Didn't expect you home so early."

Obviously.

"No swim practice?"

"Friday," I said. "We get a break before the all-day torment." If there was a perk to being on the synchronized swim team, this was it. No Friday practice. Saturday, though? That was a different story. My muscles ached at the thought of non-stop dry-land drills and endless ballet legs across the length of the pool.

"Right. Forgot." He looked like a kid caught skipping school, his thick hair spiky from a close encounter with the couch cushion. Everyone says we look alike, same wheat-colored hair, same brown eyes, his more amber, mine closer to black. Only Grandma Adele says I look like my mom.

And she only says it when Dad isn't around.

"Hungry?" I asked, going for normal. Sure, Dad blowing off work wasn't normal, but then March never was.

"I ate," he said.

Most months, we split the cooking fifty-fifty, after stuffing the freezer with all those easy express dinners and ground beef for Hamburger Helper. But not in March. If Dad got hungry, if he remembered to eat at all, he'd nuke something. *Hot Pockets* were his favorite.

Dad on Hot Pockets: *Beats an MRE.*

Because something over-processed and covered with freezer burn had to be so much better.

I headed for the kitchen, chucking my coat over one of the breakfast bar chairs. With and index finger and thumb, I rooted around in the garbage, trying to determine whether *I ate* meant *I ate dinner* or *I ate sometime today*. The winner? *Sometime today.*

"MacKenna?" This from the den.

"Yeah?"

"How does make-your-own pizza sound?"

That was standard operating procedure—as Dad might say—for nights like this. Pizza, with whatever we wanted on top. Once, I'd asked for, and got, chocolate chips. This wasn't a chocolate chip kind of night. Still, we needed *something*. Maybe artichoke hearts and extra cheese. Or barbecue chicken.

"Sure," I said.

We could suck barbecue sauce from our fingers and pretend it was spring.

We could pretend things were normal.

———

IN MARCH, Monday mornings meant escaping the house. I didn't even mind the two inches of slushy snow or the crappy parking space in the overflow lot—next to some jerk who insisted on parking his almost-but-not-quite vintage Corvette across two slots.

Maybe it was a bit of swimmer's ear, but once inside I totally missed the warning signs. A hum of excitement reverberated down the hall, a crowd gathering in the lobby. Banners fluttered. Girls squealed. Between Friday afternoon and now, prom fever had somehow infected Black Earth High School.

I so didn't want to deal with this. Not prom. Not after a weekend full of sullen Dad. Prom was too light. Too fluffy. And I was too ... on the outside of things. I backed toward the double doors, groping for the handle. Instead, I ended up with a fistful of letter jacket.

"Hey, babe, is there more where that came from?"

The guy behind me was one of those jocks everyone knew, if only by reputation. I wanted to say, "Bite me." Or introduce him to my middle finger. Or simply ask what sort of Neanderthal still used "babe." But another voice joined the conversation and all my comebacks got caught in my throat.

"Cut it out," the other voice said.

The voice stopped the jock mid-insult. It also stopped me. Its owner was someone I knew, or at least, had known a long time ago. Even so, I didn't turn around to thank him. I didn't even want to look at him. Maybe that sounds harsh, but I had my reasons. I decided a prom-crazed crowd was a better option than obnoxious jocks and the boys who distracted them.

Brad Stanley, Student Council President extraordinaire, stood at the center of the lobby. He was giving a rousing speech on the merits of prom with co-captain of the synchronized swim team, Kayla Hanson, attached to his hip. She'd corralled some other synchro girls into a makeshift group around him, including my best friend, Nissa Jenkins.

Even though Nissa was on the prom committee, she threw me a pleading glance. Her hands gripped a pink and purple cash box so tightly, the contents rattled above the din in the lobby and Brad's exaltations on prom. With as much stealth as possible, I slipped in next to her and swallowed my sigh. It wasn't that I had anything *against* prom, I just didn't have anything *for* it, either.

When at last Brad, Kayla, and the prom committee moved on, Nissa hung back and clutched my elbow.

"Don't look now," she whispered.

Which, of course, was exactly what I tried to do. She whirled me around so my back was to the gym.

"He's by the trophy cases," she said, "talking to the cheer-leaders."

Some people might refer to cheerleaders with disdain or contempt—Nissa made them sound contagious. That had more to do with who was talking to them—the same boy who defended me minutes before, the same boy whose name we hadn't spoken since he arrived in Black Earth, Minnesota after a five-year absence.

Five years. And then, there he was, in the lobby—like now—on the first day after winter break, talking—like now—to the cheer-leaders.

If you stripped those years away, magically turned us into seventh graders again, we would've dropped our backpacks and raced to him. We'd hug him, shake him, alternately threaten to punch or kiss him, until he told us where he'd been and why he left. And why he never said a word to either of us.

But we weren't twelve. And five years was a long time, long enough to build up walls—the sort that protect—long enough to convince yourself you didn't care anymore.

So, these days, I mostly pretended that the boy, Landon Scott, didn't exist, that he wasn't in my English class, that he hadn't sprouted from a puny seventh grader into some sort of lanky It Boy for the cheerleaders to squeal over.

The expression on Nissa's face shifted, less disgust, more surprise. I stole a glance over my shoulder. Landon still stood in his little fan-girl circle, but he wasn't really looking at any of them. He nodded occasionally, but held us in his sights.

I contemplated crossing that divide. The lobby wasn't that big, not really. But it felt that way. Maybe if we'd said something that first day after winter break, things would be different.

I turned from him, tugged Nissa down the hall, toward the vending area and her morning Diet Coke. I glanced at her, and she at me, and we silently agreed not to look back.

But when we reached the hall and rounded the corner, I could've sworn that Nissa did.

SOMETHING (POSSIBLY PROM FEVER) or someone (probably Landon Scott) knocked my morning off kilter. Blame the fluff or the fact I couldn't imagine myself at prom—alone or with someone else. By lunch, I wasn't in the mood for the cafeteria. I sank a little lower in my Chuck Taylor All Stars, feeling stealthy in black jeans, a British Military sweater—one of Dad's—and his old camouflaged BDU cap with all my hair tucked up underneath.

Dad on his old clothes: *About time they were put to good use.*

I think it was his way of turning swords into ploughshares, or in this case, camo into couture. I stood by the door, not moving, figuring I could slip away without anyone noticing.

"Hey." Nissa doubled back and tugged my elbow. "Come on."

Well, except Nissa.

"I don't think—" I never got to say what I didn't think. Just then, a couple of senior jocks eased past us, Lukas Jakobitz and his wingman, Tim McPherson.

Nissa batted her eyes at them; she was the only girl I knew who really could bat her eyes and not look like she had something on her contact lens. If there were such a thing as Honors Flirting, she'd wreck the curve for the rest of us. She had crushed hard on Lukas during all of ninth grade; although to be honest, she'd crushed on Tim, too. So her reaction now? Force of habit.

It got her noticed. Lukas stopped, gave us both the once over. Instead of batting my eyes, I decided to roll them.

"You girls swimming this year?" he asked, like the scent of eau d'chlorine didn't give us away.

"You know it," Nissa said. "Coming to the show?"

"Wouldn't miss it," he tossed over his shoulder, his attention fractured between us and a gaggle of varsity cheerleaders near the senior lockers.

The synchronized swimming team put on a show every year, but if Lukas had ever attended one that was news to me.

Nissa headed for a table where most of the girls from the Dolphins—Black Earth High's synchronized swim team—sat. The team was a clique of necessity. We weren't girl jocks. Just ask any girl who played softball, or ran track, or those on the gymnastics team. They'd tell you exactly what they thought of us: Not much.

Thing was, a typical synchro routine took the same amount of strength and stamina as running a mile—while holding your breath. No one could get past the costumes, the makeup, our hair shellacked with Knox gelatin, the whole performance aspect.

The synchro table looked crowded, nothing but elbows and interlocking chair legs, and squealing over some hottie of the week. Not that I had anything against hotties. I just didn't feel the need to squee over them.

Nissa glanced over her shoulder as if to say, *You coming?*

I shook my head and took a step back. If I hurried, I could grab my coat and race across the parking lot to the burger place. But this was Minnesota. In March. Fat, wet snowflakes splattered the cafeteria windows. My Chucks were camouflage and cute, but not very substantial. Canvas and icy puddles didn't mix.

I could pull up a square of linoleum in the lobby. Me, a power bar, and the odor of guy sweat—all to the sound of the thump, thump, thump from open gym. You couldn't buy that kind of ambiance. Plus, Nissa would join me eventually, if only for the jockerific view. I took another step back and bumped against some-one. That was what? Twice in one day.

"MacKenna?"

That voice again. If it was deeper than I remembered, I still recognized the boy I once called my playground savior. Nissa's mouth froze mid-word, her eyes frantic.

"Can I talk to you?" Landon asked.

I still hadn't looked at him, so I wondered which "you" he meant—me, Nissa, or both of us. I shook my head at the same moment Nissa nodded.

I made a tactical decision to head for the library. I'd regret it later, of course, at swim practice. Starvation or Landon Scott? Maybe the choice wasn't obvious for Nissa, but it was for me. I made it to the second floor landing when the sound of footsteps echoed above. Technically, I should've been anywhere but here—the cafeteria, the library, the lobby, or open gym. By the time those punctuated, teacher footfalls faded, Landon brushed past me and blocked my path up the stairs.

He stared at me hard. Then, with his index fingers, he drew a rectangle in the air. He wiped the space with what had to be an imaginary eraser.

"Clean slate," he said to the obviously confused look on my face.

"What?" I had no idea what he meant.

"I want to talk to you."

I wasn't buying it. "Three months and now you want to talk to us?" Three months? Try five years. If he wanted to erase the past, he'd have to work a whole lot harder than this.

"You. I want to talk to you. I want to, you know." He shrugged and erased his imaginary chalkboard again, as if that explained everything. "Can we go somewhere after school?"

"I'm busy."

Landon cocked his head, raised an eyebrow. His eyes were expressive as ever, a hazel shot through with green and blue. He still had those ridiculous calf eyelashes, light in color, but thick and feathery. It took everything I had to ignore the way they rested against his cheekbones when he shut his eyes.

"Busy doing what?" he asked when I didn't elaborate.

"Swim practice."

"Isn't girls' swimming in the fall?"

"*Synchronized* swimming is in the spring, and we practice because we put on a show each year and—" And it sounded dorky just talking about it.

But Landon's expression sparked with interest. That eyebrow went a notch higher and his eyes wouldn't leave my face. Of course, it might have been disbelief. When you were on the most ridiculed sports team in school, you tended to view any interest with caution.

"So, it's like what?" he said. "Dance team in the water."

Oh. Yeah. It was that. Exactly. "Never mind," I said. "It's not important."

"I think it is. That's why you don't want to talk about it."

"No. I don't want to talk to *you*. There's a difference." With that, I pushed past him and headed up the stairs to the library.

I stood on the third floor landing, my breath echoing in my ears. A flight and a half of stairs shouldn't wind me, but I panted, felt a pulse in my throat. Snowflakes pattered against a high window. When a clump of snow hit the pane, I mistook it for a footstep, and my heart leaped.

I peered down the stairs, but Landon hadn't followed me. Of course, I'd been pretty rude. Maybe this was it—whatever *this* was. Landon would go back to being Black Earth High's own golden boy and I could resume my life, free of him—like I had for the past five years.

Chapter 2

EVEN UPSIDE DOWN IT wasn't that hard to hold my breath. I was in the pool, working on my support scull, elbows locked at my waist, face submerged and warm, calves and feet goose bumping in the air. I sculled harder until the water hit below my knees. Or rather, above. I think. Either way, I was getting some serious height. I kept my form tight, legs steady, and toes pointed.

Like everyone else, I complained about the long Saturday practices. Secretly? I loved them. Early in the season, when groups were still choreographing routines and doing land drills, the pool sometimes went empty. And that was too tempting to resist.

Through my goggles, I saw fractured light and shadows floating along the pool deck. The distorted images of legs, wide and wavy, broke through the shadows. A moment later, a muffled shriek penetrated the water, so I did a tuck and broke the surface.

Half the synchronized swimming team crowded the stands, with the other half headed in that direction. One girl, in her damp suit, slithered up and over the divider that separated the pool from the bleachers. The divider was tile, about five feet tall, without a break for steps down to the pool. You had two choices: go through the locker room and take the long way around (and past the boys' locker room—no thank you) or up and over. But if you hit the edge the wrong way? *Ouch.*

I kicked to the far side of the pool where Nissa sat, her legs dangling in the water. My arms were braced on the edge when she whispered, "Oh, my God. It's *Landon.*"

I fell backward into the pool.

"What?" I shoved the goggles to my forehead, but stayed in the water.

"Shit." She crossed one leg over the other, then stuck her hands in her armpits. "I haven't shaved in a week. I look like a gorilla."

Winter in Minnesota could do that to a girl. Although in Nissa's case—with her hair more platinum than gold—she could give up shaving for Lent and no one would notice.

I blinked water from my eyes. Even with the goggles, I'd been in the pool long enough that things looked blurry. I caught little rainbows at the edge of my vision, which wasn't a bad way to see the world, except for the slightly fuzzy Landon standing near the pool entrance. His hands gripped the handles of large paper bags, the logo of the local bagel place emblazoned across the sides.

"What's going on?" Nissa scowled, then ran a finger across her lips, a futile attempt at a lip gloss check.

Chlorine stung my eyes and Landon was as fuzzy as his intentions. Most of the team crowded around him now and the chatter died as they gorged on bagels. Honestly, I was starving. If it had been anyone but Landon, I would've vaulted the tile wall and grabbed one for myself, with lots of honey and walnut cream cheese.

The team co-captains Kayla and Kylie led Coach Patti into the throng where Landon stood. He held out a bagel like an offering. Who did he think he was? And what was he trying to pull? Patti, in addition to coaching the synchro team, taught English 11, including my class and Landon's, Honors English 11. Landon constantly interrupted her with questions, asides, strange trivia.

We were always behind schedule and it was always Landon's fault. Whatever was going on, Patti would see right through it—and him.

I glanced at Nissa, prepared to share an eye roll. But her gaze never left Landon, her expression both wistful and repulsed. I wondered if it mirrored my own.

Patti took the bagel. She smiled through bites while Landon spoke and gestured wildly. Then, she and Landon shook hands.

Oh, that looked ominous. I couldn't take it anymore—both not knowing and not getting a bagel to eat. I pulled myself from the water and landed with a splat on the pool deck.

"I think we should go over there," I said.

Nissa ran a hand over her shin. She studied the nearly-invisible stubble, then Landon. After a few back and forths, I knew: Gorilla Girl was staying put.

Landon was the only one not eating. His voice echoed through the pool area its tenor all but rippling the water. I froze by the diving board. Maybe Nissa had the right idea. Did I want to face Landon now, in nothing but a practice suit faded a puke brown from the pool?

Then someone behind me snorted. I hadn't heard anyone walk over—no bare feet slapping the pool deck—but that was Constance Radley for you. You only heard her if she wanted you to.

"I can't wait," she said, "to find out which one of the mental midgets came up with this idea."

I eyed Constance warily. A little known fact: Constance and Landon were cousins. Once upon a time, she used to torment the three of us: me, Nissa, and Landon. Even in elementary school Constance was ... intense. After all these years, she still scared the hell out of me.

"Landon Scott." Constance spoke his name the way someone might say *global* and *warming*. Then she waved a hand as if that could erase him from her sight—or life.

"Forget him," she said, sounding like she already had. "I want to talk to you. Anyone grab you for a duet?"

Constance was, hands down, the absolute best swimmer on the synchro team. And yet, last year, no one voted her into an elected position. She had to try out, like the rest of us, which she did—all without smearing the immaculate kohl around her eyes. And now? Constance couldn't be asking me that. Just like Landon couldn't be standing in the bleachers, spreading around cream cheese and charm.

"It's the bone Patti tossed me," she said. "Actually, she made Kayla do it—and it practically killed her. Like I care either way."

But she did care. Never mind those kohl-rimmed eyes and fright-night hair—glossy, black, currently tucked into a swim cap. She'd placed fifth in freestyle at the state tournament, made a decent showing in the one hundred yard butterfly, but her passion was synchronized swimming. Goth meets girly. It was just a little bit weird. And, in a way, unfair she wasn't team captain with a solo of her own. She had the skill, the strength, and oddly, the elegance to totally rock it.

"So. Duet. It's mine," she said. "Don't even have to audition it. You up for it?"

I touched my chest, just below where the hem of my suit was giving me a rash. "Me?"

"Yeah, you. Who else am I going to ask?"

Someone in the stands squealed. Constance spared them a glance, then rolled her eyes. "Besides," she added, "your form has really improved since last year."

"I've been swimming at the Y." Dad and I went there during the fall and winter. He lifted weights and pounded out miles on the indoor track while I did laps and, during open swim, worked on technique.

Constance nodded like she knew all this. "I'll let Patti know you're in."

Only after she left, presumably to tell Patti, did I realize I hadn't actually said yes. But then, who wouldn't? Another squeal came from the bleachers, and I had my answer. A lot of someones, that was who. Constance wasn't popular with the other girls on the team. In fact, she wasn't popular with girls at all. But guys went nuts for her. The swim boys followed her around school and threw rose petals across her path—well, metaphorically speaking.

I think that was why girls didn't like her.

Still. Me? A duet? The thought of it tightened the back of my throat. I could taste the anticipation there—and it tasted a lot like chlorine. I took a deep breath, expecting a whiff of the pool's chemical cocktail. Instead, the scent of fresh bagels slipped past my nose. It was so incredible, I nearly followed the smell right into the water. And, I'm embarrassed to admit, I drooled.

Landon was staring at me, a bagel in his outstretched hand. I rounded the diving board and approached the tile divider, all without thinking. An expression about biting, hands, and feeding crossed my mind. So did a story about a girl named Eve and an apple. I ignored both. Denying that I wanted that bagel—possibly more than any one before or since—seemed stupid, especially once my stomach growled.

Landon placed the bagel in my palm. The crust was smooth, still warm, and he made sure to give me thick swirls of honey. I took a huge bite.

"So that's how it is."

Constance was back. With her words, a walnut lodged in my throat. Not that it mattered. My mouth was too full of honey and cream cheese to choke out a single word.

"Constance, my little sea anemone," Landon said. "You look radiant."

"Shove it up your ass."

He pulled back, neither startled nor perturbed, but perplexed, like it was impossible that someone, somewhere, could resist his charm. Then he skewered her with a look. "Sweet, as always," he said. "Bagel?"

Constance sideswiped his wrist, deflecting the bagel from its collision course with her mouth. "Why don't you tell me what you're doing here instead?"

Landon touched the hem of his T-shirt. He was wearing a vintage tee for a concert he could've only attended in utero. "Don't you girls put on a show each year?" he asked.

Constance crossed her arms over her chest.

"Well," he continued, "don't you need a host for that show?"

Generally, we were desperate for one. It was practically a synchro team tradition for a senior girl to con her boyfriend into hosting. Last year, Kayla got Brad Stanley to do it.

Bagel still in one hand, Landon held his arms wide. "Meet your new host."

I swallowed hard, pushing the lump of carbs and cream cheese down my throat, my appetite suddenly gone. On reflex, my free hand went to my stomach.

"Just don't hurl into the pool," Constance said to me. "It's a bitch to clean."

"Please." An edge had crept into Landon's voice, like he couldn't believe both of us weren't completely thrilled with the arrangement. "The show needs a host. Am I right?"

Constance sighed. "You're right."

"And from what I heard, last year's show ..." Landon let the sentence trail.

Last year? We swam great. No one had a wardrobe malfunction, at least not one that ended up on the Internet. But the narrator?

Brad was a great guy, especially if you like them hot and completely sincere, which, apparently, Kayla did. He was one of those Nordic blonds, blue-eyed, sturdy, and as bland as Minnesota wild rice soup. He was too serious about everything to be funny about anything. For a show like ours—where you had to make people forget they willingly sat on hard bleachers in nearly one hundred percent humidity—humor went a long way. Kayla offered up Brad for this year (I sometimes wondered if she arranged all his extracurricular activities), to which Patti responded with:

"Oh, thank you, honey, but we wouldn't want anyone to think we were playing favorites."

Now *that* was funny.

But it left us without a host. Until now. Landon? In my inner sanctum of swimming? The one place where I could forget everything—forget about Dad, forget about my mom, forget about me. I could lose myself in the water. When we all swam together, it didn't matter who we were.

But with Landon around, I wouldn't be able to forget. My gaze drifted to the far side of the pool. Nissa still sat, all hunched over, whispering with a few other junior girls. Landon wasn't good for either of us.

Constance stalked to the tile wall. She reached up, grabbed the neck of Landon's T-shirt, and pulled him down to eye level.

"I'm going to say this once. You will do nothing to ef up this show."

Landon eased backward, but Constance knotted her fingers deeper in his shirt. "In fact," she continued, "I'm holding you responsible for the sound quality, any piss poor lighting, and every time some asshat decides to deface one of our posters. Got that?"

"Or else what?" Landon said, his voice full of mirth. He glanced at me and winked.

Constance tugged a little harder on his shirt and then gave the pool a significant look. "You better hope you can hold your breath for a really long time."

Her fingers uncurled and he stumbled back. Amazingly, through all this, he hadn't let the bagel plop into a watery, sticky mess on the pool deck. Without another word, he brushed himself off and retreated to the chattering group of girls behind him.

I shut my eyes. My head ached. I rubbed my left temple with my free hand before confronting the world again. I discovered Constance studying me, a grin tugging at the corner of her mouth.

"I should've known those airheads weren't the main attraction."

I touched the hem of my swimsuit again, then dropped my hand, not wanting to look like I was imitating Landon.

"Yeah, you," she said. "Who else?"

I glanced toward Nissa. The other girls were half leading, half pulling her toward the bleachers and certain bagels.

"Be serious." Constance appraised me, looked on the verge of saying something, then turned her attention toward Landon. "Still," she mused, "it could be worse. I mean, he *can* work a crowd."

True, he could. When he started at Black Earth in January, he joined the Yell Club, then was quickly adopted by the varsity cheerleading squad. All during basketball season, he wound up the crowd at pep rallies. I thought about what Landon's presence could do for the swim show. Just slapping *Hosted by Landon Scott* on the posters would guarantee a full house—and funding for next year.

"Maybe it won't be that bad," I said, mostly to convince myself.

"Oh, it is that bad." Her eyes weren't on me, or Landon, but the other seniors on the synchro team. "Just not in the way you think. You better eat that bagel. It's going to be a long practice."

———

WHEN PATTI'S whistle cut through all the chatter and splashing, I nearly collapsed on the pool deck in relief. Landon had stayed for the entire practice. In fact, he still sat in the bleachers, bent over a notebook, working on what may or may not have been the show's script. His constant presence was enough to send me over the edge. As it was, it was sending me to the locker room quicker than normal.

I couldn't wait to get home. I'd stir up some creamy tomato soup and make grilled cheese sandwiches. Dad and I would toast the duet with root beer and not notice it was March at all. I was at the locker room door when my name echoed across the pool.

"MacKenna?"

Coach Patti's voice halted me. My feet skidded on the pool deck, and I turned to see the seniors and the juniors clambering over the tile wall. It was only the freshmen and sophomores—and of course, me—heading for the locker room.

I had so missed the memo on this. Had I been zoning? Thinking about Dad? Trying not to think about Landon? One thing was clear: I. Had. Screwed. Up.

And how.

Patti crooked a finger at me and I trotted across the deck. She wasn't the sort of coach who'd chew your ass in front of everyone. But she'd give you a "talking to."

"Constance told me about the duet," Patti said. "Congratulations."

I nodded, didn't say a word, tried to listen. Dad might call that reconnaissance. With everyone in the bleachers staring at me, I called it humiliation.

"Honey, you're such a good swimmer," Patti was saying—and I had zoned again, totally missed everything between *Congratulations* and these words. "I think you could take it up a level, really be competitive, but." She pushed a strand of hair from my forehead; she was in her team-mom mode. "You did this last year, too, and you're much too talented to be so shy. The team needs your contribution, and it's like you didn't really join us until April."

My chest constricted, and for a second, I couldn't breathe. I prided myself on being stealth, flying under everyone's radar. I didn't realize that made me so ... transparent.

Her eyes narrowed. She did that sometimes, studied me. I thought of the old Black Earth High School yearbooks at home, in my closet. Patti was legacy. Way back when, she'd swum on the Dolphins for all four years of high school, right here at Black Earth. At her side, in nearly all the photos? My mom.

If Patti had made the connection, I never knew.

"Join us?" she said. From most people, this would've been

snarky. Patti made it sound like the team was incomplete without me.

In the stands, Nissa sat sandwiched between Jodi and Sierra, two junior girls who took snark to new levels, two girls I could do without, two girls who spent more and more time with Nissa these days.

I pulled myself up and over the tile divider and ... *ouch*. I tried not to wince, tried not to show that any of this bothered me, tried not to mind that Nissa was totally blowing me off. Landon peered at the proceedings—and me—over the top of his notebook, and my face went hot.

Constance patted an empty spot next to her. Actually, all the spots around Constance were empty. She had that effect on people. I sat, thought about what this meant for Dad, creamy tomato soup and grilled cheese.

Dad on staying late: *Mission first, princess.*

He wouldn't even notice until I got home. That was just it. *He wouldn't even notice.* God, I hated March. It really was the worst month.

Chapter 3

IT WAS one of those endless meetings. I'd left my team hoodie in the locker room. I rubbed my feet together in a hopeless attempt to warm them. Chlorine crawled across my skin and my hair didn't dry so much as harden.

Constance's cryptic remark now made sense: We had screwed up.

And how.

The team was way behind schedule. Patti divvied up the juniors, assigning a few to each senior (which was something the co-captains Kayla and her twin Kylie should've done back in February). Patti put Constance in charge of choreography, and I was so hoping to be assigned to her.

I got Kylie, and publicity, and a headache, because stealth and publicity were two opposite things. That was Nissa's deal, convincing people to go to some show or to spend their college fund on prom.

By the time the meeting ended, I possessed not only the CD with Kylie's original artwork for the show's poster, but the awesome responsibility of finding a place to have it printed, for cheap. Real cheap. We were running out of last year's car wash money (something about girls with lots of swimsuits and car washes—we seemed to go together).

Now all I needed to do was navigate the locker room. I sometimes thought the worst part of swim practice wasn't practice at all. I didn't mind the dry land drills, stretching, or stints on the gymnastics equipment. Dance, gymnastics—I'd never been spectacular at either, but in the water I could do both. I loved the discipline of synchronized swimming, the precision. Water was the great equalizer. In the pool, we were all important. What made swim season hell was what sandwiched each practice.

Why things changed the instant we all streamed through the locker room door always threw me off guard. I could have the right suits, the right underwear, the right clothes (all of which I didn't) and still get it wrong.

Maybe it was from growing up with Dad. I just didn't get the other girls sometimes, not even with Nissa cluing me in. I always felt like I should be on patrol, rifle ready, alert for sniper fire. Which is why I did an about face. Instead of racing home from swim practice, I said yes when Constance asked if I wanted to try a few lifts. Creamy tomato soup and grilled cheese could wait.

"Ten minutes max," Patti said, "I don't know about the two of you, but I have some very important nothing to do later tonight."

That sounded like an evening with Dad.

"What are we swimming to?" I asked Constance.

Her gaze centered on the pool instead of me, almost like she was embarrassed. "Don't laugh," she said, "But it's actually from the *Mulan* soundtrack. It's the music from the scene where she cuts her hair and—"

"And takes her dad's armor and joins the Army," I finished. "I love that movie!"

"Easy there, soldier girl." Constance eyed me. "Glad you approve. Can you download music?"

I nodded. In fact, I already owned it. *Mulan* was the only Disney princess I ever had time for.

"I'll send you the choreography tonight. I want you to do at least fifty dry-land walkthroughs this weekend."

I schooled my face so it wouldn't register shock. Fifty was a lot, but we were also making up for lost time.

"At the 2:20 mark, the music is perfect for a lift. Want to give it a try?"

With only two people, we had a limited number of moves—it would be more of a boost than a true lift. Since Constance was the stronger swimmer, I was about to meet air.

Or not. We tried hands to feet and hand to hand. Constance managed only once to push me from the water. I careened sideways, but rotated at the last second, executing a belly flop so perfect, water surged over the pool deck and splashed against the tile wall.

"Girls?" Patti said once we surfaced. "Let's call it a night."

"Was it that bad?" I asked, one hand clutching the side of the pool, the other gripping my stomach. My skin stung, tendrils of pain radiating out from my midsection. I felt like I'd dislodged an important internal organ.

I expected Constance to laugh at my pathetic performance. Instead her eyes were locked on Patti. Not anger, or determination, but resignation crossed her face, and I noted how both anticipation and disappointment tasted a lot like chlorine. I wanted to apologize for not trying harder, but I didn't think she'd hear me.

"You're not fresh," Patti was saying. "Try it next week. I'll even open the pool before school."

Constance glanced at me, the look tentative, and I almost missed the question in her eyes. I nodded.

"Monday," Constance called out.

"Tuesday," Patti said. "You'll thank me later."

Constance pulled herself from the pool and padded over to where Patti sat in the stands. I treaded water for a moment, watching them. Constance tugged off the swim cap, and with their dark heads bent together, they could've been sisters—or mother and daughter.

And three was a crowd. I swam to the opposite side of the pool and hopped out near the locker room door. I stole one last look at them, wondering if it was possible to be a part of something and still feel like you didn't belong.

My skin itched from chlorine, but I skipped the shower, intent on my creamy tomato soup and grilled cheese mission. In the lobby an odd hush followed me, my arm caught in the sleeve of my jacket, the CD with Kylie's artwork clenched (lightly) in my teeth. I never heard a single footfall, didn't notice a second presence, but I caught his reflection in the gold glint of trophies in their cases, the figure shadowy and distorted.

I yelped, not a full-fledged scream, thank God, but loud enough to bounce back at me in the nearly empty lobby. The CD flew from my mouth and cracked against the floor. Heart pounding, I whirled and confronted Landon.

His eyes crinkled in amusement. "I didn't think anything could rattle you."

Well, he thought wrong. "You scared the hell out of me."

He bent down and rescued the CD. The plastic case sported a jagged crack up the center. Landon removed the CD and blew gently across the surface.

"It's okay," he said. "How about you?"

"Me?" I touched my cheek as if I could feel his breath there. My pulse fluttered in my throat before panic edged into my thoughts. Landon gripped the CD and I couldn't leave without it. "I'm ... I'm okay." I extended my hand, hoping he'd catch the hint, and added, "Thanks."

The last word sounded breathy and unintentionally sexy. Maybe that was why he didn't give up the CD. My hand hung there, limply, for so long I couldn't salvage any pride, and finally let it drop.

"The solution is obvious," he said.

My mind blanked. If the solution was obvious, then the problem was obscured by my waterlogged brain. "I don't know what you mean."

"Posters, for the show." He held the CD just out of my reach. "I should've suggested it during the meeting, but I was in the zone." He used his free hand to mimic writing.

In that moment, he looked different. Or rather, he looked liked the Landon I'd known back in elementary school—my playground savior, here to save the day. Maybe it was the lack of people—girls mostly—who crowded around him. Here, in the quiet lobby, I could see our shared past, and it made me wonder about the future.

"Use me," he said, blowing any traces of nostalgia from my thoughts.

"What?"

"Use. Me." He pointed to his chest. "Do I have to spell it out for you?"

Uh, yeah. He did.

"Landon *Scott*. *Scott* Industries. You know, the Midwest's premier printing emporium? We can do it for free."

"Free?"

"And in color," he added, rushing his words like a used car salesman.

Dad on free stuff: *Nothing's ever free, princess. Remember that.*

And when you added free to Landon Scott, the sum no doubt equaled trouble, most likely, trouble for me.

"We have a school discount program, if that makes you feel better," Landon said, "but there's no reason to use it. Come on. How can you go wrong with the owner's son?"

Oh, let me count the ways.

"I was thinking of using my dad's employee discount." Actually,

I had no idea if Dad even had one, plus, he managed the Scott Industries IT help desk, not at all connected to the printing part of the business. Dad wouldn't be any help at all, but I wasn't about to tell Landon that.

"And my discount is one hundred percent." Landon still held the CD out of my reach. He jerked backward when I made a grab for it and spun around, complete with a flourish. Sure, he'd make a great host, but he was also a great pain in the ass.

"I have to think about it," I said.

"You have to think about free?"

"Yeah. I do. Now, can I have my disc back?"

"I don't get it," he said, his gaze on the CD. "No strings, promise. It has nothing to do with—" He looked up and hit me full on with those incredible hazel eyes. "Us."

"There's an us?" Not for five years there hadn't been.

He passed me the CD. "That depends."

"On what?"

Landon didn't answer. Instead, he strolled across the lobby. When he reached the double doors, he pushed through them backward, his eyes on me.

"Let me know what you decide," he said.

The doors whooshed closed behind him.

For a full minute, I stood in the lobby, clutching the CD so hard, a second crack appeared in the plastic beneath my fingers.

———

ON THE WAY HOME, I missed the turn for the grocery store. We didn't have cheese. We didn't have bread. Tomato soup, we had— the low sodium variety. Dad claimed he could tell the difference, but he never noticed when we went all healthy choice for dinner. My head still pounded, but I stopped at a mini-mart and paid too much for Velveeta slices and stale Wonder Bread.

When I pulled into the driveway and saw the white Toyota

Corolla behind Dad's Blazer, I forgot about tomato soup and my headache. Even the confrontation with Landon faded. I left the groceries in my Jeep and took the front steps two at a time.

Inside, it hit me. Mac and cheese. A hint of pie crust in the air. Dad loved Key lime, but this smelled like pumpkin (my favorite). I inhaled and let the aroma wrap around me. Everything felt warm, filling, and right.

Grandma Adele met me halfway between the living room and kitchen. Dad calls her our Rock of Gibraltar. Once, as a Christmas present, he gave her one of those *She Who Must Be Obeyed* coffee mugs.

All she said was, "Paul, *really*." But she uses it all the time.

With a hug, Grandma Adele breathed me in. When I was little, I'd crawl into her lap after swim lessons, still dripping from the pool. She never pushed me off, even though I ruined countless dry-clean-only-or-else silk blouses and wool dress slacks (Grandma Adele didn't do business casual). One time, while she threaded my braids through her fingers, her breath warm against my damp head, she said, "Your mother smelled just like this."

She didn't mean for me to hear—never mind remember—those words. But I did. So sometimes, like now, I let her hold on tight for as long as she wanted.

She steadied me by the shoulders, then ran a finger along my cheek. "You look tired. How was practice?" She led me into the kitchen with the slightest pressure on my back and the promise of food for days. Grandma Adele was the only reason we survived March.

Dad was in the kitchen, being good (slicing ham) and bad (wearing his *Parental Advisory—Explicit Content* T-shirt). He always threatened to pull it on for parent-teacher conferences. To which Grandma Adele always said, "Honestly, Paul."

"Hey, princess," Dad said when I walked in, but his voice sounded a little strained.

I glanced at that day's mail on the table. Underneath the bills and junk, something large, black, and glossy lurked. Everything I'd planned to say about swimming, the duet, even Landon's reappearance, slipped back down my throat. All I could think was: *It came.*

A few weeks ago, during a covert, two a.m. internet search—fueled by optimism and too much Red Bull—I requested an Army ROTC brochure. I wasn't sure how the conversation with Dad would go. Now that it was here? Everything from today felt trivial. This was real life—my life—and it started now. Or at least after the macaroni and cheese.

I glanced at the brochure, then at Dad. He kept his head down, his attention on carving the world's thinnest slices of ham. I didn't have to see his face to get the message. Something was wrong. Very wrong. I rubbed chlorine from my eyes, then inspected the kitchen, like that would help me discover what was up.

"MacKenna, honey," Grandma Adele said, "I made a double batch of tuna and pea hot dish. One's in the fridge and the other's in the freezer for later."

I hated tuna, but I forced down the casserole of the damned since Grandma Adele claimed it had been my mom's favorite. Then, one day, I found Dad spooning the leftovers into the toilet.

"Your mom didn't like it either." He shrugged. "But she never told your grandmother that."

From then on, we had a secret agreement about the hot dish. In a way, it was like the three of us shared a secret—me, Dad, and my mom.

"I can't believe how it disappears around you two," Grandma Adele said now.

Any other time, Dad might've winked at me. Ham sliced, he prowled the kitchen, no doubt seeking out other items to cut into teeny, tiny pieces. Even Grandma Adele noticed his search-and-destroy mood. She shoved a stack of plates in to his hands.

"You set the table," she ordered. "MacKenna's tired."

I never ate so much macaroni and cheese in my life. Mega portions, on top of that bagel from Landon until I wondered if there was some form of carbohydrate-induced coma. If nothing else, that would make listening to whatever Dad had to say easier. If it meant Grandma Adele—our buffer zone—staying longer, I would've eaten the tuna and pea hot dish—both pans.

But she left, as always, with another hug and a kiss to my forehead. Then it was the two of us and whatever the March wind had blown in.

———

SOMETIMES I WONDERED about life with Dad. I knew he wasn't a typical father, but then I wasn't a typical daughter—whatever that was. I could tell you about the Battle of Dunkirk (May 26 to June 4, 1940) and how to snare a rabbit (something Dad learned in Ranger School). Oh, and I was a pretty good shot, too, with both the .22 caliber pistol and rifle.

When we stopped watching cartoons, we watched the History Channel. World War II or The Civil War—battles that didn't come close to touching him, yet somehow reminded him of everything.

Why he didn't turn off the television and forget about it weren't questions I'd ever asked myself. He'd been wounded in combat (shoulder, AK-47 round, Somalia), had lost his wife (my mom, Humvee accident, Kuwait), yet couldn't turn away any more than he could forget. If you stripped that part of him away, you risked stripping all of him away.

Now he tugged the ROTC brochure from beneath the rest of the mail, like a magician pulling a tablecloth out from under dishes —it was quite a feat. Another time, and I would've clapped.

"Mind telling me what this is?" he asked.

Given his mood, I expected some sort of offensive maneuver, and that sounded like a trick question. Dad was former infantry. When you're infantry, former or otherwise, that was what you did. You attacked. You laid down suppressive fire.

The idea to tell the truth crossed my mind, that I was hopped up on caffeine—or hope—and that maybe, just maybe, we could talk about the things we never talked about. The Army. My mom. And what this meant to me. But the truth? In March? My stomach churned and my better sense told me to play it safe.

"They're sending them out to everyone," I said, going for casual. "Nissa got one from the Marines. Think the Corps has regulation lip gloss?"

That should've made him laugh, but it didn't.

"Strange," he said, "because at the start of the school year, I put you on the do not contact list."

Oh. Did I screw up. And how.

"If the school district is handing out personal information, maybe I should call them—or a lawyer."

I gave my head the slightest of shakes. My throat felt tight, so did my stomach. I wished I hadn't eaten all that mac and cheese. Any moment now, I'd coat the kitchen floor with it.

I looked at Dad, I mean, really looked at him, the set of his jaw, how tense it was. He threw the brochure onto the table between us and it sat there like an accusation. Over the years, I'd picked up on Dad's moods, knew what was wrong without him saying a word. But I had totally missed this message.

"So." Dad crossed his arms over his chest. "Mind telling me what this is?"

This wasn't a fight I was going to win. It wasn't even a fight; it was an ambush. And I'd walked right into the kill zone. Trying to explain wouldn't help. Not now, not during March.

Defeated, I shrugged. "A brochure?"

"No." He dug around in the junk drawer and pulled out a butane lighter. Brochure in hand, he stood at the sink and touched the flame to one corner. "It's kindling."

Fire crawled up the sides, curled the edges, obliterated a tank. After the hint of sulfur, a synthetic odor filled the kitchen— nothing woodsy or natural, but a stench from charred ink that made the back of my throat raw. The fire alarm shrieked. I jumped.

Dad jerked. The flame brushed the curtains before he dropped the brochure into the sink.

Nothing smoldered; nothing crackled cheerfully. Fire tore up the curtains' ruffled edges, licked the side of the spice cabinet and curled around the window frame. Dad groped for the fire extinguisher. I palmed the kitchen table as if blind, searching for something, anything. My hands wrapped around Dad's cup of morning coffee, still half full. I flung the liquid at the window.

And hit Dad full in the face.

A second later, he yanked on the faucet. With the spray nozzle, he drenched the curtains and soaked half our kitchen. The fire alarm still screeched. I climbed onto the table, reached up, and pulled out the battery. Then I sat, panting, coughing, working the smoky taste from my mouth and sudden tears from my eyes.

Dad cleared his throat and spat into the sink. "Fuck."

Yeah, Dad swore. Sometimes, Dad swore a lot. And since first grade, we had a secret agreement about that, too. He wiped drops of coffee from his eyebrows, then eased the soggy ROTC brochure from the sink and walked from the kitchen.

The front door creaked open. A minute later, it clicked shut. I held my breath, half hoping he wouldn't come back to the kitchen, half hoping he would. When his footfalls faded down the hall, I knew that I wouldn't see him until morning.

At the front door, I stood on tiptoes, peering through the top portion of the window, the glass cold against my nose. I almost slipped outside, wondering if the brochure needed some sort of post-mortem. Instead, I trudged back to the kitchen. The room looked gray, the smell of damp ashes heavy in the air.

Scorched earth.

That was a military tactic where you destroyed everything the other side could use while you withdrew from an area. Well, he'd done that, all right; he'd left me with nothing. It was like discovering a bridge you needed to cross had washed away, and everything you ever wanted was on the other side. For several minutes, I stood at the kitchen door, immobile, the toes of my shoes just touching the tiled floor.

Screw it. I wasn't the one who set the house on fire. I marched into the kitchen and slapped on the stove's overhead fan. I mopped the floor and scrubbed the counter until all the coffee and Gatorade stains vanished and my eyes stung from the scent of Comet. The stainless steel gleamed, and I left the kitchen immaculate.

Almost.

The curtains remained—the whole scraggly, limp mess—barely tethered to the rod.

———

ON THE WAY to my bedroom, I froze, halfway between the stairs and the front door. What did you do when the enemy launched a surprise attack? You called for reinforcements. In seconds, I had my jacket, my keys, and was locking the door behind me, all without scribbling a note to Dad.

I drove through adjoining neighborhoods, the March air cooling my cheeks, the rumble of the Jeep comforting, my path haphazard. If I wasn't so tired from swimming, I'd drive forever. But I was beyond exhausted, and that winding trail led to Grandma Adele's.

"MacKenna, honey," Grandma Adele said when the front door swung open. She wore a blue robe, her expression more concerned than surprised. "Come in."

We sat in the kitchen. Grandma Adele made hot cocoa—the real kind, measuring out the sugar, and unsweetened cocoa, a dash of cinnamon and vanilla. Sweet steam filled the room. I breathed it in and inhaled even deeper when she set a mug in front of me.

"Let me guess," she said. "This has something to do with your father."

I nodded, my eyes on the swirl of melting marshmallow in my cup.

"Yes, well, I suppose that makes sense." Grandma Adele's sigh chased the steam from her own mug. "What is it this time?"

So I told her about the ROTC brochure, about how I was interested in the Army. I told her about everything except the kitchen fire. That sounded a little too crazy, even for Dad. I didn't want her to worry more than she already did.

"I see," she said. "So, he's being a bit of a bear."

"A rabid bear."

Grandma Adele laughed, but grew serious. She pushed her mug of cocoa away. "Has your father ever spoken to you about your mother and her time in the Army?"

I shook my head. What I'd gleaned about my mom's life, I'd collected in snatches—a stray comment here, a sentence there, all things Dad never meant to say. My mom was like a puzzle with so many missing pieces, I couldn't imagine the whole.

Grandma Adele studied not so much me, but the air around me. "You'll be eighteen soon, and letting go isn't going to be easy for him," she said, her words quiet and slow. "None of this is, which doesn't excuse his behavior."

"Grandma, please don't say anything to him about—"

"I won't mention a word, promise. However, the Army is a big decision, and I don't think it's ... fair that you go it alone or unarmed."

Ironically, she sounded like Dad. He was forever talking about going into this or that situation armed or unarmed. If she started talking about operation orders and ruck marches, I'd have to keep an eye on both adults in my life.

Instead, she said, "Don't look so worried. I—well, I think it's best if I showed you."

I followed her from the kitchen and down the hall. If you could pick the perfect house for your grandmother, it would be Grandma Adele's cottage. Throw rugs adorned hardwood floors as if someone had casually—but artfully—scattered them there. No doilies to knock out of place or potpourri to spill, since she hated both. Everything smelled warm here, the sort of warm that made you feel good even when the temperature hit ninety outside.

And it was the only place where pictures of my mom hung on the wall.

We ended up in the guest bedroom, which is where I slept when I stayed over. Perched on a bureau, a china doll kept a care-worn teddy bear company. The doll had been a gift to me from one of Grandma Adele's ancient neighbors, the sort who thought all little girls wanted china dolls and not air rifles for their birthday. Mr. Bear had belonged to my mother—too precious and tattered to leave his spot for the bed. Even now, I still hoped Grandma Adele would give him to me someday.

From under the bed, Grandma Adele tugged a wooden box with rope handles. The wood was painted dark green, and the handles looked rough, not something you'd want to cart around without gloves. She placed the box on the bed and motioned me to take up the spot on the other side.

"This, or so I've gathered is an Iraqi ammo crate, although honestly, how would I ever know?" She exhaled a half laugh, half sigh. "And you'll see why it isn't the sort of thing I can ask your father."

I blinked, trying to comprehend how Grandma Adele had ended up with an Iraqi ammo crate. She swung open the lid on its hinges. Inside, a dingy aluminum teapot took up a good portion of the space. Dents mottled the sides and if anyone had ever drunk tea from the thing, I would've been surprised. Next to the teapot, a thick stack of letters—secured with knotted rubber bands—shared space with scattered postcards, a photo album, a map. Everything about it smelled old and dry, a fine layer of grit covering everything.

Grandma Adele removed the teapot and turned it so it caught the light. "I also gather that these were a very hot commodity. It's an Iraqi teapot." She handed it to me. "It was also your mother's."

The teapot nearly slipped from my grip. My ... mother's? I

looked to Grandma Adele, unable to speak, silently willing her to continue.

"This." She gestured to the crate and the teapot in my hands. "Was among your mother's ... things, her personal effects. At the time, your father was in no shape to deal with them, and he's never asked." As she spoke, her fingers came to rest on the items in the box. "I pulled out the photographs years ago, they were mostly of you, but otherwise, nothing's changed since the day this left Kuwait."

She handed me an envelope. "These are the pictures your mother took over there. I always thought I'd put them in the album, but ..." She touched the album's dark cover and sighed.

I knew then what I wanted. It was this crate and the things inside. I cradled the teapot, the urge to keep it—to *steal* it—fierce. As with Mr. Bear, Grandma Adele would keep this too. Years ago, I'd come to terms with that—the wanting without resentment. As much as I longed for my mother's things, I needed Grandma Adele's love more.

She eased the teapot from my grip and returned it to the ammo crate.

"Thank you for showing me this, Grandma. Can I look at it again sometime? I mean, when Dad isn't around."

She hefted the crate to her lap, and sat that way for a long time, a hand caressing the lid's wooden slats. Then she looked straight at me.

"If Paul won't tell you about your mother, then I suppose she'll have to do it herself." With that, she shoved the crate at me.

Chapter 4

ON MY WAY home joy and disbelief crowded my thoughts. The crate sat next to me, on the passenger seat. I almost locked it in place with the seatbelt, but decided that was going too far. Still, I touched it now and then as I drove and let my hand rest on the lid for the full length of a stoplight.

Before I'd left, I promised Grandma Adele that I'd return the crate soon—well, someday.

"It's okay, honey," she'd said. "It's yours now."

"Are you sure?"

She patted my cheek, then tweaked my nose, like she used to do when I was little. "Yes. Just know that it wasn't the easiest decision I've ever made."

A spate of tears filled my eyes and she brushed them away. "Shh. There comes a time when every mother needs to let go of her daughter, and a time when every seventeen-year-old daughter needs her mother."

So I'd left Grandma Adele's knowing that I carried my mother —or a piece of her—in the form of an Iraqi ammo crate with rough rope handles.

Only when I reached the driveway did I realize I didn't have a plan for getting the crate inside. If Dad had heard me leave, I was toast, especially since I didn't bother to call from Grandma Adele's. I killed the engine and lights quickly, then sat while the Jeep grew cold. I felt the March air in my fingertips that rested against the crate's lid and on my cheeks, where my skin was still tender from tears.

It was stupid to sit in the cold and risk getting sick in the middle of swim season. I eased from the Jeep, then took silent steps to the passenger side, unwilling to leave the crate by itself. As an afterthought, I grabbed the CD with Kylie's artwork, along with the abandoned bread and cheese from earlier.

I left the crate on the front porch and cracked the front door for a quick reconnaissance. If Dad was awake, I'd wait until he went back to bed. If he was asleep, I'd return for the crate.

Inside, the house felt quiet, a hint of smoke still lingering in the air. No TV from the den and Dad's bedroom door was closed. I doubled back for the crate.

I was halfway up the stairs when a floorboard creaked in the hallway below. My heart rate doubled in a flash, my palms wet against the crate's rope handles. I teetered on the step and held my breath.

"Princess?"

I cringed. At least Dad wasn't *so* mad he wouldn't call me *princess*. Of course it wasn't *me* who almost burned down the kitchen tonight, but my pulse pounded so hard in my ears I couldn't think.

"You went somewhere?" he asked.

"Just to Grandma Adele's." My voice squeaked and I swallowed, trying to sooth it. "Hope that's okay."

"Uh, sure," he said, his tone contrite.

Ha, I thought. There were lots of things I never told Grandma Adele, and he should know I wasn't a tattletale. I gripped the rope handles tighter and the crate bounced against my thighs. Clearly, there were things I never told Dad.

We stood like that, not talking, but not *not* talking either. After the night we'd had, that was something. "I'm kind of tired, Dad," I said, "from swimming."

"Oh, of course, princess. Go to bed. Good night."

"Good night," I said.

Maybe it was silly to take the steps by two at that point. Maybe I should've thought about traces of ice and mud clinging to my Chuck Taylors. All I know is one giant step later, I went soaring forward, the crate coming with me. Its lid flew open, smacking me in the forehead. The teapot spilled out and landed on a step with a clatter. I dropped the crate to stop the teapot from rolling down the stairs. The wood hit the landing with a solid thud.

No way Dad didn't hear that.

He pounded down the hall. I peered over my shoulder and saw his barefoot on the second step from the bottom.

"Princess? You okay?" Another step. "What the hell was that?"

I couldn't let Dad upstairs. He'd recognize Iraqi *anything*. And that conversation would go from bad, to worse, to terminal. I groped for something else, another explanation, an excuse. Then my gaze fell on Kylie's CD, the case open on the step above me.

"Sorry, sorry," I said. "It's just props."

"Props?" He sounded perplexed.

"For the swim show. I had them in the Jeep. I meant to bring them in earlier."

If he didn't laugh, then at least his tone was lighter. "Go to bed, princess. And maybe think about sleeping in tomorrow."

My legs wobbled. I sank to the stairs and sat there long after he left. I hated lying to Dad, and during March, I did a lot of lying. But that was about survival, not important things. I looked at the crate. Was this survival? Or was it important? Neither, I decided. This was a secret, like the tuna and pea hot dish, only this one I shared with Grandma Adele and my mom.

The aluminum teapot glinted dully in the light from my room. I realized, belatedly, that Dad must have headed upstairs earlier and turned on the light so I wouldn't have to grope in the dark.

I shut my eyes, feeling like the worst daughter ever.

Then I contemplated the things—my mom's things—on the steps. I carried the teapot to my room, then came back for the rest. I placed the letters and empty photo album back into the crate, scooped up the spilled photos and postcards, trying not to peek at any before I had the chance to really look at them.

One by one, I removed the items and placed them on my comforter, all lined up—dress right dress, as Dad would say. There wasn't much here. Some photos of people I didn't know, most of them looking as sandy as the background. Lots of "any service member" mail—paper snowflakes from elementary schools, all sorts of cards—but none of it personal. What, I wondered, did Grandma Adele expect me to find? My mom wasn't here in this crate. I didn't know why I expected her to be.

I plopped onto the bed and something shifted inside the crate, a dry scraping like wood against wood. I jostled the bed again, and again, that light scraping sound came from the crate.

I sat up and peered inside. Only then did I notice the bottom of the crate looked odd. Without thinking, I curled my fingers around the center panel and tugged. A splinter shoved its way into my thumb, grit coated my hands. Under the false bottom, I discovered a spiral-bound notebook with lined pages filled with uneven rows of neat handwriting.

A journal. My mom had kept a journal.

And suddenly, I couldn't breathe.

———

I FLIPPED THE PAGES GINGERLY. The paper crinkled under my touch. It was dry and yellowed and even smelled old. Inside the front cover, I found a calendar for 1991, with a black X through each day, abruptly cutting off at March 25th.

Instead of speeding up, my heart seemed to slow, each beat carving a new ache in my chest. My fingers trembled against the cover. A wave of dizziness swept over me and I felt pinpricks against my cheeks.

Then, I pulled myself together. I had a journal, my mom's journal, and I was ninety-nine percent certain that not even Grandma Adele had read it. So at last I had a secret—a secret with my mom —and I didn't have to share it with anyone.

Pre-Deployment:
December 1990

The New Girl

I stand in the German rain,
staring up at the building where I'd work
if we were staying here.
Where I'd have time to learn my job
if we were staying here.
Where I'd get to know the soldiers—their strengths
and weaknesses. I'd earn their trust.
If we were staying here.

I leave the keys for Paul
and take the trolley home.
He'll only read the truth on my face.
He always can.
He'll only worry for me.
He always does.

The only thing worse than being the new lieutenant
is being the new lieutenant in a unit going to war.

I stand in my government-issued quarters,
staring at the walls I planned to paint green
if I were staying here.
Where I'd watch my baby girl take her first steps
if I were staying here.
Where I'd cuddle her each night, learn her secrets and dreams
if I were staying here.

I clutch MacKenna close and wonder
what it will feel like
when she's no longer there to hold.

The only thing harder than being a new mother
is being a new mother about to deploy to war.

Puppy Chow

Here's how I meet Master Sergeant Collier:
He has his jump boots propped on a desk
so I can see how worn his soles are.
And that desk is a demarcation line.
Me on one side, a green lieutenant.
Him on the other, a Vietnam vet, a man
with more years in the Army than I have
on the planet.

He pops Puppy Chow into his mouth—
not the snack with powdered sugar, but
bits of kibble you feed dogs, the sort that's
dryer than the desert.
His crunching grates against my ears.
I feel it in my jaw, and the meaty smell
makes my stomach roll.

One question forms on his lips, which are dusted
with all things a puppy needs.

Hungry, LT?

But it's not really a question. It's more like:
A dare.
A test.
My fate.

I eat the Puppy Chow. I really do.
A handful that's not too big
and not too small, the size that says:
*I take your dare, but don't push it—**Sergeant**.*

Sometimes it's better to be hardcore
and stupid,
than prissy
and smart.
But it's never clear which one is which
until much too late.

Mission Always

The Army has a motto:
Mission First. Soldiers Always.
When MacKenna was born, Paul changed it to:
Mission First. MacKenna Always.
This is how we both ended up
Thousands of miles away from her.

———

AFTER READING those first three poems, thousands of thoughts to match those thousands of miles tumbled in my head. Because that was what they were—free verse poetry. At least, I was pretty sure of that. We did a section in Honors English on the war poets of World War I, and I wondered if those same poets had inspired my mom to write this journal.

I worked to make sense of the few things I knew with what she'd written. I remembered Grandma Adele telling me how my parents had been stationed in Germany, and how she'd come over to take care of me so my mom could go back to work, go back on active duty.

I'd always imagined my mom as beautiful—all gauzy and perfect. Not real. Not someone like me, someone who kept secrets from Dad. Not someone I longed to help, no matter how many years stood between us. I wanted that, more than anything. I ran my fingertips along the journal's cover. Okay, so maybe I couldn't help my mom, but maybe she could help me—and Dad.

Maybe, with her help, I'd finally understand everything I needed to about my life.

———

IT WAS FRIDAY, an early release day, the kind where they scrunched each class into half hours and let everyone go early for spring break. That afternoon, in my spot at the kitchen table, I found a new pair of Pumas and a gift card to Jerome's Java, the local coffee place. And yeah, I knew it was a peace offering. The charred remains of the curtains still hung in the kitchen window. We'd both been too stubborn to take them down, never mind put up new ones.

Maybe I'd swing by Target, pick out something *not* on clearance, something very Martha Stewart, something with a puffy valance to hide the shadow of smoke behind the curtain rod.

Something flame retardant.

But it was one of those rare Minnesota March days where the sky looked like spring and the air was doing its best to catch up. It was warm enough—and dry enough—to run. And if my run took me by the strip mall with the Army Career Center? Well, I could stop and look at the posters, couldn't I? I pulled on my new shoes and was out the door before I could talk myself out of it.

Once there, I realized that talking myself inside the Army Career Center was a whole different issue. If by crossing the threshold, would I also cross from secrecy to betrayal? Staring at the cardboard cutouts of soldiers seemed to be the better option, or at least the most neutral one.

I stood there, oddly immobile, while the whoosh of bicycle wheels sounded behind me. I stepped closer to the window to let the cyclist pass, but the whooshing halted right behind me. In the window's reflection, I caught a hint of a black and red biking outfit. A black helmet. Serious black sunglasses. This guy thought he was too cool for words.

Then he unsnapped his helmet and palmed it. When the glasses came off, I realized this guy was also Landon. He inched forward with barely a muscle twitch showing beneath those second-skin cycling tights. So few people could get away with that look. But on Landon?

Well, I wasn't going to think about that.

"You serious?" he asked.

I spared him a glance. "About what?"

He rolled his eyes and gestured at the cardboard cutouts with his sunglasses. "This. This is … big."

Like it was any of his business. "I'm just window shopping."

Landon snorted. "They probably see a lot of that."

This time, I turned away from the window to stare full on at him. That biking outfit was something else. I couldn't decide if he biked because it suited his lanky frame, or if he'd developed all those lean muscles from biking.

Either way, I wasn't going to think about that.

"Once you cross over." He shrugged. "That's it, you know?"

That very thought had stilled my hand from opening the door and walking in. I turned back to the window.

"O-kay." Landon slipped the sunglasses back on, "Why don't we talk posters for the show instead?" He peered over the top of them at me—or at least my reflection in the window. "I'll throw in matching programs, for free."

I spun, abandoning my possible future for the here and now. "You're kidding," I said. Generally, we ran programs off on the school's copier and they always looked faded and old, like we left them out in the sun.

"I never joke about printing. It's far, far too serious a subject."

"What do I have to do?" I asked, because something this good had to have strings.

"Give me the CD."

"And ...?"

"By today."

"Today today?"

"Now would be good."

"It's at home."

He swept his hand wide, indicating the route I'd taken to the strip mall. "Run if you want. I can keep up."

He did, not that my two legs were any match for his two wheels. Much to my relief, when we reached home, only my Jeep was in the driveway. An empty house would make this exchange so much easier. Landon coasted around the driveway, then stopped in front of me.

"It's inside," I said.

He raised an eyebrow. What did he want? An invitation? Considering the look in those hazel eyes, I guessed he did.

"Would you like to come in?" I asked with mock politeness. "Our tap water is the freshest on the block."

Landon swung off his bike. "Lead the way."

In the kitchen, I dug two bottles of water from the fridge. Our tap water might be fresh, but the bottled stuff tasted better.

"Nice place," he said, craning his neck. "When did you guys move?"

"Eighth grade. My dad got tired of renting."

"Manly." He eyed the curtains. "But with that rustic touch."

Yeah, that pretty much described our house, right down to the mess hanging in the kitchen window. Heat pricked my cheeks. Damn. I'd forgotten about that.

Gravel crunched in the driveway. I glanced at the stove clock and saw that, yes, while it was early, it could be Dad. Yet one more thing I'd forgotten.

Dad charged in. He was in a mood, too, probably geared up for the full-fledged rant on his drive home. It was Friday, and March, and I pretty much expected something like this. Usually, it beat coming home to find him listening to the playlist from hell. Today? With Landon at our kitchen table? I wasn't sure which was worse.

"Hey, princess," Dad said. "You won't believe—" He stuttered, a full body stutter, like a power surge flooded the neurons in his brain. He looked at me, then Landon. I saw him add an item to his mental "things to talk to MacKenna about" checklist.

"Dad," I said. "You remember Landon."

I didn't bother to add *Scott*. How many Landons could there be in Black Earth? By the way he shrugged off his jacket and loosened his tie, I could tell the name didn't register.

"Get this, princess," he said, gearing up for the performance with no clue who sat in the audience. "I show up early to a meeting today, which means I was freaking on time."

Oh, yeah. I knew where this was going. This was the punctuality rant, Dad's major pet peeve. It had something to do with the Army and pushups.

"So, guess who's late to his own meeting, the one he set up, the one the rest of us had to attend—or else?"

"Dad—"

51

"I'm telling you, this *never* happened when old man Scott ran the place."

"Dad—"

"He'd stand in the lobby every morning," Dad continued, totally oblivious. "If you came in a second after eight, he'd take your name and kick your ass—metaphorically speaking."

"Sounds like my grandfather," Landon muttered.

"Dad!"

Dad glanced up, eyes startled.

"You remember," I said each word slowly. "Landon Scott."

Dad looked unfazed, but that also had something to do with the Army and pushups. Still, instead of slipping off the tie, he tightened the knot. He nodded at Landon.

"It's been a while," Dad said. "Didn't recognize you."

"It's good to see you again, sir. I see Scott Industries is treating you well."

I nearly choked on the water in my mouth. As it was, I sputtered and drops soaked the front of my fleece jacket.

Dad and Landon did this thing where they stared at each other. You know how they say men can't communicate? Well, maybe they didn't speak, but I'm here to tell you: There was a whole lot of communicating going on just then.

"So," Dad ventured. "You're at Black Earth High for good?"

"Unless my dad ships me off again." Landon cocked his head and gave Dad another odd look. "Don't worry, sir. He doesn't know I'm here."

Dad morphed again. He was now Paul Meyers, professional parent. "Where does he think you are?"

"I'm pretty sure he doesn't think much of me at all."

Dad pulled at his tie again, but the line of his jaw softened, a little more Paul Meyers, a little less Avenging Dad.

"And I should be going," Landon added. "MacKenna, you have the CD?"

Numbly, I nodded. Here was a dilemma. Leave Dad and Landon

alone together in the kitchen or forgo full color posters and free programs for the swim show. I decided to run to my room—fast. I tripped back down the stairs, knocked my elbow on the railing, and crashed into the kitchen doorway on my way back, all the time, the CD clutched in my hand.

"Here." I gulped in a breath and handed it to Landon. "And thanks."

"Hey, don't mention it. See you at practice." Landon nodded at Dad. "It was good to see you again, sir."

He left, with—I realized belatedly—the only copy of Kylie's artwork. The front door clicked closed and Dad stared in its direction, not looking at me—intentionally, I could tell. Then he said, again to the door, and not me, "Refresh my memory, princess. Is this the same Landon Scott that vanished after seventh grade?"

I nodded, reluctantly. True, Landon had vanished, never returned to school after Memorial Day weekend, never returned any of our calls, not mine, not Nissa's. Finally, his mom, with zero explanation, ordered us to stop calling.

"That's what I thought." Dad rubbed his temples. "Do I need to refresh your memory?"

I'd cried a lot that summer. Nothing about Landon's disappearance made any sense. Even now, I probed that memory gently because the hurt lingered, the wound unhealed.

"He's the host for our swim show," I said at last. "It's nothing, really. I barely talk to him except for that."

"How about no talking? Is that an option?"

I laughed, a coil of tension releasing inside me. All at once, I was glad I hadn't walked into the Army Career Center, that everything was still the same.

"I'd take that option if I could."

Dad pulled me close for a quick hug. He smelled of starch and cooking oil. Fridays were popcorn day at Scott Industries. Dad was one of the few brave enough to run the ancient contraption that popped the corn. When he let go and grinned down at me, I could see the start of spring in his eyes. I knew then: We'd made it through another March.

Dhahran:
January 1991

Land of the Free (Haircuts)

The place to find the cheapest haircuts in the Khobar Towers
is the fourth floor apartment of Tower D.
I should know because Paul wields the scissors, and his haircuts
are always free.

Soldiers try to give me their place in line.
I wave away their offers, not wanting
to sandwich time with Paul
between two privates.

The line snakes. Paul's platoon sergeant smirks.
He thinks it's ridiculous that Paul and I
pretend not to be married. He rolls his eyes, mutters,
Officers, and shakes out an unfiltered Camel from the pack he carries
in his ammo pouch.

The sun slants low in the sky, and when my turn
finally comes, afternoon light fills the apartment,
floods the balcony, turning clouds of cigarette smoke
a tarnished gold.

Paul sees me and the scissors snip shut.
He holds himself to impossible standards
while in uniform.
No PDA goes without saying,

but if he can run his hands over every single
scalp in Echo Company, there's no reason why
he can't touch mine.

Still, the price of this haircut may be more
than I am willing to pay.
But I sit in the folding chair.
I shut my eyes.
I hold my breath.
Beth, he says, *Really?*
I nod, tugging my bangs to my nose, hiding
behind my excuse. I only wanted to see him.
But I can't tell him that, not in so many words.

He pulls a strand of hair, then another.
It's like cutting spun gold. And his voice is softer
than the smoke on the balcony.

Two stories above, someone stabs the buttons
of a boom box, and the first notes mingle
with the smoke.
Paul's scissors snap closed.

That song. The unofficial anthem of everyone
in the Khobar Towers,
although I'm sure I've never heard it
before coming to Dhahran.

But you can't walk a block without cheap speakers
distorting Lee Greenwood's voice, or someone belting out,
God Bless the USA!

I'd pull on a gasmask, Paul says, *but I'd still be able to hear it.*
Paul's patriotism has never been sentimental, and I'm glad to see

my soldier cynic hasn't lost his touch with either words or scissors.

But by the time the song fades, and the Islamic call to prayer
takes its place, the evening sun can barely crest the balcony rail.
A single shaft of light slants through the balcony doors
and illuminates the bits of gold scattered
around the folding chair. And I find myself wondering
how much more of us will be left behind.

Chapter 5

WE ATE at Grandma Adele's that night, which gave me enough time to sneak in another poem. I'd tried to read them fast, read the entire journal straight through, but after I gobbled down those first few poems, I was struck with the thought: I only get to do this once. The first time through. The first time getting to know my mom. So as tempting as it was to rush, I rationed the poems.

That night at dinner, I kept staring at Dad, wondering how on earth the words *spun gold* had ever left his mouth. He stared right back, probably wondering how—after five years—Landon Scott had ended up in our kitchen.

It was close to nine when I pulled Dad's Blazer into the driveway. The headlights illuminated a shivering figure on our porch. Sure, it was warm, especially for late March, but going without a coat wasn't an option. Unless you were Nissa, in which case it was mandatory. A coat would crush the delicate, mostly see-through top she wore over the delicate, mostly see-through camisole. And even in the dim porch light, it was pretty clear she'd opted to go braless.

Dad exited the truck, scowling like he had a migraine. "Nissa?" he said.

"Hey, Mr. Meyers." Nissa jumped up from the porch steps. "I was wondering if I could borrow MacKenna."

"You want to *borrow* her?" Dad sounded amused.

"There's this party, and my mom's on a date and has the car, and MacKenna—"

"Is a great designated driver," I finished for her. It was the reason I was driving the Blazer, since Dad drank a few beers at dinner.

But that wasn't what Dad zeroed in on. "How's your mom doing?" he asked.

"Good, good," Nissa said, plucking at her blouse. "She really likes this guy."

"Even though he doesn't own a car."

Dad's comment flew right over Nissa, but he skewered me with a look that meant: *Date a loser who doesn't own a car and I'm locking you in your room until you're fifty.*

Dad could be judgmental.

Inside, he rummaged through the coat closet and pulled out an old physical training sweatshirt, a gray one with a zipper that split the word Army in two.

"Boys like a bit of mystery." He handed Nissa the sweatshirt. "Trust me on that."

We headed upstairs since Nissa insisted I change. She flopped on my bed and adjusted the sweatshirt cuffs. They were so frayed it looked like silver fringe dangled from her wrists.

"Your dad is completely adorable." She dropped her voice an octave. "Boys like a bit of mystery." She burst out laughing. "As if."

"He's a riot," I said.

"Still." Here, she sighed. "It's too bad ... he, I mean they never—"

"Yeah. I know."

Back in grade school, we had regular "Parent Trap" sleepovers where we watched both movies over and over again and plotted our own version—to trap Nissa's mom with Dad. We made elaborate plans for a new shared bedroom that was sure to come from this glorious union, and we tried a few times to get Dad and Nissa's mom together. Nissa's mom seemed more than willing. Dad grimaced like he was undergoing a root canal. Later, I realized that when it came to single (and good-looking) men, Nissa's mom was always willing. Something, I guessed, Dad knew all along.

From my closet, I pulled a skirt and the stretchy camisole that matched Nissa's. We'd gone in together on a buy one, get one free sale. Hers was bubblegum pink, mine olive green. I added a canvas shirt I'd found at the Army-Navy surplus store, and the ultimate accessory: My knee-high Chuck Taylor pleated silk shoes. They were my absolute favorite. I rationed wearing them, since finding a replacement pair would be expensive if not impossible.

"You're kidding," Nissa said. "Could you show a little skin?"

I rolled up the sleeves of my shirt.

"Ha, ha. Seriously, don't you want to meet someone?"

I thought about that. I mean *really* thought about how showing some skin—or going braless—upped my chances of meeting someone, and what sort of someone that would be. "No. Do you want me to get out of the house?"

Nissa made a face. She'd heard the patented Grandma Adele lecture on how dressing like a slut does not empower you. Dad had his own version, one he liked to give in various clothing stores in the mall, in his military command voice.

"What is this?" he'd say. "The skank-in-training department? I refuse to let my daughter dress like a tiny whore."

Shopping with Dad? A blast. He and Grandma Adele were a united front when it came to clothing. The day he handed me a credit card and let me do my own back-to-school shopping was one of the happiest of my life.

I adjusted the camisole and unbuttoned a few shirt buttons. "So?" I asked Nissa.

"Here," she said, "sit." She shook out her purse and cosmetics rained down on my desk. With me captive in the chair, she went to work. "Close your eyes ... pucker ... hold still already."

And so on. After five minutes, she offered up the compact with its little mirror. Nissa had a knack with makeup. Me? A little gloss, a little mascara, but anything more, and I'd end up venturing into Bozo the Clown territory. But this? Looking back at me? Almost amazing.

"Thank you." I meant it too. I could never look this good on my own.

"You know," she said, "it makes you look like ..."

She let the sentence trail, but I knew how it ended. Nissa had been to Grandma Adele's plenty of times, and I heard the echo of her unspoken words.

Like your mom.

I almost showed her the journal then. But bracelets jangled on her wrists and she was close to chewing off all her carefully-applied lip gloss. Party now. Journal later.

Downstairs, Dad sat in the den, TV tuned to The History Channel. In the kitchen the coffeemaker grumbled and sighed. I contemplated keeping Dad and the First World War company. Instead, I poured a cup of coffee and set it on the table next to his chair.

"I'll be good in a couple of hours," he said. "Phone charged?"

I pulled it from my knapsack purse and held it up for his inspection.

"Call if you need anything," he added.

"You shouldn't drive," I said.

"Couple of hours." He took a sip of coffee and winced at its heat. "I'll be good to go."

We had a deal, or rather, a "no bullshit" deal as he called it. Dad never pretended parties—especially those Nissa dragged me to—weren't what they really were.

"There's nothing you can do at one of those that will upset me," he always said.

The first time he told me this, I must've given him a *for real* look, because he laughed.

"I'm serious, princess. I've been seven flavors of stupid. I'm not going to hold it against you if you're one or two." Then he paused and considered not me, but our ceiling. "I just want you home safe."

We did all this without painful discussions or pledge signing. If I needed to, I could call. It was that simple.

"Go," he said now. "Have fun. Keep an eye on Nissa."

"That's going to be the hard part."

Out in the driveway, my Jeep was like ice, even with the hard-top. Dad had gotten a deal on it, so I had both covers, the soft-sided canvas and the hardtop.

Dad on soft-sided, canvas covers: *Sucks during a Minnesota winter, princess.*

He was right about that. I cranked the heat but Nissa shivered, despite Dad's PT hoodie.

"You are so lucky," she chattered more than said.

I knew she was talking about the Jeep and not necessarily life with Dad.

"So, are you pumped?" she asked.

"About?"

"The party," Nissa said, sounding cold and annoyed. "It's going to be the best. It's got to be. It's Lukas's last one."

She believed, and kept on believing, that the next party, or dance, or whatever, would be the one. The one for what I never figured out. What were we—or maybe it was just Nissa—looking for? I didn't think we'd find it spouting from a keg on a sticky basement floor.

Sometimes I missed the other Nissa, the one who constructed false bottoms for her pencil cases (to hide lip gloss), the one who didn't care quite so much about parties and boys. (Although, honestly, it was hard to remember a time when Nissa hadn't been boy crazy.)

So, no. I wasn't pumped or anything else about this party, not even the very last Lukas Jakobitz spring break blowout—or whatever the thing was called.

I'd started the turn for the newer sections of Black Earth when Nissa grabbed the wheel. The Jeep swerved, my heart revved, and for one black second, we skidded sideways toward someone's Lexus.

"What the—?" I began once I'd regained control.

"Sorry, sorry." Nissa's apology came out with panting breaths. "I forgot. I told Sierra and Jodi we'd pick them up."

I stopped the Jeep. "What. The. Hell."

"Come on, they're not that bad."

"Are we talking about the same Sierra and Jodi?"

Nissa rolled her eyes. "People change."

Well, maybe *people* did, but I wasn't so sure about those two. Back in eighth grade, they whispered about Nissa's bargain basement wardrobe. In grade school, they labeled Landon a "retard" because he was in remedial reading. They told me I was going to hell because Dad never took me to church. Call me cynical, but I didn't think they'd changed all that much since then.

"Please." Nissa gave me a sly look. "I'll be your best friend."

I laughed, couldn't help it. Popularity, boys, parties, *prom*, it meant so much to her—and going along didn't hurt me.

"Okay," I said at last. "But they have to sit in back." The back seats were like blocks, and in this weather, blocks of ice.

"Done," Nissa said.

The second I pulled into Jodi's driveway, the two of them burst from the front door. Back in grade school, Jodi had a mass of red curls that she now wore ironed flat. That, I thought, must take her two hours every morning. She was short, petite, and a killer in field hockey. She wasn't a bad swimmer either. If she didn't slavishly follow Sierra in everything, I might actually like her.

Sierra was one of those Nordic goddess types, tall, blond (but not as blond as Nissa, and personally, I think Sierra resented that). She double dipped, not in girls' swimming and synchro, but gymnastics—and acted like she was doing us all a huge favor by being on the team.

Nissa hopped out and pulled back her seat. Sierra gave her a look, but Nissa merely shrugged. A wave of perfume shoved its way in first, followed by gasps and exclamations.

"Oh, my God, MacKenna, you're the best," Sierra was saying. "My mom is such a bitch. She knows Lukas always has a spring break party and she took away my car keys anyway."

Jodi made a sympathetic huffing noise.

"Why'd she take away your keys?" I asked. From what I remembered, Sierra's mom was actually pretty nice.

"I just told you, she's a total bitch." Sierra didn't say *duh* but it was there in her tone. "Maybe she's going through menopause. How should I know?"

Jodi and Nissa giggled. I had the sudden urge to drive off a cliff. Actually, what I wanted to do was stop the car, swing around, and get right into Sierra's face. Then I'd say: *At least you have a mom. At least she's more than splinters in your palm, more than some old teapot, more than poems about to crumble into sand.*

I knew better than to give Sierra that kind of ammunition.

"Maybe it was that D in Chem," Jodi added a moment later. Then, "Ow! That hurt."

I'd like to say we drove the rest of the way in either companionable silence or scintillating conversation. But, we didn't. After they catalogued every junior on the synchro team (present company excluded), they started in on the seniors.

"I seriously think Kayla and Brad haven't done it yet, and they've been going together for how long?" Sierra asked—us or the air, I wasn't sure. It didn't matter, because she kept talking. "I'm telling you, that's not natural."

"It's not actually any of our business, either," I said.

Silence crashed inside the Jeep. If not for the dirty look Nissa threw me, it would've been wonderful.

"Then there's Constance," Sierra continued, seemingly undeterred, "but there's a reason she hasn't done it."

Jodi burst out laughing and even Nissa snickered.

"Oh, that's right, you're swimming a duet with her." Sierra leaned forward between the front two seats. "Good luck with that." She treated me to a blast of hot air and perfume.

Again, I found myself thinking: What. The. Hell. I glanced at Nissa and she mouthed, "I'll tell you later."

Great.

WHAT WAS NORMALLY a ten minute drive felt like ten hours. At last we turned into the subdivision where Lukas Jakobitz lived, the sort where it was difficult to tell the McMansions apart. I leaned forward and squinted as if that would help me figure out which house was his.

Lukas hung with mostly obnoxious jocks, although he occupied a subset—obnoxious jock who was okay if you got him alone. Sadly, Lukas Jakobitz was almost never alone. He always had a crowd—of friends, fan-girls, and hangers-on working their way up the Black Earth High social strata. So naturally, his was the house surrounded by the most cars.

We crunched icy grass on our way to the back deck. A keg sat in one corner, cups on a nearby picnic table. Wingman Tim McPherson manned the spigot. Nissa dragged me toward him and certain beer while Sierra and Jodi ducked inside. Tim siphoned off a beer. Foam slopped over the rim and he licked it before handing the cup to Nissa. She giggled, batted her eyelashes, and for a moment, he clearly forgot my existence.

"You?" he said to me, sounding startled to find me standing

there. He raised a plastic cup, presumably one he hadn't licked—yet.

Ew. No thanks. I shook my head. Alcohol zapped my endurance, completely. Dad had let me try beer, and once, wine at Christmas. It took me a week to recover my stamina. How the jocks did it, I never understood. Technically, Black Earth High had a zero tolerance policy. In reality, I think most everyone regarded it as just a technicality.

"Aw, come on," he said. "I made it myself."

Nissa giggled again. I managed an eye roll. I tugged her across the deck, toward the kitchen door. She did this two steps forward, one step back thing, always turning to look at or say something to Tim.

"He's a contender," she whispered when we reached the door.

"A what?"

"For prom."

"King?" I doubted Lukas would let someone else into his spotlight.

"*Date*. For prom."

We stepped inside, the warm air clinging to my skin after the cold. In the kitchen, bags of chips and plastic soda bottles lined the counter. Two guys were concocting drinks from vodka and orange soda, but most everyone was downstairs. The bass from the music vibrated through the soles of my feet until I felt it in my jaw.

"So, you're what?" I said. "Taking prom date applications?"

"Look, these guys would wait until the day before prom if they could. So you gotta, you know." Here, Nissa shrugged. "Be prepared. Speaking of which, MOA road trip?"

By which she meant, me—and the Jeep—and the Mall of America.

"There's nothing on the racks around here," she added. "So?"

"So what?"

"You, a date, a dress."

The beat from downstairs shifted, the relentless thump, thump,

thump from the bass mellowing into an almost melody. Apparently a bunch of jocks took that as their cue to leave, because a moment later, the stairs and kitchen were filled with them and Nissa's high-pitched giggle, her question about prom forgotten.

Lukas, still sober enough to play host, wrapped an arm around my waist and Nissa's, then pulled us close. He wore the legendary spring break T-Shirt, an old Hanes Tee two sizes too small, which meant being treated to every pec ripple and ab flex. On the front, penned in Sharpie, were the words:

My parents went to _____ and I didn't even get a lousy T-shirt.

Below the blank were the following:

Barbados

Aruba

The Seychelles

Costa Rica

This year's destination appeared to be Mykonos in Greece. If the Jakobitz knew—or cared—that Lukas threw the biggest party of the year the second they entered international air space, it wasn't clear.

"Two of my favorite girls," Lukas said now, probably because we were the only two girls in the room.

I slipped out from under his arm and shot Nissa a look. Normally, I wouldn't leave her alone in a room full of guys, but she sat on the kitchen counter, swinging her legs and holding court. I left her to sort out all the prom contenders and headed downstairs.

I paused at the foot of the stairs, my eyes adjusting to the reddish glow—someone had draped a cheerleader's "spirit" bandana over a lamp—and saw Landon. He stood on the far side of the room, behind a long, floral couch that separated the high end stereo from the masses. He wore the cuffs of his oxford shirt rolled, his expression all studious, as if selecting the right kind of make-out music required his full attention.

I decided that diverting his attention was the last thing I wanted to do. And I wasn't about to join Sierra and Jodi who stood near one of the speakers. So I played wallflower, inching my way along the paneling. I was nearly out of his line of sight when I spun and crashed into someone.

"Whoa," Constance said. "There's an exit if it gets that bad." She pointed at the basement door that led out to a patio.

My mouth refused to work. My mind, on the other hand, worked overtime. Gossip from the Jeep flooded my thoughts and a stupid blush heated my cheeks.

"Man, this sucks ass. And he." She pointed at Landon. "Isn't helping."

A few more jocks had migrated downstairs. One was in a heated debate with Landon about the state of the music. From where I stood, neither boy looked to be winning.

"What are you doing here?" I asked. This wasn't her crowd; it wasn't really mine, either. The question popped out of my mouth, but Constance didn't appear offended.

"I promised Sam I'd chaperone ... babysit ... make sure they—" She gestured at a few freshmen swim boys huddled in a corner. "—didn't drink more than two beers each." She studied the boys for a moment, and one of them gave her a wave.

Sam Avery was captain of the boys' swim team and president of the Fellowship of Christian Athletes. He was one of those guys so totally unobtainable—physically, morally—that most girls in school had stopped trying. Still, he could part the rowdiest group of jocks like Moses parting the Red Sea.

"I figure this is one of those things you got to experience, just so you know it isn't what everyone says it is." She turned back to me. "You?"

"I own the car."

Constance laughed. "And you're too nice to tell Snake Eyes to fuck off."

Snake ... Eyes? Sierra whirled around at that moment, her face pinched, her eyes dark, small, and, I realized now, close together. Yeah. Snake eyes.

"That's mean," I said.

"But oh, so true. Look, if she were a guy, she'd be pulling the wings off of flies. Instead, she does the symbolic equivalent to the freshmen class. And there's nothing I hate worse than a bully. Next year on the team is going to suck if you guys don't reel her in."

"Thanks for that day brightener."

"Don't mention it." A thoughtful look crossed her face. "I was thinking of asking Patti if I could come back as an assistant coach."

"I thought for sure you'd swim at college." The second the words left my mouth, Constance's face closed off. It was such a stupid thing to say. The synchro team wasn't a competitive team. We were good, but no way could we compete with clubs in the Twin Cities, never mind on a national level.

Except for Constance. I'd watched enough competitions to realize she could swim at that level, assuming she had unlimited resources and money. And, of course, she didn't.

The gooey make out music cut off, leaving the basement in a strange kind of quiet. Muted footfalls echoed above our heads before a half squeal, half shriek filled the silence.

Constance wrinkled her nose like something reeked. "Looks like she found some prey."

I turned to see Sierra and Jodi talking to Landon. Sierra brushed her nails against his bicep. My stomach lurched, then settled back down. I turned away from them to find Constance contemplating her freshmen charges, still hunched in the far corner.

"We've got practice tomorrow," she said. "You need to be on."

Without another word, Constance left me standing there. She nodded at the swim boys, who followed her from the basement like a litter of puppies. And if someone thought to bother one of them, a look from Constance had them rethinking that.

I gave the room a quick scan—Z-pattern, like Dad had taught me—but no person or group looked inviting, never mind safe. A cheerleader had commandeered the stereo and some Top 40 pop tune poured through the speakers. I caught Landon's frown, and got caught—period.

Our eyes locked. The perturbed expression faded, replaced by something I couldn't name. With two huge steps, he reached my side before I could escape.

"Want to go somewhere to talk?"

I stared at him. When that didn't work, I crossed my arms over my chest and stared even harder.

"What?" he asked.

"That is such a line."

A grin tugged at the corners of his mouth until a dimple appeared in his left cheek. Oh, I'd forgotten about that lone dimple. If Helen of Troy had a face to launch a thousand ships, Landon Scott had a dimple to break a thousand hearts. Back in grade school, I used to make him smile, all so I could run my finger along that hollow. I curled my fingers into fists to keep myself from doing it now.

"Okay," he said. "It's a line. What of it? I do want to talk."

One pop tune shifted to another. Landon's dimpled vanished and he looked like he just swallowed lukewarm beer from the keg.

"And I really don't want to do it here," he added. "Come on." He reached for my hand, but at the last second, pulled back.

My legs appeared to be under Landon's direct control, because I followed him, up the stairs, through the kitchen and past the jocks, and finally, to the Jakobitz's living room. Only then did my legs wise up. Not even the most obnoxious jock strayed into the Jakobitz's ultra-white living room. No one sneaked in for a quick make-out session. No one crossed the threshold, period. Except Landon, who barged in like he lived here. In truth, I'd never seen Lukas barge in like he actually lived here.

"I think this room is off limits," I said.

"Which makes it the perfect place for talking."

I remained at the threshold as if a velvet rope held me back. The room looked like it could be a museum diorama. Just call it: *Early Twenty First Century Conspicuous Consumption.*

"Please." Landon stood by the fireplace. "It's too cold for a walk, and I want to ask you about the Army."

I crossed my arms over my chest. "What about it?"

"Why do you want to join?"

"What makes you think I do?"

"Because no one stands outside Army recruiting for fifteen solid minutes just for the hell of it," he said.

"What? Were you timing me?"

He raised an eyebrow. "So?"

"Why don't you tell *me* something," I said. "What's up with you and your dad?"

His expression froze and I knew I'd hit a target, maybe even a bull's-eye. My subconscious must have been working overtime, mulling the cryptic comment Landon made in our kitchen.

I'm pretty sure he doesn't think much of me at all.

I didn't know a lot about Mr. Scott. Sure, Dad complained about him. I had a vague memory of Landon's dad on the sidelines of Little League and soccer games. And a lot of yelling. I remembered a lot of yelling from those sidelines.

Landon stood there, not moving, not talking. The choice was mine now. I could walk away, find Nissa, and go home. Or, I could talk to Landon.

I took a single step into the room.

"I know I don't have to tell you this," he said while I picked my way across the ice-white carpet. "But there is a war going on, two of them, last time I counted."

"And?"

"And I'm pretty sure you've thought about that."

I halted, my feet on the tile in front of the fireplace. A hint of soot hung in the air. For a room OCD as this one, a cheery fire, the promise of s'mores seemed impossible.

"Which means," he continued when I didn't say anything, "that you've probably made the connection. War." He held out a hand. "Military." Landon held out the other, then he clapped them together. "I don't think you've missed the obvious."

Of course I made the connection. I made the connection every damn day.

"What about you?" Landon asked, softly. "What's up with you and your dad?"

There, in that strange living room, I found myself confessing. I could barely see Landon's eyes, yet there was something about them, about him, that compelled the words from me—a memory of past, whispered confessions, the secrets we shared. Five years melted away and he was again the boy I could say anything to. I told him about the fight with Dad, about the ROTC brochure, about why charred curtains hung from the kitchen window.

He didn't offer a solution, didn't tell me everything would be okay. He did what he'd always done. He listened.

"What about you," I said, when I ran out of words. "What about you and your father?"

"It's nothing."

"A whole five years of nothing? I don't believe you."

Here, Landon laughed, loudly, too. "Ever break someone's heart?"

I didn't know what to say, so I shrugged.

"Ever do it with your own?"

Now I really didn't know what to say. In the quiet, a shadow crossed the entrance to the living room. My pulse raced. Landon merely tucked his hands into his pockets and looked serene.

"MacKenna?" Nissa sounded incredulous. "What are you—" Her gaze darted, from me, to Landon, and back again. "—doing?"

No one spoke. A rumble of voices came from the kitchen. Hip-hop music filtered through the air, and the scent of soot mixed with Nissa's perfume.

"I want to leave," she said, the order sharp, non-negotiable.

So did I. Confession might be good for the soul, but it made my legs tremble like I'd just run a marathon.

On the way through the kitchen, I spotted Sierra with her lacquered nails wrapped around Tim's arm. No wonder Nissa was pissed. Right then, I decided Snake Eyes could—and probably would—find her own way home.

Landon walked us out, an arm linked with mine and one with Nissa's. He was so tall now, lanky, almost skinny, the sort of guy a jock might push around, but it'd been all high-fives and fist bumps back in the kitchen.

No one said it was like old times. It wasn't the start of something new. We weren't twelve and the three of us loving each other unconditionally seemed bizarre. If anything, it was like the sad refrain of a song you could barely remember.

When we were inside the Jeep, he walked to an almost-but-not-quite vintage Corvette. I started the engine, but let the Jeep idle, and felt like I was doing the same. Nissa stared through the windshield.

"So," she said, her voice tight, hands planted on the dash. "You and Landon."

"We were just talking."

"Huh."

"About the Army." I sighed, gave her the Cliff Notes version of Dad, ROTC, and Landon catching me outside the Army Career Center.

"Really? The Army?" she asked, her voice softer. In the dark, it was all I had to go on. I drew in a deep breath, then exhaled, gratefully. We were still friends, despite Landon, Sierra—despite everything.

"Practice is going to suck tomorrow," Nissa said as I pulled from the subdivision.

That it would, and how. I glanced at the clock. "Today," I corrected. "It's going to suck today."

Nissa groaned. "The party was probably a bad idea."

I clamped my mouth shut. I knew it would be this kind of night. No matter when we left, these parties always ended the same way, with Nissa depressed and me tired. I didn't have the heart to say *I told you so*. I just wished I could help her find what she was looking for.

Chapter 6

DAD LUMBERED TO BED–GRATEFULLY–WHEN I got home.

"It's late," he warned me before leaving the den.

"I know. I need to hydrate before I go to sleep."

It wasn't a total lie. I huddled in the swivel chair in front of the computer and gripped a mug of my special blend: heated Lemon-Lime Gatorade and decaf green tea—enough electrolytes and antioxidants for anyone.

Something had sparked in my thoughts during that conversation with Landon. Why bother with recruiters when there was the internet?

One mug of tea later, my mind overflowed with possibilities. On the screen in front of me, I had an application for an Army ROTC scholarship. Maybe Dad wouldn't listen to me, but he might pay attention to money, especially in the form of a full-ride scholarship. This was it—the answer I'd been searching for. I felt like letting out a big laugh, loud enough to wake Dad.

Then I read the essay question. The application called it a personal statement, but it amounted to the same thing. The joy I felt iced over, then splintered. This part mattered. I'd have to hit it just right. Only, I didn't know what that was. The only person who knew was the one person I could never ask.

Depressed, I checked email (nothing), then logged onto Facebook. A bunch of kids were posting texts from Lukas's, making it sound like the Best. Party. Ever! I wondered if things were fun only because other people said so. When I refreshed the page, Landon's image appeared on the sidebar.

I'd be lying if I said I'd never searched for Landon before. I had, right after he returned to Black Earth. And yeah, I'd spent plenty of time staring at his profile picture. Tonight, when I clicked on mutual friends, the first person listed was Nissa.

A wave of nausea hit me, and the massive amount of tea I'd drunk grumbled in my stomach. Friends? Since when? I clicked through to Nissa's profile, then spent a frantic few minutes clicking more, and more, and more until I found the answer. November, of last year, two months before Landon had returned to Black Earth.

What. The. Hell.

She'd found him first? Or did he find her? Why hadn't she told me? For that matter, why hadn't he? I reviewed everything Nissa said or did over the last three months, ever since Landon barged his way into Black Earth High. That earlier relief—the idea that yes, we were still friends—soured. Clearly, I didn't know everything about my best friend.

I shut everything down and headed upstairs. I wanted to forget about it all—parties, and Nissa, and Landon, school, the internet. I wanted something real.

I wanted my mom.

Before

January 1991
The Tactical Operations Center

Smells like damp sand and musty canvas
and the best French roast coffee
you've ever tasted.
We call it the TOC—as in tick-toc,
or Tee-Oh-See
Because this is the Army, and everyone knows
it's better to use letters
than actual words.

The TOC (or Tee-Oh-See) has treads like a tank,
but not the armor of one.
Antennae sprout from the roof
like a garden of spindly weeds.
It's a neon sign, one that says:
Shoot Here First.

We'll lumber across the desert,
the perfect target for a stray Iraqi
with a rocket-propelled grenade.
My first thought is: *I hope we don't meet one.*
My next thought is: *We probably will.*

The Best Part of Waking Up

The only way to get the best
French roast in the battalion
is on a strictly
need-to-know basis.

Master Sergeant Collier needs
to know you.
He needs to know
you're worthy.

The list of who can pour a cup
without asking is short and way
above my pay grade.

The soldiers call it heaven in a canteen cup,
and when Master Sergeant Collier is feeling
generous, everyone gets a sip—if they're lucky.

I sometimes wonder what would happen if the percolator
tipped and spilled across the desert.
We'd all rush forward,
lap up the coffee
before the last drops
sank into the sand.

And I wonder how it is that the best part
of my day is something
I can't have.

In Which I Exchange Words with Master Sergeant Collier

Master Sergeant Collier: Ma'am, you do any sports in high
school?
Me: I swam.
Master Sergeant Collier: No wonder you can hold your breath
through all this shit.
Me: It's the fine art of holding your breath.

Master Sergeant Collier: You been listening to any RUMINT
lately, ma'am?
Me: Rumor Intelligence? Never do.
Master Sergeant Collier: Sometimes it's true.
Me: And sometimes people don't know what to do with their mouths.
Master Sergeant Collier: So are you saying I shouldn't listen to
the rumors about you?

Breakfast in the Desert

The field mess comes to life
while the desert is still cold.
Pans clang; pots scrape.
Where they get water for boiling
and scrubbing and cooking,
I don't know.

The soles of combat boots grate
against the metal stairs,
three steps up into the cavern
of griddles and steam,
of melted butter on grits,
and sizzle of bacon fat.

When I close my eyes, I might be
anywhere.
Denny's, the officers' club, home.

I bypass pancakes and hash browns,
preferring an egg the cook plunks on my plate
with tongs.

For one moment, it's the cleanest thing
in this desert.
I crack the fragile shell
on the stock of my rifle.
Inside I discover a trail
of sand.

Sand. In everything. Even breakfast.
And I wonder how much salt
I will need to add
to fool my molars.

———

SATURDAY MORNING, I stood poolside, shrouded in my Dolphins hoodie. The poems I'd read last night left me unsettled. Nothing about my mom's deployment seemed fair. The second I thought that, I heard Dad.

Dad on life: *Sometimes, princess, life just isn't fair.*

Even worse, my eyelids felt heavy and I blinked away what seemed like a pound of grit. The only consolation was, judging by the red, sunken eyes and ratty hair, practice was going to suck far, far worse for Jodi and Sierra.

Today our tech crew arrived. In fact, Josh Wylie, our guru of all things technical, was unwinding cords and schooling his two new freshmen recruits on the finer points of dropping the underwater speakers. I knew then this day couldn't be all bad.

It may sound strange, but there's no better place to listen to music than underwater. Dad always laughed when I told him this, but he'd never tried it. A few brisk laps to something upbeat and

I'd wash away all my doubts about Nissa, worries about the Army, my mom, Dad, and anything to do with Landon.

Except Landon chose that moment to fling open the door to the upper deck. As the host, all he had to do was show up for dress rehearsals. But here he was. Kayla preened and actually pulled off her Dolphins hoodie before going over to talk to him. Coach Patti gave him an indulgent grin and what looked like a stern, no messing around, waggle of her finger.

And, as if on cue, the rest of the team executed a synchronized sigh.

I stood on the far end of the pool deck, near enough to the tech boys to hear them grumble. Josh's ears burned bright red. He was a junior and we stole him from the drama club every spring. Secretly, I thought it was the other way around. For Josh, the synchro show was *his* show.

"What the hell is he doing here?" Josh said now.

No one spoke. At last, I offered up, "He's hosting the show."

Josh grunted. "Is he swimming in it too?"

Landon landed with a splat on the pool deck, feet bare, cargo pants rolled to his knees.

"It'll be okay," I said to Josh, hoping that it really would be. Maybe the tech boys and the junior class It Boy could peacefully coexist.

Landon marched along the pool deck, leaving the slightest impression of his feet on the tile behind him, until he reached Josh, the underwater speakers, and a mass of coiled cords that the tech boys guarded. Josh flattened a palm against Landon's chest. He even shoved, a little. In the halls of Black Earth High that wasn't the sort of move Josh could get away with—except with the other techies. But here?

Here, it worked. Landon skidded backward, a perplexed frown on his face.

"It's like watching a nature show," a scratchy voice said next to me.

I pulled back my hood so I could look at Nissa. "Do you think they'll battle it out for dominance?"

Her giggle morphed into a cough. "God, I feel like shit this morning. You?"

"I'm okay." I eyed her. "Not hung over at least."

She held up a hand. "I know, I know. It's stupid to drink during swim season. I only had that one beer."

"With extra spit—that probably did you in."

Nissa made a face. "Two-faced jerk."

Okay, so Tim was still a sore spot. Mentally, I moved him to the "do not discuss" list, figuring at some point, he'd do something cute and all would be forgiven. That was how it usually worked with Nissa, which meant things were the same. My gaze flickered between her and Landon, who was now helping to unroll the speaker cords. Well, mostly the same. Maybe at some point, I'd work up the nerve to ask Nissa about Facebook. Maybe it really wasn't that big of a deal.

"MacKenna?" My name echoed through the pool area. Patti waved in my direction. Next to her stood Constance. I hurried over, my stomach jumping.

"As soon as Josh has the speakers dropped," Patti said, "I want you to try the duet. The musical cues might help with the timing of the lift."

"You better warm up," was all Constance said to me.

I stretched and tried not to obsess about performing the routine in front of everyone. We took our place on the pool deck and waited for the first strains of music to filter through the speakers.

What we got was Landon.

"Hey, man," he was saying, apparently to Josh. "Can you hook me up with something hands-free. This thing is a pain in the ass."

"Landon ..." Patti's warning tone reverberated across the water.

"Sorry," Landon said. "This thing." He shook the microphone and feedback screeched through the pool.

"This thing restricts my ... creative movement."

Constance shifted, hands now on hips, a glare to freeze the pool centered on Landon.

"Boys," Patti called out. "You can work on that later. Right now, we need the music for the Mulan number."

Constance had choreographed an extensive deck routine, one that demanded I pay attention, and not screw up, and not pitch into the pool a second too early. The moment I hit the water, I forgot everything else. The music was like a cocoon. Between it and the water, nothing bad could happen. I hit my marks; Constance and I swam in unison, like we were really two halves of the same person.

On the lift, I held my body tight, extended my leg at the pinnacle, then re-entered the water with barely a splash.

I didn't have to ask. Patti's grin said it all. We'd done it, which meant we could do it again. Scattered applause echoed in the pool area, and Kylie met us at the pool's edge for high fives. I was pushing myself from the pool when Patti called the next number.

"Sierra? You girls ready?"

"Of course," came Sierra's reply.

My arms went stiff, palms planted on the pool deck. I froze, half in, half out of the water. At the opposite end, Jodi stood with Sierra, flanking her left side. On her right, arms raised in a flourish, stood Nissa.

No one pulled a routine out of thin air. Constance and I had started late, but she was Patti's favorite, and we were willing to swim overtime to perfect the duet. But Jodi, Sierra, and Nissa? No way they just came up with this. This arrangement—or whatever it was—had been going on for a while. And Nissa never said a word about it.

Sierra narrowed her eyes at me. I shoved myself from the water. The deck felt off kilter, slippery, as if it would send me sliding into the pool. I backed up, so the tile wall was flush against my spine. I hugged my arms and forced myself to watch the entire routine. No lift, but they executed some advanced stunts and were mostly in sync. I hated myself for wanting it to be awful.

At noon, we ate lunch in the stands, since dressing and then rushing across the street to the burger place was a pain. On the first row of benches, Nissa sat with Jodi and Sierra, their heads bent over a slightly soggy notebook. While everything told me this was a bad idea, I approached them anyway.

"We're busy," Sierra said, even before I had a chance to sit down. "Our routine." Here, she shrugged. "You know how it is. Needs to be perfect."

Nissa ducked her head and wouldn't look at me. Constance was talking to Patti and again I was struck with the mother/daughter vibe—struck lonely, struck dumb. I retreated to the very top tier of the stands, in the far corner where the tech boys sat.

"Is it okay if I sit here?" I asked the two freshmen, Dylan and Matt.

They stared at me as if I'd made the request in Latin. Then they shifted, with a crinkle of paper lunch sacks and clunk of aluminum water bottles.

"Uh, sure, yeah," said Matt, whose cheeks did this amazing techno-color transformation from pale to pink to the same blazing red as his MP3 player.

I gave myself a quick once over, just to make sure I wasn't exposing a body part I shouldn't. The Dolphins hoodie fell below my hips, so I didn't think that was the problem. I tried a few conversation openers (*What classes are you taking? Did you work on the fall play?*) without much success. When Landon and Josh pushed past us, a large cardboard box suspended between them, I sighed with relief. All the boys gathered around while Josh pulled first one, then another microphone from inside.

"Hands-free," Landon said.

"Sound quality," Josh countered. "People will actually want to hear you—for some reason."

Josh directed Dylan to stand at the pool entrance and then stationed Matt in front of the girls' locker room.

"The girls take their cues from your narration," Josh said, his voice all teacher stern. "They need to hear you, too."

"Right. Got it," Landon replied, his tone not nearly as contrite as his words. He toyed with his microphone, the world's worse padawan learner.

The gigantic pace clock on the wall ticked off thirty seconds before Josh's exasperated huff filled the pool area. "You have to *talk* if we're going to test the microphones."

Landon looked at the mic as if it were a foreign object. "What do you want me to say?"

"I don't care. Just keep talking."

"In that case, tell me, Josh, how long have you worked with the Dolphins?"

Josh scowled, but in the spirit of *keep talking* actually answered. "This is my third year." He looked toward Matt. "How's it over there?"

Matt cupped a hand around his mouth. "A little fuzzy."

Josh nodded and swapped microphones.

This continued, Landon asking reporter-on-the-scene kinds of questions, Josh switching microphones, tinkering with the settings on the sound system, the resulting conversation coming in odd waves, loud, then soft, brassy, then muted.

At last, they settled on one particular model. Josh adjusted settings, scowled some more, and absently answered Landon's questions.

"So, why the Dolphins?" Landon said, in full-on newscaster mode. "A man of your capabilities should be heading up the tech crew for the spring musical."

"Those drama turds don't know what they're missing. Dyl, how's it sound now?"

"What, exactly, are they missing?" Landon prompted.

Josh snorted. "Like I need to deal with the egos? No thanks. I like running my own show."

Oh, I *knew* it.

"With all due respect to the team, their show isn't the production number, if you will, of the play. If you're thinking college or career—"

"Screw that. The fringe benefits are worth it."

"Really? Mind elaborating?"

"Seriously? Are you blind?" In a stage whisper, Josh added, *"They're all wearing swimsuits."*

Unfortunately, a stage whisper spoken into a hot microphone isn't much of a whisper. Except for a weak burst of feedback, the entire pool went silent. Girls who'd been ignoring Josh turned to stare. I thought I saw Constance mouth something obscene, but I heard Patti. Actually, we all heard Patti, even without a microphone.

"Landon Scott, get over here right now!"

Landon's eyes went wide. He tried to hand the microphone to Josh, but Josh turned his back. Landon set the mic down on a bench, then threaded through the stands until he reached Patti, who pointed to the hallway. Constance tried to follow, but Patti shook her head and closed the door behind her.

Had we just lost our host? I saw the same question reflected in the faces of the girls around me. We were all so focused on the door, no one noticed Josh picking up Landon's discarded microphone until his voice quavered through the speakers.

"Uh, girls, I ... I want to say I'm sorry. I didn't mean it the way it sounded. You all swim real hard, and I would really hate it if what I said upset you, or made you want to quit or something, or—"

Josh's voice sounded thick, his normally ruddy cheeks stained dark. I felt a pinprick of tears in my eyes and clamped my hand over my mouth, convinced that he was on the verge of crying. I caught a glimpse of Constance pushing her way through the stands. In that instant, I knew what she was going to do, but I was closer.

I slid down the three rows of benches, cracking my tailbone on the last one. Pain spiked all the way up my spine, but I swallowed it back. I walked over to Josh, slowly, like I was approaching a wounded animal. I eased the mic from his clenched fingers, then switched off the sound system.

"It's okay," I told him. "You make us look good."

He hung his head, gaze locked on his feet. A moment later, Constance pushed past me, followed by Kylie. I took a step back, feeling suddenly extraneous, and landed on the bench. I winced, both at the ache in my tailbone and Patti's reappearance—without Landon.

I can't remember a longer or more subdued swim practice. It was like we collectively had the wind knocked out of us. Patti made us swim until four, but even she glanced at the clock at least ten times (that I counted) during the last hour. When I reached the locker room, I decided to—once again—skip the shower.

In the parking lot, Constance caught up to me and anchored me in place with her grip on my jacket.

"You, soldier girl," she said. "You have a mission."

"I do?"

"Landon. It's your job to keep him in line. Got it?"

"He's still the host?"

"Who else are we going to get? Brad Stanley?" Here, Constance rolled her eyes heavenward. "I'll keep Josh from quitting, you keep Landon under control."

"And this is my job ... why?" Maybe Constance was doing me a huge favor by swimming a duet with me, but that didn't mean I had to execute her every order. Besides, what she was saying made no sense.

"He's hosting because of you. Therefore ..." Constance shrugged. "Your job. Deal."

"Right," I said, but I don't think she heard me—or the sarcasm.

She turned, slung a drawstring bag over her shoulder, and headed for a white minivan with a dent in the side door.

Next to my Jeep, I saw the bright yellow Corvette Landon had driven from the previous night's party. The Corvette's windows were dark. No one sat inside. As I pulled from the overflow lot and onto the road, I thought the Corvette, there all by itself, looked incredibly lonely.

Chapter 7

SPRING BREAK WAS NO BREAK, and I was waterlogged from a nonstop week of swimming. Friday afternoon, I stood at our front porch, working up the strength to turn the doorknob. I had chlorine, not blood, in my veins. I felt the exhaustion clear down to my fingertips and I was hoping Dad would open the door so I wouldn't have to.

He had music going in the den when I finally managed to open the door. I felt a thickness in my throat, fatigue mixed with chlorine. If Dad had *that* playlist going, I thought I might cry. I might turn around, close the door behind me, and drive to Grandma Adele's.

One song faded into the next. The air quaked around me. Serious 80s techno-pop alternated with head banging metal, loud enough to shake the walls. Loud enough the neighbors might complain. Again.

I was five when I figured out how important music was to Dad. Whenever his mood downshifted, I went for the radio, my fingers on the dial, shooting past one station, then another, all in search of his favorite songs. I even knew what a mix tape was and could recite all the words to AC/DC's *Shook Me All Night Long* by the time I was six.

Once, I brought home a CD filled with patriotic music from Sierra's seventh birthday party. The CD had passed from girl to girl —the white elephant prize among all the lip glosses and princess tiaras—until it reached me.

When Dad started harmonizing with *The Army Goes Rolling Along*, I knew; this was better than the radio. We stood at attention during *The Star Spangled Banner* and booed to *Anchors Away*.

Then *that* song came on. With the first strains, it was like something shiny and hard washed across Dad's face. The moment Lee Greenwood sang about starting over, with his children and his wife, Dad brought a palm down on the boom box. The song skipped. A strangled *God Bless the USA* squeaked through the speakers, then nothing.

He grabbed the disc and grabbed me by the hand. Down in the basement, he couldn't grab the air rifle quite as quickly—it was in the gun safe. He dropped the CD on the floor, and it landed, shiny side up. Its surface glinted and the combination lock clicked home.

Then we went outside. He wedged the CD into an old railway tie. With a .22 air rifle, Dad took potshots until gouges, scratches, and scars marred the surface.

I stood, almost at attention, too horrified to run away, but not scared, not of Dad—maybe just *for* him. I knew this really wasn't something most fathers did. What coursed through me was one thought: *My fault, my fault, my fault.* So I didn't run and hide. Instead, I stood sentry with him.

BBs pinged and cracked against the disc. A few soared through the center hole and hit the railway tie with a muted thump. An entire box spent, Dad set the rifle down and wiped his brow. Only then did I dare speak.

"Daddy?" My voice was tiny in the silence, its quaver matching how I felt.

He looked at me, and the hard, shiny veneer cracked. That was worse somehow, my own father crumbling before my eyes.

"Oh, princess. I'm sorry, I'm so sorry." He scooped me up in one arm, carried the air rifle under the other. "I'll buy you another one. Hey." Here he kissed a tear from my cheek. "What do you say we have make-your-own pizza for dinner tonight?"

I swallowed back the sobs that clogged my throat and nodded.

"What kind do you want?"

"Chocolate chip."

It was the sort of outrageous request I could make at times like this. Dad didn't say a word. He bundled me into the Blazer and drove straight to the fancy grocery store by the day spa, bypassing our usual stop at the warehouse market. He sat me on the edge of the information desk and quizzed the lady behind it. Was there such a thing as chocolate chip pizza?

The pizza was round, the sugary sauce shiny. Melted dots of chocolate speckled its surface. It looked too pretty to cut, but we sliced the thing into pieces. I gorged until I was nearly sick. Never had anything tasted so good.

Later that night, I crept from my room, my bare feet muffling the squeaks and groans in the floorboards. Outside, a silver disk of a moon hung in the sky, its surface pockmarked and cold. I crossed the back lawn, clutching my pajama legs high. The CD was still wedged in the splintered groove of the railway tie. When I pried it free, a sliver of wood pierced my middle finger.

Inside, I slipped the CD back into the boom box. I knew it couldn't play, but something made me try. The speakers screeched and I threw myself over them, suffocating the sound. I waited, my heart pounding like Army Band drums. I lowered the volume and tried again, but all I heard was the scratchy refrain of: *Land of the free, and the home of the brave.*

I kept the CD, hid it in a shoebox under my bed. Every once in a while, when Dad wasn't around, I'd pull it out and listen to those same words, over and over again: *Land of the free, and the home of the brave.*

───────

"PRINCESS?"

Except for Dad's voice, the house was quiet. No *Pump Up the Jam.* No *Welcome to the Jungle.* No *Star Spangled Banner.* Just me and Dad, on a Friday afternoon, with the strange, silent air around us.

"You okay?" He stood in the kitchen doorway. Over his shoulder, I caught a glimpse of our new curtains, bright white with polka dots in multiple shades of spring green. A poofy valance hid the shadow of smoke behind the rod.

"I—"

He glanced at his watch, a frown brewing between his eyebrows. "You just get in?"

"I—"

Then he grinned, like he just plunked down the last piece of a jigsaw puzzle. "Hungry."

It wasn't a question. Even so, I nodded.

"What do you want for dinner?"

Chocolate chip pizza. I shrugged. "Whatever."

"I'm in kind of a pizza mood myself. Want to order something online?"

"Sure," I said. And hold the chocolate chips.

───────

AFTER DINNER, I pulled the ammo crate from under my bed, but didn't open the lid, not at first. Tonight I needed to catch my breath before I dived into another round of my mom's poetry. I needed to sort through memories—my own and my mom's—about *that* song and Dad.

What did he see when those first notes came through the

speakers? Even though I'd been right there in the living room with him, I now knew he'd been somewhere else—like that fourth floor apartment in the Khobar Towers.

The impact of linking my past with my mom's left me breathless, hollow, and yet, at the same time, a little fluttery. I removed the journal, brought it close to my face, and inhaled—dry and gritty. Every time I flipped a page, residue coated my fingers. The journal was so tiny, not even a full-sized notebook. And yet, it contained so much. I could only imagine what other questions my mom might answer for me.

———

Where Are Your Men
January 1991

The Boys' Club

In the early morning, steam rises from fifty-five
gallon drums. Old Spice and menthol
ride the breeze.

The men never falter in this ritual.
By the time the sun's heat touches
the air, all that's left behind are
dots of shaving cream on sand.

The scrape of razors sounds like grit
against metal, and that razor-burn red?
The men wear it like a badge of honor

I watch them,
my feet itching to creep closer.
Would the captain lend me

his shaving cream?
Or would I have to bring my own?

Could I kick off my boots, roll my pant legs,
and hike a foot on the rim
of the drum?

And if I carved up my legs like they do
their faces, would that be enough?
Or are there other rituals to endure
to be a member of the club?

Of Surgeons And Gunslingers

The Kuwaiti linguists gather around a
drum, part of the club, but not.
More than I am?
Less than I am?
With the steam clouding the air,
it's hard to tell.

They jockey for position, elbows and M16s knocking.
Some carry their weapons like gunslingers
from the Old West.
Others have the hands of surgeons, the M16s
too clunky for their precise touch.
None are soldiers.
All speak Arabic.
Every last one can eavesdrop when we aim
our equipment across the border
at the Iraqis.

Every last one has a reason
for being here. But those reasons,

spoken in Arabic, float on steam from
fifty-five gallon drums until the sun
burns them all away.

Where Are Your Men

When Ahmed sees me, he breaks from the group,
sets an intercept course, his aim
perfect, catching me—as always—between
the TOC and the field mess.

He launches the same question, and it strikes me, with the same
politeness:

Ah, Lieutenant, I must ask you. Where are your men?

Answers elude me.
I understand his words, but not his intent.
Today, however, I'm glib:

I didn't know I had any.

Ahmed mutters in Arabic,
the phrases both derisive and melodic.
He has put his Georgetown education on hold,
his mother and three sisters trapped in Kuwait.
The worry—that he hasn't heard anything since
the invasion—is carved around his eyes
and his mouth.

He is in this no man's land for a reason.
He wants to know mine.
The intricacies of the all-volunteer Army
are lost on Ahmed.

I'm a soldier. It's my job.

Might as well be spoken in Chinese
He still wants to know:

Where are your men?

Now he adds, as if he's given these new questions
much thought:

The ones that stay in America? Why are they not here?

Anything I can say would make as much sense
to him as women in the Army.

He leaves me with an odd, half-salute.
I forget I'm hungry. I forget I need
some field mess coffee.
Grains of sand blow across the toes
of my combat boots, Ahmed's question echoing
in the wind.

Where are your men?

What does it mean
that after all this time,
I still don't know
the answer?

———

FOR THE LONGEST TIME, I thought nothing bad could happen in
April. April meant happy; it meant my dad back to his old self, or

mostly so. Like the time when he walked into my third grade class-room, still in suit coat and tie, and pulled me out of school for the day.

We drove north in his Chevy Blazer, straight to the Mall of America and the indoor amusement park. We rode all the rides and stayed until closing. I remember that day, not so much for what we did—although for a week, everyone at school called him the Best Dad Ever. I remember his laugh, how free it was, how it reminded me of summer, sweet and warm, and full of freshly-spun cotton candy. That was just one of the many reasons I believed only good stuff happened in April.

Then I started high school.

The Monday after spring break, I was heading for my locker before lunch when the sight of Nissa and Landon had me stum-bling to a halt in the middle of the hallway. Someone bumped my shoulder and I staggered forward, but only a step. I stood there, transfixed, while Landon pulled twenty dollar bills from his wallet and handed them to Nissa. She fumbled with the cash and one bill floated to the floor. By the time he scooped it up, she held out two prom tickets.

Landon vanished into the cafeteria, but Nissa stood there, clutching the cashbox with both hands as if that was the only thing keeping her upright. When her gaze finally focused on me, her eyes went wide. Then she shrugged, as if to say, *well, what can you do?* She nodded toward the cafeteria. My stomach rebelled at the thought, and I shook my head.

Nissa headed for the door, her step lighter, something new in her attitude. Hope, I thought, in the form of two prom tickets. I wanted to smack Landon. I didn't care who he was taking to prom. Okay. I did care. A lot. But unless he planned on asking Nissa, buying tickets from her was cruel—and nothing like the boy I used to know.

Forget prom, swimming, and everything else. I had a more important mission. My scholarship. Or what I hoped would be my scholarship. I could work in the library. Or better yet, I could see if Patti, or rather, her alter ego Ms. Flynn, was in her classroom. I took the stairs two at a time. When I reached the second floor, heart thudding, I downshifted into stealth, my Chucks barely making a squeak against the tile. I was sure this was the perfect idea. Almost.

Patti sat at her desk, lunch to one side, a book open in front of her. I hated to interrupt and was about to turn around when that special sense all teachers have alerted her to my presence.

"MacKenna?" Patti sounded pleased, at least. I heard the scrape of her chair against the linoleum. "Can I help you with something?"

"I don't—I mean, your lunch," I began. "But yeah, I could use some help."

"It's stale." Patti shoved her sandwich to one side. "So, do you need swim coach help or English teacher help?"

"Well." I inched into the room, pulling out the scholarship papers from my binder. "It's English help, I guess. I'm working on a scholarship application and—"

"I don't believe it!" Patti exclaimed. For one horrible moment, I thought she meant that *me + scholarship = ludicrous*. But the grin that lit her face had me relaxing in the chair next to her desk. It struck me that how she looked, right then, was a lot like her senior portrait. It was strange to think she'd gone to school with my mom, that they swam together, that if my mom were alive, she'd be the same age as Patti.

"Finally, someone who listens on the first day of school," she said.

Now she'd totally lost me, but I nodded like I knew what she was talking about.

"I offer to help with applications and essays every year, and if anyone remembers to ask, it's in June." She beamed at me. "You just made this teacher's day."

"I was thinking about trying for early acceptance, too." I'd like to see Dad refuse me that—full ride scholarship, early acceptance, all wrapped up with awesome SAT scores. Now *that* was superior firepower.

"The written portion of all applications is becoming more and more important," Patti continued. "Along with test scores, extracurricular activities, and grades." She caught her breath as if just thinking about it winded her. "I sometimes think it gets harder and harder each year. When's your SATs?"

"After the swim show."

"Good plan. Now let's see what you're up against."

I tell you, the woman was positively giddy. "The space is really small," I said, "and we can't use continuation sheets. I tried to write something, but it's really hard to write something good and write it short."

"I have made this letter longer than usual because I lack the time to make it short," Patti announced.

I looked at her—blankly given how she laughed.

"Pascal," she said. "Sorry, English teacher moment. Go on."

"They're calling it a personal statement." I studied the paper, like I didn't already have it memorized. "It has to be all about service, and why you want to serve, and why the Army. I'm thinking a lot of kids will write patriotic stuff, but I wanted to write something really personal."

I babbled, for how long, I couldn't say. I wanted to build on the poems I'd read on Friday night, about the volunteer service and maybe even work in that question: *Where are your men?* I was about to mention the journal when I saw that her eyes had gone hard, the smile no longer lighting her face.

"Pa—Ms. Flynn?"

"Sorry ... sorry." She shook herself, then considered me for such a long moment, heat rose in my face. I felt all of six years old, caught doing something naughty. "I don't think I'm the right person to help you with this," she said at last.

Her words sank all the way to my stomach. Not the right person? Five minutes ago, she'd assured me she was.

"I think maybe your guidance counselor, or even Mr. Reed would be a better choice. You'll be in Honors English 12 next year, and I'm sure he won't mind."

I didn't like my guidance counselor and other than seeing Mr. Reed in the halls, didn't know him at all. Patti knew me, both from class and swimming. She could help me. I knew it. So why wouldn't she?

"I don't—" I began.

"I'm sorry, Beth."

Beth?

"I mean, MacKenna." Patti dropped her gaze, pinched the bridge of her nose, a frown digging deep furrows across her brow. If before she looked young enough for high school, she now looked closer to retirement. "I can't do this again."

———

PATTI WENT SILENT. She didn't explain and I didn't ask. Somehow, I backed from the room. Somehow, I found my way to my next class, hollow from shock and lack of food. I'd felt like I'd betrayed Patti, which didn't make any sense at all.

I dreaded English. Patti had a policy, announced on the first day of class. Unlike her offer (or non-offer) to help with applications, everyone heard this:

"You are all honors students," she told us. "Black Earth High's finest, at least according to your GPA. I expect a certain knowledge of English literature. Starting now."

In other words, the class spring butt (Marissa "me, me, call on me" Johnson), stealth girl (usually me), the class clown (generally Landon), and everyone in between answered questions. I braced for the worst, most obscure questions to come my way. Patti's route through the class was arbitrary, but she never missed a student.

Until today.

Behind me, Josh leaned forward and tapped me on the shoulder. "How do you rate?" he whispered. "She's been through the class three times and hasn't called on you once. Trust me, I've been counting."

I shrugged. Patti was in rapid-fire question mode. Those days usually sucked. I'd sit through class, my stomach clenched, anticipating an answer for each question. It probably got us ready for tests. It probably gave us ulcers too.

Now my stomach clenched, then dropped each time she didn't say my name. Even blowing an answer was better than this. For once, I wanted to burst out of stealth mode. I wanted to know why Patti refused to see and hear me.

I wanted to know why, after years of flying under the radar, it hurt so much to be invisible.

Chapter 8

THE POOL AREA amplified sounds in odd ways. Patti always warned us not to gasp, grunt, or groan during performances or speak above a whisper in the locker room. If you wanted to keep a secret, the pool wasn't the place to do it.

This was why, that Monday afternoon at swim practice, when Landon approached me and said, "We need to talk." everyone heard.

I was in the middle of a straddle stretch, not the most elegant position for a conversation, but I risked stealing a glance at him. Our eyes locked. The panic I saw in his gaze froze my muscles.

"Now?" I asked. Stray thoughts ricocheted through my mind. I thought of the prom tickets Landon had bought from Nissa today. Of what that meant for me and for her. No matter what Landon had to say, I knew I wasn't going to like it.

He knelt. I pushed forward, almost into a split, letting the pain distract me.

"They canceled the order," he whispered.

"They ... what?" And because my mind was so focused on

Nissa and Landon and prom, for a second, I thought he was telling me they canceled his prom tickets.

"The posters," he added. "And I don't know why. Not yet."

I fell back on my butt and tugged first my right, then my left leg to my chest. Landon pulled a cell phone from his cargo pocket. He studied it and uttered a few words worthy of Dad.

"I can't get reception in here. So I—"

He met my gaze. Maybe it was the water, or the tile, but his eyes looked nearly blue. I was well acquainted with the tricks those eyes could play. Green on the playground, dark and stormy in our old clubhouse (a garden shed behind Grandma Adele's), but always a barometer of his mood. But this blue—and the way he scrutinized me—had me perplexed.

"I'll run out to the lobby in a bit," he said. "Talk after practice?"

Numbly, I nodded.

"What do we do if—" I began.

He held up a finger to stop me. "Don't go there. It'll be fine. Trust me."

"Hey, dude," Josh called out from across the diving board. "Get over here and do some actual work."

Something shifted in Landon's face, almost like he became someone else, his grin, his posture, all of it adjusting to fit Josh's tone, like his mood was a mask he could slip on and off.

Landon raised a hand, middle finger extended.

"And stop harassing the talent," Josh added.

"Why, Josh," I said. "I didn't know you cared."

Josh only snorted.

Landon stood. Without even a backwards glance, he padded around the diving board, one knee of his cargo pants damp from where he'd knelt on the deck. He joined the other three guys where they worked to construct the platform stage.

They'd scraped together plywood and some two by fours. What they couldn't scrounge, Josh said Landon had paid for—with his own money—like the black cloth they planned to drape between supports. After Landon's first (disastrous) day, the four of them had worked out some sort of truce. Maybe they weren't friends, but they didn't sabotage each other, and if there was a pecking order, then Josh was at the top.

"Please tell me everything's okay."

I spun to find Constance, arms crossed.

"Tell me." Her gaze moved from my face to where Landon stood in the far corner. "This has nothing to do with him and the show."

For three seconds, I considered lying. But this was Constance. We were swimming a duet together. She and Landon were cousins. She'd learn the truth—somehow. And when she did?

"I wish I could," I said. "He's helping me with the posters. There's a problem with the order."

She groaned. And yes, the sound went everywhere. A few girls peered at us, then lost interest. "You're kidding me," Constance added, lowering her voice. "You agreed to that?"

I shook my head. "He made it hard to refuse."

"You wouldn't be the first girl who couldn't."

My cheeks went into nuclear meltdown at that. I opened my mouth to explain, but Constance shook her head.

"I expect nearly instantaneous updates," she said.

Absently, I nodded, an invisible pull turning me toward the stands. There, in the first row, Nissa was staring at me.

Actually, Nissa, Jodi, and Sierra all stared at me from their perch, like they were all set to watch a show. I thought about slinking off, taking the route around the diving board, and approaching the stands from the other end. Then, it hit me. Nissa was my friend—my *best* friend. And while a sneer wrinkled Sierra's nose, Nissa simply looked sad.

Constance had wandered off to talk to Patti, so I sucked in my stomach, lifted my chin, and marched over. Something weird happened then. Sierra and Jodi scooted backward, away from me. My feet, unsure, skidded on the pool deck, but I caught myself and kept up my stride. If I'd known they were so easy to intimidate, I would've tried that a long time ago.

"What's up?" I said when I reached the wall. I planted my fingertips on the tile ledge and stood on tiptoes.

Nissa stayed silent, but I followed her line of sight to where Landon worked in the far corner. If she'd been keeping secrets from me, then I'd kept this one from her.

"It's the craziest thing," I told her. "He offered to help with the posters. We were just—" I broke off, not sure I wanted to confess my full-fledged panic about the situation.

For all I know, we would've remained like that—both not talking about the boy we couldn't stop thinking about—but Patti's whistle sliced through the air. Nissa jerked back. My fingers slipped from the wall, my heart thudding so hard it hurt.

The team gathered around Patti, and I stood at its fringes. While she spoke, I searched for Nissa. She sat sandwiched between Jodi and Sierra, up high in the stands, completely out of reach.

———

PATTI ORDERED us into the pool for an endless round of drills. No routines this afternoon, just nonstop laps. First came full lengths underwater, then balancing bottles of water on our stomachs as we sculled across the pool, followed by ballet legs until even our toe muscles trembled. If Landon slipped out to make a call during all this, I never noticed.

No shower, no stealth, and my skin was still damp when I tugged on my underwear and my socks. I raced from the locker room in world record time.

Landon stood near the trophy cases, hands in pockets. When I got closer, I saw the packed display for the boys' baseball team directly in front of him, the gold reflected in his eyes and against his skin. I'd wondered about his Little League career once he'd left Black Earth. He'd been good; the sort of good other kids' parents commented on, because they were impressed, not just to be kind.

"Are you going out for baseball?" I asked, before remembering that boys' baseball had already started.

"No."

"It's not because of the swim show, is it?"

He turned from the trophies and gave me a smile that didn't quite reach his dimple. "No." Something in his expression told me he wasn't going to elaborate.

"Did you hear about the order?" I asked.

His smile faded. "By the time I called, everyone had gone home. I'll try tomorrow during lunch."

I glanced at the wall clock. "So I only have to avoid Constance for eighteen hours."

"You told her?"

"She figured it out."

"I'll handle Con too," he said. "She can't help but love me."

"Maybe because you're related?"

"Like I said." This time, the grin reached his dimple.

I stared, willing my fingers not to reach out, not to trace the hollow in his cheek. My mouth went dry; I had no words. Desperate, I licked my lips. When Landon's gaze flickered to my mouth, I realized that had been the wrong thing to do.

He stepped closer. "MacKenna."

When had he learned to say my name like that, like some soft, sexy chant? Suddenly, five years didn't matter anymore. Nothing mattered except how Landon's eyes turned gold in the glow of the trophies. He reached out and swept a strand of damp hair from my forehead. His hand stayed there, seemed to shake as if he couldn't decide to use it to tug me closer or push me away.

"MacKenna, I—"

"Hey, guys!"

The high pitched voice ricocheted through the lobby. I jumped back, panting like I was still in the pool doing laps.

"Oh, I'm sorry," the voice, now syrupy sweet, belonged to Sierra. "Are we interrupting something?"

My throat tightened, but all of me relaxed when I saw only Jodi behind Sierra. I felt like I'd dodged a bullet. Three seconds later, Nissa rounded the corner, her eyes fierce.

My feet wouldn't obey the order to step forward, to use the tactic that had worked so well before. This time, something was different. This time, *I* was different.

How did Sierra do it? Less than two weeks ago, she'd had her lacquered claws all over Tim McPherson. And yet, Nissa glared at me for doing nothing with Landon. Except, it wasn't nothing. Five more seconds and it would've been something. I knew it. I had no moral high ground, not anymore. So I did the only thing that made sense.

I headed for the exit. When I reached the double doors, I shoved through and ran.

———

I MADE it through dinner with Dad (fake Swedish meatballs) and up to my room, where I dumped all my books and homework onto my desk. Then I sat on the floor and pretended all of it wasn't about to crash down on my head. I pretended my life wasn't about to do the same. In one day:

My favorite teacher (and swim coach) had stopped speaking to me.

My best friend thought I'd betrayed her.

The boy who first kissed me five years ago almost did it again today.

As long as Landon acted like there was nothing between us— and never had been—I could too. For three months that had worked so well. What was different now?

Because really? There wasn't much to that first kiss. We'd been in our club house, just the two of us, that Friday afternoon before

Memorial Day. He'd grabbed my hand and yanked me close—so abruptly, I was about to punch his shoulder. Before I could, his dry, seventh-grade-boy lips landed on mine.

"I'll be back on Monday," he'd said, then ran from the club house without a glance behind him.

Of course, he hadn't returned on Monday, not unless he actually meant on a Monday five years in the future. And here's the thing: I never told Nissa.

At first, I wanted to talk to Landon. Then, when days turned into weeks into months, I didn't see the point in hurting Nissa even more. He'd kissed me and left us both. End of story. Or at least, it had been until he suddenly appeared for the sequel.

Instead of scaling the mountain of homework above me, I pulled out the ammo crate and my mom's journal. Right then, Saudi Arabia sounded far less hazardous than Black Earth Minnesota.

———

Rumors
January 1991

RUMINT

Here's the thing: There are rumors.
About Master Sergeant Collier.
About the soldiers in my section.
About how they chased off the last
female lieutenant who worked there.

Here's the thing: I've been warned.
Put on notice.
Offered friendly advice.
Mostly from people I don't really know.

Here's the thing: If the chauvinism exists,
I haven't seen it,
or am not very observant.
And if they try to chase me away,
where would I run to?

There's nothing but sand, nothing but sky.
I say: Let the wind steal the rumors
and blow them far across the desert.

The Best Things Come in Small Packages

The biggest box at mail call
has Felicia's name all over it.
Well, it probably says *Lieutenant Stover*,
but it's all hers and she refuses
to open it where everyone can see.
She never needs to work very hard
to unleash her inner bitch, but in this case
it's extra-special.

She plans a party—female staff officers only,
because battle lines have been drawn
in more ways than one.
I promise my soldiers I'll return
with treasures from what no doubt
will be an orgy of unwrapping, eating,
and forgetting.

Church ladies, Felicia tells us. *You should see*
the spread they do for coffee hour after mass.
Church ladies always know what you want.
Church ladies always know what you need.

Felicia's church ladies will take care of us.

Three layers of packing tape
suffocate the box. Felicia slices through
with a non-regulation knife she keeps hidden
from the colonel.

I pause to read the crumpled newspaper, throwaway
cushion for the treasures inside. I'm captivated
by the words—real American words—from
somewhere in Texas.

I don't hear the crinkle of tinfoil.
I don't smell chocolate or cookies.
I blink at the mirage of teal and blue,
at the silhouetted figure, modest
and feminine.

The entire box—every last square inch—is filled
with sanitary napkins,
the old-fashion kind,
the sort that needs a belt.

The thought of bringing a box—in all its modest glory—back to my
soldiers
is both hysterical and abhorrent.

Felicia is speechless, the happy gleam in
her eye replaced by the emptiness
of betrayal.
And if sometimes she's a bitch
then maybe it's something she learned
from those church ladies in Texas.

Chapter 9

THE NEXT DAY, I was still thinking about Lieutenant Felicia Stover and how she must be related—somehow—to Sierra Linden. It beat thinking about Landon and the kiss that wasn't. And I thought about rumors: who was saying what about my mom and how you dealt with that.

It had never been an issue for me. Black Earth High had so many drama kings and queens—an entire court's worth of royalty —that a stealth girl like me could navigate the halls unnoticed. Until today. I threaded my way through the cafeteria and felt the pinprick of collective gazes on me. I resisted glancing over my shoulder. That looked guilty. And I wasn't guilty of anything, I told myself. Besides, you couldn't see rumors—they just floated around you.

"Hey, MacKenna!" My name boomed across the cafeteria.

Landon stood in the doorway; I was at the far end, near the "better for you" salad bar. Between us, a really long stretch of linoleum. I didn't look left; I didn't look right. I didn't have to. This was rumor mill uranium and the Geiger counter had pegged the second he called my name. When I passed the synchro table, I weathered a deadly blast of radiation. It was, quite possibly, the longest walk of my life. When I reached Landon, he leaned back against the cafeteria wall.

"You want to talk here?" I made a conscious effort to avoid his eyes and then his mouth. I settled on his neck.

He glanced around, waved at someone, then shrugged. "Why not?"

Oh, for a million reasons, the most practical being that it was loud. Dishes clattered, screeches and squeals bounced off the walls, various words from crude jokes reached my ears if not his. Landon didn't move, didn't speak, but he swallowed—hard—and his Adam's apple bobbed.

"Did you call?" I asked.

"No."

So that was it. "Then—"

"Didn't have to." He held up the cell phone he had cupped in his hand. "Got a voice mail. My dad personally canceled the order."

From what little I knew of Mr. Scott, that had to be bad. "Hell."

"Yeah, something like that."

What was I going to do? What would I tell Constance? Never mind that. How on earth would I report this to Patti, especially after yesterday? "I'm in so much trouble." I sighed and tried to calculate just how much trouble and what it was going to cost me.

"How much money do you have in the budget?" he asked. To his credit he didn't even twitch when I told him.

"I'm sorry," he said. "I thought ... I was only trying to help."

"It's not like you did it on purpose."

He gave me that smile, the one that didn't reach his dimple. "I'd like to try to help fix it. Thing is, I kind of cashed in all my chips—the few I had. There's no way I can put in another print order." He tilted his head upward as if the answer to this could be found within the acoustic tile, his exposed throat incredibly vulnerable. "But my dad can."

"What does that mean?" I asked.

He returned to staring just past my shoulder. "A trip to Scott Industries after school."

"I have practice."

Landon raised an eyebrow. "Skip it."

Did I have a choice? My best—and only—option was going along with Landon's plan. "Okay, what are we going to do?"

"Talk to my dad. Let him think you've just taken over as publicity chair—"

"We don't have—"

"Just taken over for the previous chair and you're in a bind. I'll get us that far, then I'll turn it over to you."

"And I'm supposed to say what?" I asked. He was making this difficult.

"I was going to leave that up to you."

Okay, he was making this impossible. "What on earth could I possibly say?"

"Whatever it is, it'll be better than anything I could."

"I'm serious."

"So am I. Meet you by my car after school. I'm in the overflow lot."

No doubt parked across two spots.

He pushed against the wall, but made no other move to leave. All he did was inch us closer together. "You hungry?" he asked.

"I lost my appetite." About the time Landon had said *canceled* and *order*.

"You should eat."

"So should you," I countered. "So should everyone."

"I don't swim my ass off every day." He raised a hand and touched not my cheek, but the tender spot beneath my eye. "I don't have these dark circles."

Despite the cafeteria buzzing around us, despite the fact Landon had just touched me—in front of everyone—I laughed. "You don't get rid of dark circles by eating."

"Have you tried?"

"I have a Power Bar in my locker. I'll split it with you if you tell me what to say to your dad."

"And if I can't tell you what to say? Does the offer still stand?"

If I looked at it, hard and cold, I wouldn't be in this mess if not for him. But I couldn't wish him out of Black Earth, or out of my life. Something deep inside me—something fierce—grabbed on to Landon. This time, I wasn't going to let him go. But I didn't answer, didn't say a word.

Dad on staying silent: *Sometimes, princess, the best thing to say is nothing at all.*

I doubted Dad had this scenario in mind. I walked to the cafeteria door. At the threshold, I glanced over my shoulder and smiled at Landon. Then, I left.

He followed.

We ended up sitting in the junior class hallway, our backs against the lockers. I pulled out the promised Power Bar. Landon added dried mangos, a pesto club sandwich on sourdough, and a single bottle of water.

In that moment, I saw us on the playground again, our backs against the bricks of the school, Landon coming to my rescue, a stash of something edible between us. I turned my head until the cool metal of the locker touched my cheek.

I didn't say it was like old times. Neither did he. We were too old for that. But when I caught the green in those hazel eyes, and the dimple in his smile, I wondered if maybe it was the start of something new.

———

THANKS TO DAD'S endless stories about Mr. Scott, I knew I couldn't wing it this afternoon. In between classes, I thought about what on earth I might say. I walked into English in a haze, only jolting back to reality when Josh plopped down at his desk. I swiveled, feet toward the aisle. He wore his black and white drama club T-shirt, the one that said: *Black Earth High Drama ~ The Play's the Thing.*

I plucked the sleeve of his Tee. "Did you get those done at Reynolds?"

"Yeah," he said. "Sweet, aren't they?"

I nodded. Reynolds Shirt Shack had printed our Dolphins hoodies, and custom-made fleece jackets for the swim boys. "Did you guys get a deal?"

"I guess. I only paid five bucks for this." His forehead crinkled. "What's up?" he asked.

"I was just ... thinking."

"I've been trying to get Landon to join drama. Did you know he could sing?"

I cast Landon, who sat on the other side of the room, a quick look and shook my head. Just one more mystery about the boy who used to be my playground savior.

"But he won't," Josh said, "he keeps saying—"

I never learned what Landon kept saying. At that moment, Patti's voice cut through the room, silencing not only me and Josh, but the random paper rustlers and nose blowers.

"Excuse me, Ms. Meyers, Mr. Wylie? Would you care to join the rest of us?"

The rush of blood to my face felt like a slap. I turned, tucked my feet under my desk, then flipped through my notebook. The pages blurred in front of my eyes, a teardrop landing in the exact center of the first blank sheet I found. If Patti called on me, I wouldn't be able to speak. As it was, I could barely breathe.

Stupid, I thought. I shouldn't care so much. A week ago, I would've blown this off, laughed about it with Josh after class. But today it felt personal. And when Patti didn't call on me for the second class period in a row, I knew it was.

———

IN A MOVE that was either half brilliant or all crazy, I ran to the locker room after last bell. I needed to grab my Dolphins hoodie, needed to do that before the rest of the team filtered in after class.

I charged to my locker, spun the combination, and grabbed my hoodie. I whirled, ready to race outside, and crashed into Constance.

"Whoa. Going somewhere?"

"I—"

"We swim the duet." Her gaze moved to the wall clock. "In thirty."

I deflated, went from charged to crushed, all with six words. No way we could drive to Scott Industries, talk to Mr. Scott, and get back in time.

"Constance, I can't—"

"Can't what? Think? Talk? Swim?"

Pretty much all three at the moment. "I'm trying to get us some posters."

"Wait." Her eyes narrowed. "We don't have any?"

"Landon's dad canceled the order he put in."

"Shit." She stared past me, toward the showers and the entrance to the pool. "And you need to ...?"

"Landon's driving me to Scott Industries. We're talking to his dad."

Her gaze darted back to me, sure and sharp. "I hope you're the one doing the talking."

"That's what he said."

"What do you know? For once, he's right." She blew out a breath. "I'll cover for you, but I don't know how long I can keep it up. Patti was pretty cold toward you at yesterday's practice."

So. Constance had noticed. But then, she noticed everything. My cheeks flared with heat. "It's ... got something to do with ..." I

118

trailed off, not sure what it was about, not really. "School," I said at last.

"It'll be about swimming if you don't get your ass back here."

I fled, past the softball girls, past Nissa, Jodi, and Sierra—who, I belatedly realized—must have been listening in. Nissa threw me a look so cutting I swore I felt it against my skin, but I couldn't stop.

I burst from the locker room, flew down the steps, and broke into a sprint before the school doors shut behind me.

————

LANDON HAD the Corvette running by the time I made it to the overflow lot. The windows were rolled down and the almost-but-not-quite vintage Corvette blared almost-but-not-quite vintage Green Day.

Way to make a statement.

I doubled over, sucking in huge gulps of air before struggling into the hoodie.

"Dressing for success, I see," Landon said.

"I have an idea," I replied, adjusting my pigtails. "Unless you've come up with something to say to your father, I suggest you keep quiet."

He raised both hands in mock surrender. "All I'm saying is my dad likes the Junior Achievement types and they never wear sweats."

"That's part of the plan." I didn't elaborate. If Landon had secrets, then I could have a few of my own. Besides, we'd both find out soon enough whether my so-called brilliant plan would work.

Landon held open the door for me. I must have given him an odd look because I caught a flash of dimple before I slipped into the Corvette. Or, I slipped in for the first second. I was used to my Jeep or Dad's Blazer. Gravity took over. I plummeted into the leather seat, which, any lower, would scrape the asphalt. The Corvette felt tiny and vulnerable. But pretty fast and hot. We shot from the parking lot, fishtailing for good measure, and bumped onto the road that led to the onramp.

Scott Industries sat on the outskirts of Black Earth, surrounded by what had once been acres of farmland. Now sub-divisions—like the one Lukas Jakobitz lived in—sprouted where corn and soybeans once grew. The housing areas sprawled, each year edging closer to the trailer park, and further down, the nature preserve, duplexes and split-levels growing like weeds.

Landon zipped into a reserve parking place right by the front entrance. Apparently being the owner's son came with perks.

Landon threw open his door and I climbed from my side into spring air and warm asphalt, my heart pumping like I'd been caught trespassing.

"Wait!" Landon paused outside the main doors. "Your dad. He's a manager here, right?" He grinned like that fact made all our problems melt away. "This is going to be better than I thought."

I barely heard him. My heart stopped. So did my legs. So did any brain function. Dad.

Crap. *If Dad finds out . . .*

I couldn't finish that thought, so I simply banished it from my head. Besides, no one did stealth like I did. Dad never had to know. What Dad didn't know wouldn't hurt him—or me.

Inside, mirrored walls caught our eyes and splintered my pigtails into four, eight, twelve. Landon gave the security guards a mock salute, and we breezed through to the elevators. We were whisked to the top floor and exited to tinted windows and carpet so thick it swallowed our footfalls.

My bulky, hoodie-clad reflection followed my every move and I wondered what I'd been thinking. I wondered if I'd been thinking at all.

———

IN THE RECEPTION area outside Mr. Scott's office, Landon went immediately for the woman who sat behind a gleaming wood desk. He leaned in for a quick kiss on her cheek. "Hey, Nan."

Nan of the reception desk brightened as if Landon were her only son. "Oh, honey, we don't see enough of you these days."

Landon made a face. "There's a reason for that."

"If you were here more often, it might help." She gave him a sly, motherly sort of look.

"This," Landon said, ignoring the comment and the look, "is MacKenna Meyers."

Nan blinked, then a warm smile lit her face. "Paul's daughter, right?"

So much for stealth. Of course she knew Dad. He wasn't a VP, but he was a senior manager. My stomach fluttered, but I told it to shush.

"Yes, ma'am," I managed, after a deep breath.

"That military influence." She raised an eyebrow at Landon. "So polite."

"Hey," he protested. "I'm always polite."

Nan rolled her eyes, and I liked her for that.

"Well, mostly," he amended and nodded toward the door. "My dad free?"

"You can go in. He's expecting you."

"He always is," Landon muttered.

More thick carpet swallowed my footsteps. More tinted windows turned the surrounding countryside a strange blue-gray. I still looked bulky, even next to the huge, dark wood desk that dominated the room. The few scattered chairs seemed specially designed for discomfort.

Mr. Scott was on the phone, jotting something on a legal pad in front of him. He waved a hand at us, the message clear: Be quiet and wait. On his desk, a golfing trophy nearly eclipsed a family portrait. In that moment, five years disappeared. The photo was *that* old. I knew Landon at twelve, better than I knew the boy who stood next to me now. I'd cried against that plaid shirt, stared into those hazel eyes, ran my finger along that dimple.

Landon's posture shifted. His shoulders slouched and he jammed his fists into the front pockets of his jeans. His face was slack, except for the jaw that tensed and twitched. If I hadn't known him as my playground savior and Black Earth High's golden boy, I would've said he was a slacker, a stoner, someone who routinely avoided living up to his potential.

Mr. Scott hung up and stared at Landon. If Landon resembled his dad at all, it was in the jawline. Mr. Scott was tensing his own. Again, I was reminded that guys did a lot of talking without actual words.

"So, Landon," Mr. Scott said. "You needed to see me?"

"Dad, this is MacKenna Meyers. She's the ... new publicity chair for the Black Earth High synchronized swimming team."

I winced at Landon's hesitation, but Mr. Scott only gave me a cursory glance before hitting Landon with a *well, what of it* sort of look. Clearly, he was unimpressed—by both of us. Landon nodded at me. I opened my mouth and hoped for the right words.

I explained about the lack of posters. My voice came out reedy and false. If you recorded it, you could use it as an instructional example: *Now, children, this is what a lie sounds like.*

But Mr. Scott's face was placid; he was obviously not outraged at the girl spewing untruths before him.

"Can I ask you something, Miss ...?"

"Meyers, sir. MacKenna Meyers."

"You expect a gratis print job on posters for your show when we have a very generous school discount program?"

"We don't have a very generous budget, sir."

"And that's my problem, how, exactly?"

I drew in a deep breath and glanced toward Landon. He fidgeted, moving from foot to foot and refused to meet my gaze.

"Well, sir. It might actually be your problem."

The room took on a silence thick enough to swim through. Mr.

Scott didn't speak, but he inclined his head, barely a millimeter, letting me know to continue.

I stepped forward, held out my arms, and announced, "This is our team sweatshirt." I turned around to show off the back. "Every year, we have new ones made, and everyone on the team gets a sweatshirt with their name on the back."

From behind me, it sounded like Landon was choking on his own spit. I ignored him.

"The dance team has new yoga jackets this year, the boys' swim team always gets custom embroidery." After I'd talked to Josh, I spoke to every jock, every club member, anyone who ever wore a custom-made shirt for a sport, club, or extracurricular activity.

Beyond confirming the fact I'd hoped to be true, gathering the information brought me in contact with the entire social strata of Black Earth High, from the chess club to the cheerleaders. Nobody blew me off, and everyone wanted to add this or that tidbit about Reynolds Shirt Shack.

"The drama club, the gymnastics team, even the football players order practice jerseys. Do you know what they have in common, sir?"

"I imagine you're going to tell me."

"Reynolds Shirt Shack." I pulled a piece of computer paper from my back pocket. In a stealth move, I'd asked for a library pass during social studies under the guise of "research," which actually wasn't a lie. I'd printed out an entire sheet of what I hoped was pretty compelling research.

"This is an estimate." I handed Mr. Scott the paper. "Of the wholesale cost and the discount cost of the various shirts Reynolds supplies the teams and clubs at Black Earth High. As you can see, it's pretty good business."

"This might be compelling information, Miss—" Mr. Scott looked directly at me. His eyes widened. For a fraction of a second, he smiled, and I caught the hint of a dimple. "Meyers. As in little MacKenna Meyers. Paul's daughter."

Crap. Black Earth really was too small.

Mr. Scott stood, rounded his desk, and advanced. "Why, the last time I saw you, you were." He waved his hand somewhere around his knee.

I tried not to flinch, and stepping back would ruin everything. Still, we were three seconds away from a hair ruffle or cheek pinch. I needed to rethink the whole stealth thing, since it so wasn't working. Mr. Scott chuckled, although whatever he found funny was lost on both me and Landon, who swayed slightly, looking as shell-shocked as I felt.

"I'm going to have to give your old man a hard time for not bringing you around," he added.

Oh, God. *No.*

"So, Miss Meyers." Mr. Scott stressed the *Miss*. And yeah, if I'd been six, that would've been cool. "What were you going to tell me? I'm not sure I see how Reynolds Shirt Shack relates to Scott Industries."

Okay, so sure, Reynolds had a tiny space in the mall, but they'd been in business forever. "Sir, am I right in thinking a company's brand is more than the products they put on the shelf?"

Mr. Scott hitched a trouser leg and sat on the edge of his desk. "Continue."

"Every fall and spring, the school play needs programs and posters. Does Scott Industry print those?" Since I knew the answer (no, according to Josh), I kept going. "Did you know the boys' swim team puts together an entire retrospective of the season, including team and individual stats, and pictures. Does Scott Industries print those?"

Thanks to Sam Avery, I knew the answer to that as well. No. "So, I have to ask you, sir. Why have a school discount program if it isn't generating any business or good will?"

Now I did take a step back. That was it. All I had. Now that I'd said it out loud, it didn't sound like much. My pulse pounded in my ears, the roar so loud, I was afraid if Mr. Scott spoke, I'd miss it. His scrutiny went from me, to Landon, and back again. I worked to breathe. If something didn't happen soon, I'd faint.

"Jesus." Mr. Scott exhaled, but he didn't look upset. "Like father, like daughter. All right, Miss Meyers, you've made your point. Let's talk good will."

In the end, we reached an agreement. For one small line of text, four little words, hardly a sentence, the team could get colored posters and the bonus of matching programs—for free. All we had to do was add *Sponsored by Scott Industries* at the bottom of each.

And sure, there was the *Not setting a precedent here* and *Other teams can't expect this sort of deal*, and I had to promise to steer all my contacts to the new and improved school discount program once it was online. Various thoughts followed me to the door—*too good to be true* and *far, far too easy*.

Before we could leave, Mr. Scott called out.

"MacKenna, could I speak to you? Alone."

Of course. Nothing was that good or that easy. Landon's eyes went dark, his skin a little waxy. This did not fill me with confidence. The door clicked closed, and I was left with that eerie silence and the feel of my pulse beating against my throat. Mr. Scott sat at his desk now, fingers steepled, not angry, but clearly skeptical.

"So Landon is actually helping you with this show." It wasn't so much a question but a statement of disbelief.

Oddly enough, Landon *was* helping. Even I thought he'd get bored; Constance definitely did. But each night, he made us a playlist, loaded it on his iPod, and sent new songs through the underwater speakers for our endless conditioning laps. Snippets of his narration filtered through the pool area. He'd try out a line, revise on the fly, then try it out again, each time making it sound fresh. He tinkered with the electronics along with Josh, and helped build the limited scenery we used.

How did this compete with hitting home runs in Little League? How did you explain to someone that his son was like glue? We were holding it together this season in a large part because of Landon. And sure, maybe we were showing off and swimming harder since he'd been around, but even Patti admitted that everyone's form had improved.

"He's like glue, sir." After saying the words out loud, I realized that they made no sense and added, "You have every reason to be proud of him." I considered whether Mr. Scott was the ogre Landon—and Dad for that matter—made him out to be. After all, I was walking away with a free print order.

"Thank you, sir, for everything." Without waiting for Mr. Scott's reaction, I turned, slipped through the door, and shut it gently behind me.

When we left the reception area, Landon took my hand, his fingers interlocking with mine. We were quiet through the sole-sucking carpet and tinted glass of the corridor. Not a word while we waited for the elevator. Only when the doors whooshed closed, did Landon lean against the elevator wall and burst out laughing.

"I've never actually seen anyone do that to my dad before." He closed his eyes, a blissful expression on his face. "I'm never going to get tired of thinking about it, either. You did it."

"We did it," I corrected.

Landon pounced then, yanked me close. He kissed me, fast and hard, left cheek, right cheek. He let go as suddenly as he grabbed me. Breathless, I stumbled into the elevator's wall. It was seventh grade all over again.

"You're my hero," he said.

"You're my playground savior." The confession took us both by surprise. I'd never told him that before; it was always something I'd held locked inside me.

But when the elevator doors opened, and gold lit his eyes, I knew it had been the perfect thing to say. He took my hand and together we ran from the building, dashed to the car, our laughter chasing us. When the spring sun touched our faces, I felt the last five years melt away.

Chapter 10

WE HELD hands all the way back to Black Earth High. I glanced at
Landon now and then. I couldn't see the dimple in his left cheek,
but I knew it was there.

Reality hit me when we pulled into the overflow lot. Practice
was more than half over, the duet not worth thinking about. My
slot on the team, however? That was probably worth a worry
or two.

Landon took my hand again on our way across the parking lot.
In the shadow of Black Earth High, the move sent a nervous pang
through me, from the center of my stomach all the way down to
my fingertips and into Landon.

"You okay?" he said.

"I missed duet practice," I said. "I told Constance I'd be late,
but I don't think Patti is—"

"I'll handle Patti. She loves me."

"You give her gray hair."

"She still loves me."

That, sadly, was true. He squeezed my hand again. "Don't

worry. You—we—did it. We make a pretty good team, don't you think."

"We always did."

By now we'd cleared the school's double doors and stood near the stairs that led to the locker rooms. I needed to hurry, throw on a practice suit, and use all the stealth under my power to sneak into the pool area.

My foot was on the first stair when his arms wrapped around my waist. He turned me around until I stood on the step above him. My mouth was even with his and the jumping in my stomach told me what came next was either very good or else very, very bad. I held my breath.

"We could keep on being a team," he said. "All the way to prom."

All the way to … prom? For the second time that day, I couldn't think, couldn't speak, couldn't get my legs to move.

"It's why I bought the tickets," he said.

"But you bought the tickets from Nissa."

A crease formed between his brows, one so perplexed it took all my willpower not to smooth it away. How could a boy who was so popular with girls not understand anything about them?

"You bought the tickets from Nissa." I stressed each word. "She thinks it means something." I waited, but when he didn't speak, I added, "Between the two of you."

Landon shook his head. "Of course there isn't."

"You friended her on Facebook."

"She friended me, and I would've sent you a request, but I was afraid you'd block me."

Back in January, I would have. But somehow, during the last four months, Landon had chipped away at the wall I'd built around my heart. Brick by brick, he dismantled my defensives, broke through until I stood there, thinking: *Yes, I'll go to prom with you.*

Except I knew I couldn't.

"Nissa—" I began.

"Is not your friend," he countered. "I don't know what happened between you two, but take it from someone who's been watching both of you real close, trying to figure it all out."

"We're still—" My mouth couldn't form the word best or friend and Landon jumped in again.

"You're not. Seriously, she'd rather hang with Sierra. And believe me, you don't want to know what they say about you and Con when you work on your duet."

But I could guess. Landon was right. I didn't want to know.

"And why she thinks saying it so I can hear is a good idea, beats me."

Because we were all clueless when it came to boys? It was a tactic, one I'd seen Nissa use. The result? Self-inflicted wounds. Always. Like now.

"But that's not the point," he said. "The point is me and you." His exhale reached me and I saw the quick, nervous bob of his Adam's apple. "And prom?"

"Oh, Landon—"

"Is that 'Oh, Landon, yes'?"

I squeezed my eyes shut and shook my head, a single teardrop trailing down my cheek. He caught it with his thumb. His touch made me jerk and I stepped to the second stair.

"She's not your friend anymore," he said.

"But she was." The words, the accusation, streamed from my mouth. "She was my best friend, and she was here for the last five years. Where the hell were you?"

I whirled from him, stumbled up the stairs. Tears blurred the corridor in front of me. Maybe that was why the girl in the Dolphins hoodie didn't register until I barreled into her. Jodi leaped back and flattened herself against the wall, her red hair fanning all around. From the look on her face, I could tell.

She had heard the whole damn thing.

———

IN THE LOCKER ROOM, I took my time. Stealth hardly mattered at this point. So I soaked myself in the shower, drenching my suit, my hair, hoping to wash away the tears and the telltale red from my eyes. Before stepping out, I jerked the handle all the way to the right. Icy water stung my skin, shocked the tears from my eyes and thoughts from my head. If I could hold onto that state of shock for the last hour of practice, things would be okay.

I eased along the edge of the pool area, working my way to the diving board. Patti stood on the deck, at the shallow end, talking the freshmen through sculling techniques. Landon worked with the tech crew up in the stands. I averted my gaze, but not before I saw Sierra nudge Nissa in the back and inch her closer to the boys.

I hid behind the rolled up lane markers. But not for long. Constance found me, her already pale skin going a shade whiter when she saw me.

"Holy shit, tell me. No wait, don't tell me." She glanced over her shoulder and crouched. "Okay. Tell me. We don't have the posters, do we?"

"No," I said, "we do."

"Then—?" She glanced toward Landon. "Why do you both look like shit?"

"Because we got free matching programs too?"

"Seriously, what's the problem?"

"It's just." I broke off and rubbed the back of my neck. Was there such a thing as emotional tetanus? I felt like at any moment I'd stiffen up and break in half. Thank God we weren't swimming the duet today.

"It's personal," I told her. "It has nothing to do with the show. Things just got ..." My eyes had a will of their own and they flickered toward Landon.

"What did he do?"

"He didn't do anything."

"No, he did something, and you're telling me what it is." She plopped down on the pool deck, effectively blocking any escape path.

"He asked me to prom, and I said no."

Her face was a mask of disbelief. "Why the hell did you do that?"

"I ... what?"

"Why say no?" She waved a hand toward the stands. "It's why he's hosting the show, and actually busting his ass to help out. Maybe Josh does it for the view, but that's not why Landon's here."

I stared at Constance, not daring to steal another look at Landon.

"You really don't see it, do you?" Constance asked, her voice losing some of its edge.

"I see other things." This time, I let my gaze wander to the stands where Sierra had successfully nudged Nissa all the way into the corner. The three of them—Nissa, Jodi, and Sierra—were talking to Matt and Dylan, or, judging by Josh's scowl, distracting them. Landon worked on the sound system as if he were alone, not raising his head, not speaking.

"I can't go to prom with Landon," I said at last.

"Can't," Constance echoed. "Funny, but that doesn't have the same ring as *don't want to*."

I shrugged.

"You sure?" she asked.

For a second time, I went with the highly articulate shrug.

"Well, okay. I'll drop it then. But you'd better stretch. I got Patti to push back duet practice. We're up in ten."

Crap.

———

DAD WAS SITTING on the front steps, under the light of the porch lamp, when I pulled the Jeep into the driveway. Under any circumstances, this greeting was not good. Tonight? I didn't have the strength for any kind of talk. Never mind the emotional lockjaw, I ached all over from the worst duet practice ever. Constance stayed silent about it, which made it that much worse.

Sure, Dad was all casual, leaning back against the cement landing, legs crossed at the ankle, but I knew better. I thought about various offensive maneuvers but decided on subterfuge. If I could dash inside and get something aromatic going on the stove, it might distract him. An army moved on its stomach, after all.

I made it to the landing when Dad grabbed my ankle.

"So," he said, still staring straight ahead. "I had an interesting talk with Mr. Scott before leaving work today."

"Oh."

"'Oh' is right," Dad said, but he let go of my ankle.

I glanced down at him. His brow was crinkled. He looked almost defeated, even. Not as bad as I'm sure I looked, but clearly Dad was out of his element. He sat up and rubbed his face.

"Jesus, princess, I don't know where to start."

Grounding? Yelling? Would you like the butane lighter?

None of the above? I sat next to him. The cold cement soaked through my jeans, reminding me I wasn't completely dry after my short time in the pool. We stayed like that, in the circle cast by the porch light. The air grew darker, crisper. I felt the chill against my eyes and blinked to warm them.

"Why don't you tell me what happened?" Dad said.

My mind whirled with so many things that had happened, I couldn't pinpoint which one he meant. Besides, the question felt rigged, almost like he'd started reading parenting magazines (highly unlikely) or had some fiery plans for the kitchen.

"Adele thought we should start there," he added.

Or option number three. Thank God for Grandma Adele.

I gave Dad the publicity chair story Landon had concocted, figuring he'd already heard that from Mr. Scott. Why complicate matters with the truth? Then I described my impromptu Shirt Shack survey and how I used the results to convince Mr. Scott to print our posters. The matching programs, I told Dad, totally Mr. Scott's idea.

"Well, you impressed Mr. Scott. I'm dying to know what you told him."

"Basically that his school discount program sucked, only I used more words."

Dad chuckled. "Want to know what Mr. Scott told me? Anytime you want to start up at Scott Industries, you have a job."

Oh. Joy.

"They have tuition reimbursement, for undergrad, too, you know."

Thanks, Dad, for that not-so-subtle hint. I knew all about Scott Industries and their tuition reimbursement program. He'd slaved away in night classes and weekend seminars to get his MBA. We used to sit at the kitchen table and do our homework together. So, yeah, consider me informed and unimpressed.

"Tired, princess?" Dad's expression changed from amused—and maybe even a little proud—to concerned. Despite the dim light, I could still see the furrows along his brow. "Or is there something else?"

The locker room mirror had told me that I wore today—or the last few hours of it—across my face.

"I had a bad day," I said.

"And...?"

"A boy asked me to prom."

I had to hand it to Dad. Not a single twitch or muscle spasm, but I felt his entire being shift from relaxed to high alert.

"I told him no," I added, after letting him sweat for a few seconds.

"Any particular reason why?"

"I ... a friend likes him."

"Oh, princess." He tugged me close, held me tight. "If I were a better dad, I'd know what to say right now."

"If I were a better daughter, you wouldn't have to say anything."

"Stop that." He pulled back, just enough to see my face. "You are the only daughter I could ever want." He hugged me again, fiercer this time. He smelled like Scott Industries, like spray starch and recycled air and twelve hours spent in white collar hell. I buried my face against his chest and whispered:

"I'm sorry." For what, exactly, I couldn't say. Maybe everything.

Dad on apologies: *Easier to ask for forgiveness than permission, princess.*

Words to live by.

————

UP IN MY ROOM, I reached under my pillow for my mom's journal. The any-soldier mail, the teapot, and all the rest stayed in the ammo crate, but I'd taken to rereading the poems when I couldn't sleep. I'd select one and work my way through it until I could recite it by heart, write the words in the air with my finger.

————

Stars and Stripes
February 1991

Stars and Stripes Forever

Master Sergeant Collier pulls
a folded newspaper article
from his wallet.

He sets it on the field table

on top of the operations order
I'm trying to write.

The newsprint blurs. It's like a lone
cloud has passed over the sun,
turning the entire desert gray.

I can feel the questions bloom
between us—how long has he had this—
where did he get it—has anyone else (like
the colonel) seen it?

But it's his one question to me
that I must answer, the one
he speaks out loud:

How do you do it?

The Stars and Stripes
January 5, 1991

First Lieutenant Elizabeth Grey is one of the new breed—a wife, a
mother, and a soldier currently deployed in support of Operation
Desert Shield. She has the same responsibilities and carries the
same weight as the men around her.
Absently, her hands come together, and Lieutenant Grey cradles a
phantom baby. "It's strange," she says. "Even with all this." She
hefts the rucksack on her back. "I still don't know what to do with
my arms."

MacKenna's Toy Box

Before MacKenna was born,
Paul built her a toy box.
He painted it too, in jungle
green and startling blue,
with monkeys, giraffes, lion cubs
and hippos.
I can see them now, all marching
around a tree with fronds
so long, they sweep the ground.

I keep that image of the box
in my mind. Everything about MacKenna
is in there.
I can remove those things, one by one,
examine them, inhale them, hold them close.

But I can also put everything back inside.
I can close the lid.
I can lock it tight.
And then I can write an operations order
that will take us into Iraq.

The only thing that doesn't fit
inside the box are all the questions,
like Ahmed's *where are your men?*
And Master Sergeant Collier's *how do you do it?*

Because no matter how much space there is
inside that box,
there isn't any room
for doubt.

Master Sergeant Collier: You know, ma'am, no one would've blamed you if you had stayed home.
(*I would have.*)
Me: Could I raise a daughter to do the right thing if I refused to?

When Master Sergeant Collier speaks
I wonder if he's heard me at all.
Or maybe he's heard me too well.

Master Sergeant Collier: I'm thinking Lieutenant Meyers is one hell of a lucky guy.
Me: No. I'm the lucky one.

My First Cup of Coffee

Master Sergeant Collier: How is it, ma'am?
Me: Now I know what heaven will taste like.
Master Sergeant Collier: Jesus, ma'am. It's not that good.

I can't find the words to explain
just how wrong he is
about that.

———

IT TOOK me forever to realize my mom was telling me a story. Okay, maybe not me, exactly. But I could feel the story building, not only in the words she put on the page, but the ones she didn't. Each poem had weight, like each time she wrote one, it cost her something.

But even as I thought it, part of me couldn't help but feel light. All these words. And they were mine now. It was like after all these years, my mom was able to tell me a bedtime story.

Chapter 11

I POSTED notes for Nissa on her Facebook page. She deleted them. I sent her private messages. She ignored them. All my calls went into voice mail, all my text messages to wherever unread texts go to die. I constructed a dozen scenarios for what Jodi could've told Nissa (and Sierra). Then I realized something.

This wasn't my fault. I had told Landon no. By Friday, I decided that acting like nothing had changed was the best strategy since nothing actually had. It was all rumors and gossip and none of it was true. I used this fact to navigate the cafeteria. It propelled me forward; it was my shield, my armor.

It was a really stupid reason to sit at the synchro table.

The mood at the table was glacial. I sat, pulled out my lunch, and tried to ignore the overly-loud crackle of aluminum foil. I leaned across Jodi like she wasn't there.

"Hey, I brought your favorite." I pushed the bundle filled with Grandma Adele's molasses spice cookies toward Nissa.

"I'm not eating sugar until swim season is over," she said, shoving the foil back at me.

A few cookies scattered. One skittered past my outstretched hand and plunged to the floor.

"I guess those Skittles are sugar-free then." I eyed the industrial size bag centered between them. Jodi froze mid-chew, shrugged, and popped another handful into her mouth.

I felt slightly ill at the thought of Grandma Adele's spice cookies crushed beneath the foot of some football player, but I didn't feel foolish. I just felt sad. I collected the cookies worth saving, tucked the rest of the food into my lunch bag, and stood. "I think I sat at the wrong table."

I was almost through the cafeteria door when I heard my name. Once, twice. Really loud. I turned to see Constance waving me over. Only when I reached her table did I hesitate. Outside of swimming, I never talked to her. One, she was a senior and I never saw her in class. Two ... well, she was Constance Radley. I'd be lying if I said she still didn't scare me a little.

"It's more comfortable if you sit," she said, pushing a chair out with a foot.

So I did.

Sam Avery and a couple of senior swim boys filled the rest of the spaces. Two had a pocket-sized Bible between them. Constance had a copy of *The Grapes of Wrath* open to the last page.

"Sam's trying to explain the symbolism to me," she said, "but he's having a hard time saying the word breast."

A flush traveled up Sam's face. Since he was still shaved bald from swimming at the state tournament, even his scalp turned pink.

For the rest of lunch, I pretended the glares from the synchro table didn't bother me. I pretended the synchro table didn't exist, or the techie table, for that matter, where Landon now sat. He'd elevated the status of the tech crew to a new kind of cool. So many people made a deliberate detour to that out-of-the-way space, I was surprised they hadn't worn a path into the linoleum.

"You know there's a name on that chair you're sitting on," Constance said a minute before the bell rang.

Okay, I admit it. I actually swiveled and craned my neck to peer at the back. Constance burst out laughing and gave me a *gotcha* look.

"It's yours," she said.

The bell rang.

"See you tomorrow at practice. Remember, we're swimming the duet early."

I nodded, but sat a second longer, letting the crowd thin. My chair. For the first time in days, something felt right. And I had to wonder: Did my mom feel like this when Master Sergeant Collier handed her that cup of coffee.

———

CLASS NUMBER SATURDAY was the single worst Saturday of the entire synchronized swim season. It was always in April; it always meant the show was right around the corner; it always reminded us how we were so not ready. It was also the day we lugged all the extra equipment—lane markers, starting blocks—into the storage bay.

There was an unwritten rule that only underclassmen did the grunt work. Even so, I worked with a group of freshmen to heave the lane markers through the double doors. I was already damp, already winded from practicing the duet. But, I was one of the few upperclassmen around. There'd been another party last night, but apparently Nissa no longer needed my Jeep to get to those.

I heaved a section of lane marker to the girl next to me. We laughed at the sweat running down our faces and watched as the lane markers snaked into coils and out of the way.

"Glad to see you could make it, girls." Patti's voice was cold enough to freeze the deep end all the way down to the concrete bottom.

I peered over my shoulder in time to see Nissa, Jodi, and Sierra slink into the pool area. They'd drenched themselves in the shower, but they weren't fooling anyone.

Landon chose this moment of ice to barge into the stands.

"Hey, sorry I'm late," he cried out. "I stopped for the posters and the programs. Take a look."

Josh manned the spotlight and was sweeping the beam in an experimental path across the water. He caught sight of Landon and trained the light on him just as the poster unfurled.

"What do you think?" Landon asked. "Personally, I think it's one of the better examples to come out of Scott Industries."

Kylie had fashioned a Hollywood red carpet premier with *The Dolphins Cinema Splash* in the marquee. It was 1940s glamorous. Up close the lines softened and wavered. If you stared long enough, you discovered what the picture really was: A close-up of an aquarium, complete with tropical fish.

"Nice job."

This was Constance. She stared not at the posters, but at me.

"He helped," I said.

"Don't sell yourself short." She eyed me, then Landon. "He isn't."

"I have to tell you," Landon was saying. "MacKenna's the reason we have posters and programs. She convinced my dad to revamp the school discount program, and she did such a good job, we got our print run for free."

"Free?" Patti choked out. She gave me an appreciative glance—the first look in ages that acknowledged my existence.

"In fact, the new discount program launches next Monday. My dad would like to include the poster." Landon gave the sheet a light shake. "In the portfolio of examples. With Kylie's permission, of course."

Kylie could've doubled for the spotlight, she glowed so much.

"But thank MacKenna," Landon added, "not me."

Okay, sure. We were the synchronized swimming team, but

how everyone else coordinated the simultaneous head swivel was beyond me. My cheeks heated under the scrutiny and for a crazed second, I wished I hadn't done anything at all.

"Publicity chair next year," Landon was saying, mostly to the air. "She's a natural." Like this particular cake needed the extra frosting.

Kylie inched closer, took the poster from Landon, and gazed at it. Then she glanced up and locked eyes with me.

"Thank you," she said.

"If there's any left over, will you autograph one for me?" I asked.

Her expression was guarded, like she was bracing for a cruel joke. "You're kidding."

I gave my head a shake so hard, my pigtails slapped my cheek. "When you're a famous artist, I'm going to sell it on eBay."

Kylie laughed, but she continued beaming. It seemed like such a small thing: Nice posters for the show. Normally, we'd print something up on colored poster board and call it done. But having a vision for the show—*our show*—*Cinema Splash*, was special. It was like the football team wearing their jerseys on game days, or the cheerleaders and their uniforms.

When Patti announced it was time to start the class numbers, Kylie invited me to sit with her, Kayla, and the other seniors. I hesitated, feeling oddly on edge. Nissa, Sierra, and Jodi threaded their way to the far end of the stands, once again positioning themselves by the spotlight and engaging in what was clearly the game of the week: breaking freshman boys' hearts. I wanted to say I belonged there, but couldn't get myself to even consider it. But defecting to the seniors? Alone?

"I'm not going if you're not," I whispered to Constance.

"Do I have to like it?"

"No," I said. "But you could try it."

She sat with the group—at the very, very edge. This togetherness thing? Maybe we could both get used to it.

We endured the freshmen's *Surrey with the Fringe on Top*. Patti stopped and started the number so many times, the rest of us in the stands had a week's worth of earworm. The sophomores struggled through *Stars and Stripes Forever* with a bit more finesse.

During their last run through, I pulled off my Dolphins hoodie and slipped over the tile wall. The juniors were doing *Greased Lightnin'*. The number was energetic, and fortunately, short. We planned to strut out in fake leather jackets and the deck work included plenty of hip thrusts. It was bound to be a jock pleaser.

I was on the pool deck, in a straddle stretch, when I heard someone say, "What's this deal with Landon?"

I craned my neck upward. Nissa hovered over me, hands on hips.

"What?" I said.

"What's going on with you and Landon?"

Now she wanted to talk about it? Five minutes before we were supposed to swim? This was crazy. She was crazy. And I was crazy for wanting to hear her out, despite everything.

"Because I know you," she continued, "and I don't think you did what he said you did."

My mouth went dry and what felt like a rock formed in my stomach. I pulled my legs to my chest and hugged my knees. So maybe Nissa was right. Normally, I didn't put myself out there. But now that I had, I saw that—sometimes—it was worth it. Even if it did have consequences.

"Landon helped me get the posters," I said. "I told you that. We worked together. End of story."

"So making him think you wanted to go to prom was just part of the plan?"

I blinked a couple of times. Was *that* the rumor going around? "I don't know what you're talking about."

"The rest of the school does. It's all over the place."

Obviously. "Funny, but I don't know what the rest of the school knows."

144

"That you used him, that you—" Nissa's voice cracked and she broke off.

Sierra and Jodi stood off to the side, not part of our conversation, but clearly within earshot of it. I still sat, knees curled into my chest, that imaginary rock still weighing me down. Slowly, I slipped my legs beneath me and stood, the damp tile unusually hard beneath my knees. Nissa didn't offer her hand to help me up.

"I'm thinking that a month ago, you would've believed me over the school." I nodded toward Sierra and Jodi. "You would've believed me over them."

The sophomore number ended, the music and lights cutting off at once. In the hushed dark, someone muttered, "Bitch."

And, of course, the word went everywhere. The lights went up and Patti gave us all a hard look, then said, "Juniors, places please. You're next."

We streamed along the pool deck and scrunched into the small opening just inside the doorway to the girls' locker room. We lined up by height, which put Nissa in front of me, Sierra behind, guaranteeing that the rest of swim season was going to be hell.

Nissa jerked backward and I stumbled into Sierra who struck my shoulder with the palm of one hand. Not hard, just bitchy. But I was already off balance. On the damp tile floor, my feet slid. I fell.

The first strains of *Greased Lightin'*—complete with revving engine—filtered through the locker room door. All the other girls filed out. No one bent down. No one helped me up. I staggered to my feet, pushed open the door, and hurried to catch up with all the strutting and hip thrusting going on. I needed to be in line before we dived into the water. We cascaded, one after the other, like they did in those old Esther Williams movies.

I slipped again, but caught up in time to dive in. We swam through a few formations and did some synchronized leg work, then went into the layout for the wagon wheel.

A wagon wheel wasn't something you'd see in competition, but was practically a team requirement if you had enough girls in a routine to pull it off. Each girl hooked her feet beneath the chin of the one in front of her, then the first girl in line dived backward, swam beneath and hooked up with the last girl in line. Then, it was circle time. The audience loved the stunt and it never failed to get applause.

It also never failed that sometime—during rehearsals or the actual show—someone got kicked in the face.

Sierra's feet gripped my chin. She squeezed hard enough I felt her toenails against my throat. We went around once, twice. At first, revolutions in a wagon wheel were a little scary. If you didn't break the surface, you snorted in water or waited for the next time around to breathe. And when the girl gripping your neck was trying to choke you with her feet? I stole what breath I could.

At last we broke the wheel and transitioned to the next stunt, more snappy arms and legs before we did a lift. Sierra frog kicked away, her foot crashing into my face.

A blur of bubbles blocked my vision. I lost my nose clip. Water burned the back of my throat, my lungs. I surfaced, blinked chlorine and tears from my eyes, and gulped air. Then, I smiled. Because that was what you did when someone nailed you in the face during a routine.

We pushed Jodi—the smallest—up and out of the water. The lift was our big finale. At the edge of the pool, the freshmen girls (who Patti had instructed to "watch carefully") clapped. So did Constance and a few seniors lounging in the stands.

I barely heard them. The lights went up and I dog paddled to the edge of the pool, under the shadow of the diving board. All I wanted was a space to choke out the water I'd inhaled. At the pool's edge, someone grabbed me and pulled me from the water. That someone plopped down on the deck and tugged me all the way into his lap.

Landon.

He smoothed the hair from my face. His fingers were like fire, my cheeks ice. I choked, coughed, possibly drooled. Water burned my lungs. Landon's fingertips burned my skin.

"Jesus," he said. "I can't believe you kept swimming."

"It's just." I coughed some more. Pleasant. Ladylike. Sexy. Not. "It's what you do."

"You kick each other in the face, too, I suppose."

"It was an accident."

"No," he said, slowly, "it wasn't."

No one purposely screwed up a routine. Not at the end of the day. No one would sabotage their own class number, make practice last that much longer. Not even Sierra Linden.

"I was sitting on the wall." He gestured toward the stands. "She looked back and made sure to kick you in the face."

I tried to push away, but he held on tight. "I'm soaking you," I said.

"I don't care."

"I—" The next words lodged in my sore throat. Bright red drops splattered on Landon's shirt sleeve. He wore a frayed oxford over the almost-but-not-quite-vintage Green Day concert Tee, his favorite, I guessed. Mine, too, and I didn't want to get it bloody. I swiped my nose, bringing away a handful of water and blood.

"You're bleeding." Landon shrugged off his shirt, wadded it up, and held the cloth beneath my nose, gently. He shifted slightly, his lips grazing my hair. Only then did I realize that everyone—the tech crew, the team—was staring at us.

Patti clambered over the tile divider and hurried across the pool deck, first aid kit clutched in one hand. Her voice was low and sweet. At first, I didn't understand her. At first, Landon wouldn't let me go.

"It's okay," Patti said more to him than me. "I need to make sure she isn't hurt, check for a concussion." She extracted me from Landon, although how—exactly—wasn't clear, and led me over to the stands.

"Go help Josh," she told Landon.

He refused to move, my playground—or poolside—savior, until I gave him a quick nod.

For the rest of practice, I sat next to Patti. My nose eventually stopped dripping blood. I winced with each check of my pupils from a tiny flashlight Patti had in the kit, and suffered a probing inspection of my nose.

This was the Patti I remembered. Team mom and best friend rolled into a strict—but usually cool—teacher. Part of me wanted to stay safe and secure in the stands and part of me wanted to run like crazy, away from all of this.

Patti gave me a cold pack for my nose and ordered me to stay in the stands for the rest of practice. I tried to catch Nissa's eye, but she never looked my way, not once, not even when Constance, and Kylie, and Kayla hopped the wall to check on me.

While the rest of the team swam, I thought about the Nissa everyone else didn't know, the one who was a whiz at chemistry because she created homemade makeup. The one who could take bargains from Target and Goodwill and turn them into something that looked like it came from the pages of *Vogue*. I missed the girl who always picked me over Sierra and Jodi. I missed the girl who'd seen Dad at his worst—and still liked us both.

WE WERE nine the year of the *Daring Daughters* campout. Even the name was beyond stupid. Just thinking the words heated my cheeks with shame. These days, I simply referred to it as the campout from hell, and Nissa would know what I was talking about.

Here's the thing: Dad had saved the campout. If not for him, we would have been soaked, starved, and stranded. He helped set up all the tents, pounded in stakes, then started the campfire. Plus he made a mean hot dog and awesome s'mores.

He marched us around—me, Nissa, Jodi, and Sierra—and called

cadence, put us "at ease," and said, "Smoke 'em if you got 'em," which made us giggle. Everyone wanted to be in our group, and Nissa called him "her dad for the weekend."

He was like a camping rock star.

We ate, because of Dad, and it was actually cooked through, too. At night, he'd crawl out of a warm sleeping bag to check on scary noises. When the ladle Sierra's mom was using snapped in half, Dad repaired it with duct tape, then made everyone laugh by tossing the roll in the air and saying, "It fixes everything."

Although later, when just the two of us gathered wood, he sighed heavily, thick branches in his arms, his gaze on the other adults around the campfire.

"Promise me something, princess."

"Sure, Daddy."

"Never be fucking useless."

In the morning, he made coffee in a press pot for all the other adults. They drank like he'd provided them with the elixir of life.

I don't know what changed, or rather, what Dad did. Did he let a swear word fly, or call another adult on some bullshit? Since this was Dad, both scenarios were possible. Or did someone overhear us in the woods? I remember he'd set us up with plastic laces to make lanyards. Sierra and Jodi scrambled for the pink, purple, and sky blue, but Dad pulled out a stash of silver just for Nissa. I wove black and yellow together, because it matched the Army Ranger T-shirt Dad wore with old BDU cutoffs.

When I finished, I couldn't wait to give it to him. I ran around the campsite until I found him at the fire pit, feeding the coals more wood. I skidded to a halt just as Sierra's father stepped into the circle.

"Hey," Sierra's father said, "war hero."

The words sounded right, but the tone was all wrong. This was a man I'd seen gulp down three cups of Dad's coffee just that morning, slap him on the back, and tell him he was a life saver.

Dad glanced up, took in both me and the man. I held out my lanyard.

"Thanks, princess." He took it and tucked it into his pocket. "Why don't you go make one for Grandma Adele?"

I nodded, still not understanding. Arms crossed over his chest, Sierra's father stared at Dad. I think it must've been some sort of ultimatum, but about what, I never knew.

That night, rain beat against our tent, the noise quick and fierce, like frying bacon. Lightning brightened the dark canvas, then thunder rumbled the earth. Somehow, Dad slept through all this. Only when the storm had passed, only when soft drops plunked against the tent sides, did he sit up.

He sat up and shouted, his voice filling our little tent. At first, one word reached me: *Fire.* I jerked around, not smelling smoke, not seeing flames. Only damp air, wet ground, and the freshness after rain.

"On the roof!" Dad thrashed, fought his sleeping bag, kicking, punching. "He's on the roof!"

While Dad fought the war in his sleep, I peered through the tent flaps, certain another adult would come. They knew we needed help. Any moment, I thought. Any moment.

No one came.

Except Nissa. She huddled in a red rain slicker with big yellow smiley faces on it, stood right outside the tent door. I gave her hand a quick squeeze then went back to Dad.

"Daddy!" I cried, over and over again, trying to wake him. "Daddy, you're dreaming. Wake up."

When I think back on it, how loud he was, how loud I was, my face soaked with tears, I still can't believe no one but Nissa heard us. I eased close to Dad, low to the ground, cautious.

"Daddy? It's me. MacKenna."

Dad threw an arm out. I know he didn't hear me. I know he didn't see me. His knuckles caught my cheekbone. The impact stung, launched me toward the ground. I sat there, smearing my face with tears and mud. All I could do was watch him. I knew wherever he was, I didn't exist, wasn't a part of that reality. Strange thing was, no matter how much my cheek ached, that was what hurt most of all.

I crawled to the tent flap and peered through. Nissa was still there. She took my hand, squeezed it, and stayed until Dad settled into uneasy mutterings. I climbed back into my sleeping bag, but if I slept I don't remember. In the morning, when Dad saw my face, he blanched.

"Princess? What happened?"

"I don't know." I shook my head, then shrugged, to prove I really didn't. "A tree branch?"

He knelt in front of me, probed the bruise with his thumb. I winced, but didn't pull away. "You'd tell me if something happened," he said. "Right?"

I nodded.

Later that night, we headed over to Grandma Adele's for a welcome home dinner. We were finishing up dessert when the group leader called. The ice cream was melting in my dish, but I couldn't take another bite. No one had to tell me that the troop leader calling during dinner, and calling Grandma Adele, was weird.

She stood next to the stove, phone pressed to her ear, her eyes flitting from Dad to me and back again. The high pitch of quick, panicked sentences filtered through the receiver, but I caught no meaning behind the noise.

"Of course. Yes, I see." She pursed her lips; her expression hardened. "Well, can I say that you're not only making a mistake, but your … understanding, not to mention compassion, is severely lacking." With that, Grandma Adele hung up.

Dad and I both stared at her.

She sighed. "It seems the group appreciated your help on the campout," she said to Dad, "but no longer wants you on the roster of parent leaders."

"What the fuck?"

"Paul—"

Dad held up a hand, warding off the lecture. "Sorry, princess," he said to me.

Yeah. Like I hadn't heard Dad swear before.

"Did they say why? I mean—" He looked lost. This was territory he couldn't navigate, not even with a compass. "—I don't get it."

"Neither do I." As truthful as Grandma Adele was, this sounded like a lie.

"Well, if they don't want Dad," I declared, "I don't want them." Who cared about *Daring Daughters* anyway?

Dad rubbed the stubble on his jaw. He hadn't touched his ice cream either, and we now had two bowls of sweet chocolate soup. "Princess, you sure?"

I thought about Sierra's father, the sneer when he said *war hero*, how it sounded worse than the swear words Dad used. How no one came to help us in the middle of the night. I thought about how they swilled Dad's coffee, let him put up tents and build fires, and how they didn't even bother to thank him.

"I'm sure," I said.

"Well, we could still go camping. Would you like that?"

I nodded.

"Nissa can come along, plus, this way." The spark returned to Dad's eye. "We can take Grandma Adele."

"Oh, no." She marched toward the table, a woman on a mission. She grabbed both bowls of melted ice cream and headed for the sink. "Grandma Adele goes nowhere without indoor plumbing—or air conditioning."

But she did. She cooked on a camp stove, made our popup camper cozy, and played endless rounds of crazy eights with me and Nissa when it rained. Dad did all the heavy lifting and slept too soundly at night to dream.

I thought by the start of school in September, no one would

even remember the campout, never mind mention it. Then I saw Sierra Linden on the playground, her gestures contorted, spastic, shouting, "He's on the roof!"

I rushed forward and broke through the crowd, Landon right behind me. I'd told him about Dad and the campout, of course, and we swore to keep the secret to ourselves.

I cocked my arm back, all set to knock Sierra to the ground. Maybe I'd hit her twice, once for me, and once for Dad. Nissa grabbed my wrist. Landon threw his arms around my waist. I strained against them, then a thought made me go boneless. I sagged against Landon's arms, barely able to hold myself upright.

In a flash, I saw the consequences—the principal's office, the phone call, explaining why I'd hit Sierra in the first place. But the worst of it? Explaining how, while dreaming, my own father had hit me. No one would understand he didn't mean to and didn't even know he had. So I walked away, let Sierra Linden call me names, call Dad names. Those were consequences I could live with.

———

AS I SAT and watched everyone swim, I wasn't sure about the consequences anymore. I shivered, wondering if that was shock, because every time I trembled, Patti twisted around to check on me. Applause drowned out the final strains of *Singing in the Rain*. The senior number was usually one of the best in the show, and this one, choreographed by Constance, was exceptional.

I waited until everyone had filed into the locker room. Truthfully, I waited for Nissa. She vanished through the door without looking back.

I stood, my legs shaky, and was about to hoist myself over the tile wall when Patti said my name. Her voice was quiet, the tone like something I wanted to call motherly.

"Can we talk?" she asked.

I nodded and sat back down.

"It's about your essay," she said but closed her eyes. She clenched her hands together, not exactly like she was praying, but pretty close. "Actually, it's about your mother."

I didn't dare move, breathe, or speak.

"We were friends in high school."

"I know," I said, "I have her yearbooks. My Grandma Adele gave them to me a few years ago."

Patti's expression went from somber to a mixture of amused and mortified. "Oh, good Lord, the yearbooks! I can't even imagine what I wrote. Wait—" She held up a hand. "I can imagine and I don't want to remember."

I'd read every last inscription in my mom's yearbooks and Patti's confused me the most. All in-jokes and shorthand, like the emails and texts Nissa and I sent (or used to send) to each other. You'd have to be one of us to decipher it.

"It's been a long time." Patti's smile was the best thing I'd seen in days. She looked less frazzled, more like her team-mom self. "As I was saying, your mom and I were friends. When I saw that you wanted to join the Army." She broke off and in the quiet pool area, her sigh traveled across the water. "It upset me."

I got it. I mean, after all, it upset Dad, right? That didn't stop me from wanting it, and despite Patti's refusal to help, I'd been chipping away at the essay, a word here, a sentence there.

"But it wasn't fair to take it out on you." She studied me as if through me, she could somehow reach my mom. "I'm thinking this isn't a whim, that it means something to you."

"It does," I said.

"Now, I try to keep my personal politics and beliefs out of the classroom, but you know I'm a pacifist, right?"

"So's my Grandma Adele."

Patti actually laughed. "In which case, I might not be the expert help you're looking for."

I needed help finessing words, not with the content. "I think you can help me. I know what I want to write, just not the how." A thought struck me then, fast and hard. My mom had paid for college with an ROTC scholarship, and Patti might know something about that. "You wouldn't know what my mom wrote, would you?"

"No. Beth kept some things to herself."

Like the poetry? I wondered if Patti knew about that.

"She did send me your birth announcement."

My entire body went on high alert. I stared at Patti, willing her to say more.

"I brought it in ... I mean, would you like to see it?" She gave me a sheepish smile. "Consider it a peace offering."

I nodded in what I hoped wasn't a crazed manner and inched closer. Patti rummaged in her tote and pulled out a folder. From inside, she removed a card that had a border of green and white stripes. In the center was a photograph, a scrunched up baby face, a tiny fist, with my date of birth and full name in silver script.

"I remember Beth telling me that you were a fighter, someone who wasn't going to take the crap that this world can dish out. Maybe that's something a mother knows, because I think she was right."

I didn't feel like that girl. "Thank you," I said, my voice clogged. "For everything."

"My pleasure. Now why don't you go get dressed and get a hot meal into you. Send me your essay any time. No promises I can help, but I'll take a look. You have my email?"

"Swim team roster," I reminded her.

I thanked her again. Whether she realized it or not, she'd given me so much more than I'd ever hoped for. A piece of my mom, a piece of her that only Patti knew.

I followed Patti from the pool, opting to take the long way around to the locker room. I padded down the hall, my toes cold against the linoleum. The locker room door thumped behind me, nearly silent.

At first, all I heard was Nissa's voice, her words garbled, like she was speaking a foreign language. And like a foreign language that you've maybe studied for a semester, I started picking out words I understood: *Landon, MacKenna, hate*.

I stood and listened like my life depended on it.

Chapter 12

THIS WASN'T A CONVERSATION I should overhear, but my feet—like solid ice against the floor—refused to move. A quick, hot sweat washed over the rest of me. Chlorine prickled against my skin, and I fought the urge to vomit.

I could see the first bank of lockers to the left, a flutter of shirts and jeans, doors opening and closing. To the right, I caught a glimpse of Jodi next to the entrance to the showers. She glanced backward from time to time, peering into the space, standing guard for when I came in from the pool.

I almost hated to disappoint her.

A crash shook the second row of lockers. A muffled sob. And then, "I hate him."

The flutter of clothes died as girls clutched jeans or a hoodies to their chests. Jodi looked on wide-eyed. No one else moved, afraid to let on they were eavesdropping on a pain so personal, it hurt to witness.

"I hate, hate, hate all guys. All of them. But most of all, I hate him."

My bedroom walls had absorbed those words a dozen times

over, every time some guy picked another girl over Nissa, every time no one asked her to a dance. A hallway diss, a bad party, and me always with the same refrain.

"Screw him. He isn't worth it. They deserve each other."

Only now, Sierra said those words to Nissa. I felt as though I'd walked into a very odd and very wrong alternate universe.

"It isn't fair. Even from the start, it wasn't fair. I met him first, but it was MacKenna he always wanted to play with, because MacKenna climbed trees, MacKenna could shoot a gun, MacKenna wasn't afraid of leeches." Nissa's tone went sing-song and snotty, almost like we were back in elementary school.

I remember telling her not to chase Landon. "Don't try to kiss him," I'd always say. "Boys don't like that."

Up until middle school, I'd been right, too. Then it seemed Nissa had all the answers about boys—at least temporary answers —because some of them did like to be chased and didn't mind when you kissed them. Except we never understood the rules to this new game, so it never lasted.

And she was right, at least, about the leeches. I was terrified of wasps, but after Dad poured salt on a leech stuck to my foot and I watched it shrivel up and die, I only felt sorry for them. It was like I'd done that to Nissa somehow, poured salt all over her dreams. Now I had no choice but to witness the aftermath.

"I was the one who friended him on Facebook," Nissa said, her flow of words unstoppable. "I wanted to welcome him back, but she wouldn't have anything to do with him. I'm never speaking to either of them again."

I swayed a little on my feet and realized I'd locked my knees. I bent them carefully, silently, and wriggled my toes. My muscles twitched from standing so still. My heart burned with shame and sorrow.

"What a bitch." Nissa fairly spat the sentence. "Did you know—?"

"Enough." Constance padded into view, her damp hair soaking

up the fluorescent light, the black strands taking on a greenish hue. Her gaze darted—briefly—toward me, but her stride remained smooth. "Why don't you consider not speaking *about* either of them? Trust me, it will make things a lot easier."

"Eff off, Radley." This was Sierra.

"Seriously," Constance continued. "This over-sharing with the whole school makes us all look pretty fucking unbalanced."

"Who cares?" Sierra said. "It's just us in here."

"Hello. The window." Constance paused just long enough for everyone to confirm that, yes, one of the upper windows was cracked open. "Boys' baseball also has Saturday practice. I'm sure they've enjoyed this emo-coaster ride you've been giving them."

As if on her command, the sound of sneakers scuffing against asphalt, along with a few rude remarks, floated into the locker room.

"Assholes," Constance muttered. "Like we don't have enough problems."

"Why don't you ..." Sierra began.

A few things happened then. Kylie caught my eye, her expression a mix of sympathy and horror. I decided that I really needed to go home, and to do that, I needed my clothes. But most of all, this needed to end. Not even Constance could do that, not at this point. But I could. So with a persistent buzzing in my ears, my mouth parched and foul tasting, I stepped all the way into the locker room.

Everything stopped.

Jodi's mouth hung open and she threw a quick look at the showers, as if she expected me to appear there as well. Sierra smirked like this made the whole emotional breakdown complete. I couldn't think of a time when I loathed her more.

Nissa ducked her head, turned toward her locker, and started shoving a soaked towel into a drawstring sports bag. I took a step forward, but Constance touched my shoulder and gave her head a shake.

"I think it's over," she said.

Maybe. But I couldn't abandon eleven years of friendship. The thought of it choked me. My nose still ached from where Sierra had kicked me. I pressed it gently and the shot of pain cleared my head enough that I could walk over to Nissa. It was like slogging through waist deep water. I perched on the bench next to her, gingerly, like I was approaching a feral animal. Nothing rash. No sudden movements, and everything would be okay.

"I don't know what I did," I said at last, quietly. The other girls could hear us, but I was going to make them work for it.

"That's the whole problem," Nissa said. "It's not something you can change. It's just the way you are and the way I'm not."

"There isn't anything to change," I insisted. "I'm not going out with Landon. He's not taking me to prom."

"Go. Don't go. It doesn't matter either way."

"Nissa." I reached out a hand, but like that feral animal, she scooted back, a fierceness about her.

"Constance is right." She closed her eyes for one long moment. I thought I might see tears because I felt them in my own eyes. But when she looked at me again, her eyes were dry, tinged red not from tears, but chlorine. "It's over."

"But—"

"Please." She punched a few toiletries into her bag, slammed her locker door, and spun the combination.

"I'm sorry," I said. My cheeks were damp and I didn't care who saw it. "I didn't mean—"

"You can't help who you are," she said. "And he can't help who he is." She slung her bag over her shoulder and headed for the locker room door. "And I can't help hating both of you for that."

I tracked her footfalls across the tile floor, while girls scurried back to their lockers, pretending they hadn't been eavesdropping. Sierra jab Jodi in the ribs and they both rushed through dressing and raced from the locker room.

I remained on the bench and sensed things slowly return to

normal around me. A splash of water in the sink, a toilet flush, giggles that didn't sound cruel. My muscles tightened, my feet went beyond icy. I still didn't move.

"Hey." Constance sat on the bench next to me. "You okay?"

I looked at her.

"Sorry, stupid question. Do you ...?" She trailed off.

I glanced at her again, because Constance always had an answer for everything.

"Did you know," she began again, "that I used to be jealous of you?"

"Me?"

"And Nissa. All three of you. You guys had something special, the sort of friendship only kids in mystery books have. So, yeah. I was jealous. I mean, what did I have?" She gave her shoulders a cavalier shrug. "Except attitude."

I almost laughed. "Maybe if we weren't so scared of you—"

Constance shook her head. "Naw, you three belonged together. But I wondered, even back then, which third wheel would fall off. You and Landon—"

I rubbed my face with my hands. "Don't."

"You and Landon," Constance said again. "Fill in that blank however you want. But right now? Come on."

She dragged me up by one arm and steered me toward my locker. I dressed without showering, and wondered idly if there was some sort of world's record for not showering after swim practice. We left the locker room together, the last two out.

In the lobby, she headed for the front doors. "Want a lift to the overflow lot?" she asked.

"No, it's not that far."

"See ya Monday, then."

"See ya," I echoed.

Halfway down the corridor, I realized, belatedly, that I should've thanked her.

———————

OUTSIDE, I inhaled the scent of warm, new grass, the earthy smell that comes from those first spring days when the ground soaks up the heat. I tried to rid my lungs of residual chlorine and closed my eyes against the bright light. When I opened my eyes, I saw a flame yellow Corvette in the overflow lot—and Landon. He leaned against my Jeep, arms folded over his chest, head tipped back as if to catch the full force of the afternoon sun.

I walked a slow, deliberate pace to my Jeep. When I was three steps from Landon, I let the backpack with all my swim stuff slip from my shoulder and into my hand. I dug in the side pocket for my keys.

Landon didn't move. "Boarding school," he said.

"What?"

"You asked where I'd been for the past five years. I was at an all-boys boarding school."

Oh. "I'm sorry."

"Yeah, so am I."

"I need." I jangled the keys at him.

"I don't think you should be driving."

"I'm fine," I said. "I don't have a broken nose or a head injury."

"I wasn't talking about that. I meant after."

After? As in the locker room?

"Tell me you don't hang out with the boys' baseball team."

"Wish I didn't, sometimes. Like today."

Oh, God. He'd heard it all. I could tell by the odd mix of pity and sorrow on his face. It was all out there, from Nissa's over-share to my pathetic attempts at fixing things.

"I'll drive you home," he said.

"It's been an awful day." I clutched my keys tighter. "I want to go home, I want to get there in my own car, and I want to be alone."

He pushed off the side of the Jeep and stepped forward. "I don't think you should be alone." He took another step. "I think you need someone." A third step. "And I think you need them right about now."

He'd close the space between us, and my feet refused to move even as my head screamed, *Run!* I went to suck in a gulp of air, then stopped, taking slow, shallow breaths instead, so Landon wouldn't see me panic.

"I'm sorry about today," he said. "I never thought things would get so ... crazy."

Honestly, neither did I, although in retrospect, maybe I should have. I needed to move, before things got even crazier. The air between us shimmered, our combined heat warming the space. I could get to my car now, I thought. Sidestep Landon, jump in, and peel out of the parking lot.

Except I wanted his warmth more.

"Are you ...?" He raised a hand, the move so tentative that I held still. His fingertips grazed my nose, my cheeks, my lips. I felt my eyelids flutter and my swim bag hit the ground. I concentrated on my breathing, as if the second he touched me, I'd forgotten how.

"Are you okay?" he said, voice so soft, so close, it felt like a caress.

Everything stilled around us. If cars drove past, I didn't hear them. If someone left school, I didn't see them. Landon's fingers came to rest on my lips. I closed my eyes, caught a hint of the boy I remembered, warm nutmeg and the sharp scent of sweat. Days on the playground, evenings at the park. Running fast and hard, not to escape, but because we were free.

"I'm fine," I whispered against his fingertips.

The warmth between us sparked without warning. His body met mine, and he kissed me then. Everything dropped away. I dropped away, my knees buckling. His arm caught me around the waist, his free hand cupped the back of my head. I slid my arms around his neck and had to trust he'd keep me standing.

He did.

When at last, he pulled away, sunspots danced before my eyes. I felt dizzy, and breathless, and like one of those silly girls on TV who go all limp just because some boy kisses them. Apparently there were physical consequences to kissing a boy—or maybe just the right one.

"Let me drive you home," he said.

That knocked the dizziness from me. My muscles stiffened and standing on my own was a possibility again. "I can drive myself," I declared. Sure, I *sounded* tough, but I still hadn't pulled away, so it probably lacked impact.

A grin bloomed across his face, slow and easy at first, until at last, the dimple appeared. "Okay, but you have to go to prom with me."

"I have to ... what?"

"Will you go to prom with me? Please? I've been thinking about this since seventh grade—"

Whoa. "Really? I don't remember you being so emo."

Landon threw his head back and laughed. "Okay, in seventh grade, I figured we'd just make fun of everyone else going to prom and then go play computer games." He shrugged. "Then, I got older."

"Will you tell me about—I mean, will you tell me what happened?" I didn't add five years ago. We both knew what I meant.

"I will, just not right now, okay?" He jerked his head as if shaking off the whole idea of it. "Enough drama for one day."

"Before prom," I told him. "You have to tell me before prom, or I won't go."

That dimple flashed again. "So that's a yes, right?"

It was. I couldn't change my mind, even if I wanted to. *You and Landon*, Constance had said. *Fill in that blank however you want.* So I did.

"Yes," I said. "I'll go to prom with you."

———

I SUPPOSE there are appropriate responses to accepting a prom invitation. Making out in the Black Earth High School overflow parking lot probably isn't one of them. And interrupting said make out session to fight? Not on the list either.

Yes, after all that, Landon still insisted on driving me home.

"Look, you got kicked in the face and in the stomach—figuratively speaking. I really don't think you're in any condition to drive."

He had a point. My head still swam and my legs had that unstable, wet noodle feel to them. "I don't want to leave my Jeep." It seemed so vulnerable sitting here alone. And while I didn't think Nissa would be vindictive, I had doubts about Sierra.

"I'll come back for it," he said. "Even if I have to walk."

I laughed at that and gave in.

Dad barely glanced up when the flame yellow Corvette pulled into our driveway. But his grip tightened on the rake handle, and the rake itself traveled the same path, once, twice, until I'm sure whatever he was trying to do to the lawn was beside the point. His jaw tensed; and I knew: This would not be easy.

Landon bounded around the car before I even had a chance to open my door. He helped me out, although I really didn't need it. Still, it was a good excuse to touch him, the sensation an intoxicating mix of old and new. His warmth, I remembered. Landon ran hot, always felt like he had a fever. Grandma Adele had stuck the thermometer in his ear countless times, only to stare at the readout, bemused.

"You're normal," she'd tell Landon.

"Oh, no you're not," I'd whispered. And we'd be off, Landon chasing me around the yard.

His touch felt so reassuringly the same and ... different. A little dangerous. A lot grown up. I wanted to spend at least an hour studying his hands, looking for the boy I remembered, figuring out where he'd changed.

But not with Dad standing over us, clutching what might be a lethal weapon.

"Hey, sir," Landon said. He went from close contact to putting an arm's length between us as we walked to where Dad stood in the center of the lawn. "I drove MacKenna home today. She got kicked in the face—"

"What?" The rake plopped to the ground and Dad launched himself forward.

"I'm okay," I said.

Dad was in full combat mode and I knew there was no stopping him. He clutched my chin, tilted my head upward, and commanded, "Open your eyes," when I squinted against the sunlight.

"Patti checked for a concussion." About a dozen times. "And I don't have any symptoms of a head injury."

Dad grunted, clearly unimpressed with Patti's first aid abilities. "Inside," he said.

We marched into the house. I thought Dad might shut the door in Landon's face, but he relented at the last moment. In the den, Dad settled me on the couch with an ice pack wrapped in a semi-clean kitchen towel. Then in half infantryman and half nerd mode, he began stage two of Operation MacKenna Head Injury.

He went online.

I closed my eyes, relaxed into the sofa cushions, muttering answers when Dad barked, "Nausea? What year were you born in?" And so on.

"Mayo Clinic," Landon said. "It's the best."

I opened my eyes enough to squint at Landon. For a moment, I thought he meant for Dad to drive me all the way to Rochester, which in itself might have been a sign of a head injury. When Dad's fingers clacked against the keyboard, I realized we were only traveling as far as the Mayo Clinic's website.

More questions followed, at which point both Dad and Landon came to some sort of agreement that didn't involve a hospital emergency room. Dad sat on the coffee table across from the couch, leaning forward, arms braced on his thighs.

"You okay, princess?"

"It was a rough day," I admitted.

He brushed a few strands of stiff, chlorine-encrusted hair from my forehead. "You might consider a shower."

I gave a short laugh.

"Hungry?" Dad asked.

All at once, I was starving, my body hollowed out from the day's events. I wanted to fill it with everything warm, spicy, and savory. "Orange chicken and Pad Thai," I said.

"I'll get it." Landon popped up, Corvette keys rattling.

Dad glanced at me, an eyebrow raised, a *we're talking about this* look on his face.

"That sounds great," I said over Dad's shoulder.

"Back in twenty."

Landon sprinted from the house. In the quiet that followed, Dad studied me.

"So," he said. "You and Landon?"

That seemed to be everyone's phrase for the day.

"Anything I should know?" he asked.

"You mean besides the fact we're going to prom?"

"Prom. Interesting." His words were bland, but I sensed a tension behind them. "Landon wouldn't be the same boy who asked you the other day, would he?"

I nodded.

"And the other girl?"

"Nissa." I squeezed my eyes shut as a single tear made a track down my cheek. Dad eased my clenched fists open and tucked a wad of tissues between my hands.

Dad on tissues: *If one helped, fifty could mend a broken heart.*

"It's been a while since we've seen Landon," Dad said. "He's not twelve anymore."

Oh, yeah. I sighed to myself. I'd noticed.

"People change, princes, and not always in a good way."

I gave him another nod and swallowed hard.

"And Nissa?"

I tried to explain, what I did, what I didn't do, how nothing worked, how despite everything, my best friend had slipped away from me. Dad handed me another wad of tissues.

"I'm sorry, princess," he said. "I'm sorry things didn't work out the way you wanted them to. And I'm really sorry I have to state the obvious here."

I peeked at him from behind a gauzy shield of blue Kleenex.

"Landon's done at least one favor for you, by my count. This is going to sound old fashioned, and I suppose it is, but when a girl has a rich boyfriend who does her favors, it has a way of coming back to bite her in the ass."

My brain hadn't made the *Landon = boyfriend* connection yet. Sure, he asked me to prom, but plenty of people went to prom and never spoke to each other again. Leave it to Dad to work out the rest of the relationship math.

"And he's spoiled," Dad continued, like he had a very long list he couldn't wait to recite, "and used to getting his way—"

"Landon's not like that," I said.

"I just don't want to see you hurt. And—" Dad coughed, although it sounded forced. "I want to make sure you're ... safe."

Blood rushed to my cheeks so fast, if I hadn't already been lying down, the force would've knocked me over. Not *the talk*, not after everything else that had happened today. We hadn't actually had the talk yet—that had been Grandma Adele's territory, which she'd tackled after plying me with half a dozen OMG, My Body's Changing type of books. That had been bad.

The talk with Dad?

Excruciating.

"Dad ..." I began.

He raised his hands. "I know, I know, princess. I just don't want to see you hurt in any way. Seriously, today?" He tapped his chest. "I thought I'd be making a trip to the ER along with you."

"I'm fine," I said for what felt like the hundredth time.

"In that case." Dad tugged one of my pigtails. "You want to wash off some of that chlorine before Landon gets back?"

———

I LOOKED ONLY MARGINALLY BETTER after my shower. My nose was swollen and dark circles gave me a raccoon-like mask that would only get worse before school on Monday. I went heavy on the scented shower gel, the matching lotion, and body spray, so at least I smelled better. Sort of.

I headed downstairs, the tang of promised orange chicken leading me to the kitchen, the sharp spiciness of Pad Thai hitting my lungs as I walked through the door. My stomach growled—loudly. I would've been embarrassed except the room was empty. So was the den. So was the entire house.

Only when I returned to the kitchen did I glance through to the mud room. The door to the garage was open, and I caught the barest hint of flame yellow. Barefoot, I picked my way across oil spots and crumbling asphalt.

My Jeep was parked behind Dad's Blazer, and I wondered how they'd managed that bit of magic. But front and center, taking most of the space in our driveway was the Corvette, the hood popped, Dad and Landon hovering over it like the engine was some grease-slicked newborn. It was another one of those alternate universe moments, this one more bizarre than horrible. Two guys, one muscle car, and presto, instant male bonding. Landon saw me first, his eyes meeting mine, his smile down-right evil. Dad turned from the car—briefly—and held out an arm.

When I reached his side, he wrapped that arm around my shoulder and squeezed. "Feel better?"

"I'm okay," I said.

"Good, good," he replied, a bit absently, his gaze focused again on the Corvette. "Have you seen this, princess?"

"Actually, I see it every day at school."

"Incredible," Dad said. "Vintage. And it's in awesome shape."

I'd never seen him gush before.

"Almost vintage," Landon said, his tone modest. "And it's in okay shape."

"Are you kidding?" Dad stood back and shook his head at the marvel that was Landon's car. "It's—it's—"

"It could use a good road workout," Landon said. "I've been busy with the swim show and haven't had the chance." He pulled the keys from his pocket. "Want to take it for a spin, sir?"

The keys struck Dad's chest and he caught them one handed. I watched his gaze flicker between me and the Corvette.

"I don't have a head injury," I told him, "so you wouldn't be an awful dad if you drove it around the block."

He was dying to, I could tell. He kissed my non-injured head and let out a whoop. Honestly, he was a big kid sometimes. Landon shut the hood and Dad had the Corvette backed up and in the road faster than was probably legal.

In the haze of exhaust, I said, "I hope the cops don't stop him."

"It made him happy, didn't it?" Landon circled his arms around my waist, pulled my back against his chest, and nestled his chin on my shoulder. I felt complete, like after all this time, this was exactly what was missing.

"It did." I sighed. "Maybe too much. He … he isn't always so —" Reckless? Weird? Alternating between hard-ass Dad and a sixteen-year-old with his dream car?

"He'll be fine," Landon said. "Plus, this does wonders for me. I'm still the entitled, rich brat, but now I'm one with a little street cred."

I spun in Landon's arms. "Oh, God, he didn't say anything, did he?"

He laughed. "It's dripping off him. I can't believe he left us alone."

Actually, now that he mentioned it, neither could I.

"So, that gives us what?" Landon grinned down at me. "Twenty minutes?"

"Fifteen," I said. "If we're lucky."

"So? What do you want to do?"

Chapter 13

WHO SUGGESTED IT, I couldn't say, but I think Landon must have. We left the food and plates scattered on the table, easy enough to pick up and start serving when Dad walked through the front door, which I locked.

We crept down the hall, Landon's fingers threaded through mine, both of us in stealth mode, although with Dad gone, it was silly and unnecessary. But it was a reprise of years before, when we sneaked down another hall, in another house. Once we reached the bedroom, I tugged him inside, flicked on the light, but kept the door open a crack.

The bottom drawer of the nightstand held what we wanted—or so I thought. It'd been a while since I'd gone on one of these raids. I knelt, eased the drawer open, and did a quick scan of the contents. Disturb nothing. That was the first rule. I'd learned that the hard way when I was ten.

The drawer was filled with junk. A Leatherman utility knife. A sweater. An old flash drive. Some floss, because apparently Dad believed people had dental emergencies in bed. I unfolded the sweater, an old Army one, one far too small for Dad, one with the initials *EG* inked on the label. There, tucked inside the olive-drab green wool, was a silver picture frame, the sort that unfolded to reveal two photographs.

The photo on the right had been taken a short time after I was born. In a hospital bed, propped up by pillows, my mom held me. Dad leaned over her, looked as though he meant to kiss both of us at once.

"Did you ever figure out what this is?" Landon pointed to the other photo.

Dad wore his dress blue uniform, my mom, something strapless and white, and considering this was the late 80s, incredibly simple and elegant. No Princess Diana sleeves for her. They both looked too young. They both held the most essential of GI items. "It's a dog tag exchange," I explained to Landon. "They're trading Army ID tags."

"That's a tradition I haven't heard of."

"I don't know if it really is one."

"So, did you ever … I mean, do you have her dog tags now?"

"No." I'd searched the ammo crate, a couple times over, in case my mom had hidden a tag in there, or one had lodged between the slats, even as I knew how futile the search was. I never dared ask, not Grandma Adele, and especially not Dad, but oh, how I wanted one.

"You look like her, you know," he said, "That's why I wanted to … I mean, now that you're older, I can really see it. The hair and eyes, those are your dad's. But here." He drew the back of his fingers along my cheekbone, his touch so light, I hardly felt it. "And here." He blazed another trail along my jawline and lips. "That's your mom. For what it's worth."

A lot. He had no idea how much. I wanted to tell him that, but couldn't. All I could do was shake my head, try to shake his touch from my skin and the tumbled and confused thoughts from my mind.

"You guys don't talk about her," he said, as if reading those thoughts.

"Things got worse after the second Iraq war started."

Landon cupped my shoulders and I leaned into his chest, resting my head against his heart, letting its beat reassure me.

"We better get back," he whispered. But his mouth inched toward mine. "Your dad will be home soon."

My eyelids fluttered. I wondered how the boy whose arm I used to sock on a regular basis could make me go knock-kneed and mute. At some point, after an intense kiss, the silver frame wedged between us, Landon said, "I really don't want to get caught making out in your dad's bedroom. I value my life more than that."

I laughed, pulled away long enough to tuck the frame carefully among the junk in the drawer. We laced fingers and hurried to the kitchen. We were scooping rice onto plates when Dad's key scraped against the lock of the front door.

———

DESPITE THE ENDLESS DAY, I was too antsy to sleep once Landon left for the night. But since Dad's expression wavered between *How cute—MacKenna has a boyfriend* and *We really need to talk about this*, I made my escape upstairs.

Prom. I heaved a sigh. It was something you'd totally tell your mom about. I had no idea if my mom was clothes obsessed or not. But seeing the wedding photo today reminded me that she could pick a dress. It was a side of her I'd never see in the journal. That didn't stop my hand from feeling around under the pillow and pulling it out.

———

The List
February 1991

175

The List

Cull the battalion is the official order.
How do you tell someone they're not
going to war?
It's harder than you think, harder,
possibly, than telling them they are.

It's telling them they're not good enough,
not soldier enough. They didn't make
the cut.

You can tell them it's logistics.
You can tell them that thirty
Kuwaiti linguists mean
thirty American soldiers
stay in Saudi Arabia,
at Log Base Echo.

And those thirty American soldiers can tell you
it's bullshit.

Cull the battalion.

Yesterday, Captain Redding gave me the list
of all our soldiers going into Iraq.
My name isn't on it.

The Temperature of Told You So

Felicia stands behind me in line,
her *I told you so* hot against
the back of my neck.
Hotter than the desert sun.

Hotter than my shame.
Told you he's a chauvinist pig.

I played the game of bros before hos
in this strange world where I am both
and neither.
I played the game and lost.

Felicia steps in front of me, stealing
my place in line—and I let her.
Because she is going forward. Into Iraq.
And I am not.

In Which I Exchange Words With A Chauvinist Pig

I'm working in the TOC—while I still have a job
to do—when a heavy hand lands on the back
of my chair, one that makes the legs
sink into the sand.

Only Master Sergeant Collier can anchor a chair like that.
Only Master Sergeant Collier would dare to, with an officer
sitting in one.

Master Sergeant Collier: You listening to RUMINT again,
ma'am?
Me: Never do. What I need is in this operations order.
Master Sergeant Collier: Not all of it.
Me: Like what?
Master Sergeant Collier: Your name.

In Which Master Sergeant Collier Says Most of the Words

Master Sergeant Collier: There was never any question, ma'am, about you going, so Captain Redding never told you. Same way his right arm isn't on the list.

Me: Was I supposed to read his mind?

Master Sergeant Collier: Yes, but there wasn't time to send you to training for that ... ma'am, I won't lie. Before you got here, the section worked. I think we did a pretty damn good job, too. But now? With You? We do it better. You're our glue.

Me: So I went from new to glue?

Master Sergeant Collier: What do you know. The LT's a poet.

In Which I say Three Words to Master Sergeant Collier

Master Sergeant Collier: Ma'am, there's no way I'm going forward without you, but if we get into the shit, I want you to stick by me. I'll get us out alive if I can. But if I can't ...

Master Sergeant Collier doesn't waste things.
Not food
Not ammunition.
Not the slightest gesture.
When his hand touches his pistol, I know what he means.
I know he deserves an answer.

Me: Sergeant? Don't miss.

———

CHOOSING SIDES ALWAYS HAD CONSEQUENCES. For me. For my mom. I could see that so clearly now, could see her standing in the desert with Master Sergeant Collier agreeing to *what*, I wasn't quite sure. Some sort of pact? I held the journal against my chest, my heart beating so hard, I could feel the thump of it through the cover. I wondered how something so small could contain so many landmines. Was this it, or were there more?

And if there were, would I be able to take it?

———

LUNCH ON MONDAY sent me into overdrive. Actually, I'd been in overdrive since homeroom, or more accurately, since Landon texted me:

See ya at lunch?

And I'd replied with:

Yes.

Why lunch should feel any different than making out in the Black Earth High overflow lot, I didn't know. But it did. I wasn't hungry. My mouth was dry, but I couldn't drink. I approached the table where Constance and the swim boys sat, caught Landon's eye at the techie table, and the resulting flash of dimple melted away the jitters.

Even so, my hands still shook. I was filled with anticipation, like it was Christmas, or my birthday. Landon scooted his chair next to mine and proceeded to combine our lunches like we used to do back in grade school.

"I see," Constance said around a bite of raw carrot, "that you've filled in the blank."

I shrugged, but I'm pretty sure my smile gave me away. My cheeks hurt from the strain of it.

"I'm going to be cool at practice," Landon announced, handing me some dried mangos.

I thought about that for a moment and said, "You're always cool."

Constance made a gagging noise, the disgust plain on her face. "Please, the rest of us are trying to eat."

"No, I mean." Landon opened his thermal lunch sack and peered inside, as if the words he needed were stashed in there. "I'm going to be ... cool. You know, not—"

"He's not going to pull you from the water and let you bleed all over him," Constance said.

"Professional?" I suggested.

"Yeah. That. I'm going to be totally professional. No one will even know we're going to prom."

"Oh, you're kidding me." Constance cast him a look so disdainful, I nearly choked on the mango. "Just so you know." She turned to me now. "I don't do dress shopping, so don't even ask."

"You need a dress!" Landon said, too loudly. A few of the tech boys glanced over, eyebrows raised. "Sunday," he added. "We'll drive up to the Mall of America."

"I can get something in town." A road trip sounded like overkill. Plus it reminded me of the one Nissa wanted to take. I missed her so much. Maybe my mom was better off without Lieutenant Felicia Stover, but was I better off without Nissa? I didn't think so.

"Tell her," Landon said to Constance.

Just then, Josh waved an arm over his head, clearly trying to get Landon's attention.

"I'm being hailed." Landon left, letting Constance, of all people, to explain the necessities of proper prom-ware to me.

"You can't buy one around here." She pried open a package of all-natural, organic mush and proceeded to spread it across some rice crackers. "If you're going to prom, at least do it right." She cast a glance toward Landon. "He may be annoying, but he's got a hot car. Enjoy it."

Sam Avery, who sat to her left looked befuddled, but whether it was from her statement, or the odd lunch she was concocting, I couldn't tell. He looked like he might say something, but a scrape of chairs stopped the conversation. The table rocked and we had three new arrivals: Jodi, Sierra, and Nissa.

"Hi!" Sierra sang, giving the word at least two syllables.

"Leave," Constance growled.

Sam put a hand on her arm, but she shook her head. "There's no sense in being nice to some people," she told him. "Trust me."

"Con," Sam said. "You haven't even given them a chance."

"Yes." Sierra cocked her head, her blond hair swaying. "You haven't even given us a chance, and we're just concerned about MacKenna and all."

My insides froze at this. I thought about pushing back my chair, maybe joining the techie table, or just making a dash for the girls' bathroom, but couldn't move.

"How's your dad doing?" Sierra leaned forward, hands clasped together. She looked so sincere, but then so did a cobra before it pounced on its prey. "I hope he got the professional help he desperately needs. You read so many things these days about how veterans just—"

"Shut the fuck up." Constance's voice was low, but we all heard her.

"But I was just—" Sierra began, then stopped and rummaged around in her bag. "I printed a few things off last night, about post-traumatic stress." She tried to pass the papers across the table, but I refused to take them.

Constance, on the other hand, had no problem snatching them from Sierra, wadding the paper into a ball, and throwing it back at her. The paper ball bounced off Jodi's head and into the path of some oncoming jocks. A Nike connected with the crumpled paper and it went shooting across the cafeteria. I tracked the trajectory until I lost sight of it in the combined forest of human and table legs.

"Really, Constance," Sam said. In his eyes, I caught the hint of both disapproval and surprise. "She's just concerned."

"She's just a bitch." Constance sighed, heavily. "Sometimes I really hate my own gender."

"That's not what I heard." Sierra said it in a near whisper, only meant for Constance and, of course, me.

But a flash of pink washed across Sam's cheeks. He moved to stand, but Constance calmed him with a deft hand to his arm. "Please. Like I care," she told him. "She's the only one here who thinks it's an insult."

A strange quiet settled on the table. Around us, chatter rose and fell, odd snatches of conversation floated into my ears, all of it disconnected. Sierra had blindsided me. I sat, mute and stupid. Once, long ago, I'd tried to explain dad to the kids at school. Worse, I'd tried to explain him to Sierra. Even back then, she was the sort of girl who could take your words, twist them into something ugly, then spit them back at you, while making everyone else think you'd said them that way to begin with. I had no words to give her now. I wondered if that was worse, to go down without a fight.

Landon returned, scooting his chair across the cafeteria floor. He crashed into the table with so much noise and joy the rest of us flinched. His gaze went from me, to Constance, then darting across to Nissa, Jodi, and Sierra in quick succession. I heard him swear under his breath.

He leaned forward, just slightly, just enough to put an arm around the back of my chair. Nissa glanced up at that. For a moment, it was like the rest of the table wasn't even there, the rest of the school, that too, was gone. Just the three of us sorting things out without ever speaking.

Nissa broke the spell by standing, her movement so quick, her chair shot from behind her. She gave everyone a final, disgusted look and left. She walked across the cafeteria and sat down at the synchro table. Sierra and Jodi exchanged glances and followed, also without saying a word.

"It's a beautiful day," Landon said, his voice making the rest of us jump. "Want to sit outside?"

I did. I wanted to escape. I wanted to be far away when that wadded up bunch of papers came flying back over the cafeteria. On our way out, though, I stole a look over my shoulder at the synchro table. Something about the whole thing made me wonder. I'd seen the disgusted look on Nissa's face, but I hadn't felt it. In fact, it hadn't been aimed at me—or Landon—at all.

I wondered just how miserable you had to be to hang out with people you didn't even like.

———

TRUE TO HIS WORD, Landon was cool at practice. Before anyone dipped a toe into the water, he queued up a new playlist, dug around on his platform stage for the wireless mic, and sang along. His falsetto rippled across the water while he hammered his way through Rhiannon's *My Umbrella*. During the Righteous Brothers' *You've Lost That Loving Feeling*, he got down on his knees and serenaded Constance. That lasted for as long as it took her to cuff him upside the head.

"So, tell me, soldier girl, what do you call this?" she said to me, after escaping Landon's undying devotion. "A diversionary tactic?"

He'd moved on to some boy band tune and urged the freshman girls to clap along. They only blushed, shook their heads, and giggled behind their hands, all of them in the throes of a major crush.

"I guess," I said to Constance. Honestly, I wasn't sure what he was doing, but considering everyone was grinning, and no one was throwing me nasty looks, I didn't care.

Plus, Josh had been right. Landon could sing. Voice, talent, no shame. "Why isn't he in the spring musical?" I asked no one in particular, but Constance answered.

"Do we really need to go over that again?"

The music stopped but Landon looked downright devilish. God, I knew that expression, the naughty ten year old about to do something very inappropriate. And he did. He let his cargo pants drop to the pool deck. A moment later, he pulled his T-shirt over his head. The resulting squeal was like nothing I've heard outside a rock concert. He was, fortunately, wearing a pair of blue and orange swim trunks, the colors so obnoxious they made my eyes hurt.

"You have to admit," Constance said, "the boy knows his audience."

I caught the hint of admiration in her tone—not that I'd ever call her on it. Landon pestered Kayla and Kylie into the pool and insisted they teach him how to do a ballet leg.

"Patti's going to love this," Constance observed.

I glanced toward the stands where Patti stood, looking as though she'd just arrived, the air of the classroom still clinging to her. But she had a hand clamped to her mouth, her eyes lit with amusement. Maybe after Saturday's emo-coaster ride, we all needed a break.

And I realized that after today, this would be all anyone would, or could, talk about. At least ten girls had their camera phones out. By the end of practice, Landon's swim routine would be all over YouTube and Facebook. How could I not adore someone willing to humiliate himself for me—and do such a thorough job of it too?

He floated past, Kayla on one side showing him how to scull. Landon winked at me, but I barely saw it. What I focused on was his chest, not the lean pecs, although they didn't go unnoticed, but the scar near his left shoulder.

A scar. One that hadn't been there five years ago.

For a second, a wave of dizziness swept over me. Scars, I knew. Scars, I understood. Dad had one, a neat little scar on his left shoulder, above his heart, and an angry, ragged one from the exit wound on his back.

Landon laughed and joked with the twins. Couldn't they see it? I wondered. Didn't they notice? Landon Scott had a scar. I didn't know what it meant except that it was part of the whole mystery of why he'd vanished.

"Hey." Constance touched my shoulder, her voice low.

"You okay?"

"I'm ... I'm going to sit down," I said. I staggered toward the stands and somehow managed to pull myself over. There, I collapsed on the bench.

"MacKenna, honey, you okay?" This was Patti, right next to me. Yes, with the first aid kit. She was already reaching in to pull out the flashlight.

I rolled my eyes and she laughed.

"I suppose your dad's been checking?"

"All. Weekend. Long," I said, giving each word emphasis. "I just didn't eat a lot at lunch."

Patti nodded. "Oh, I meant to ask in class. Your essay. Have you finished a draft yet?"

"Almost," I said.

"Send it and we'll talk about it this weekend. Sunday maybe?"

I nodded, but my sigh betrayed my true feelings.

"Sit out for a bit and rest," she told me. "I need to get Landon out of the water and everyone else into it."

Grateful, I slid from the bench and sat with my back against the tile wall, hidden, alone, my thoughts filled with scars—Landon's and Dad's.

I don't remember much before I was three, but what I do remember revolves around Dad, a tattoo, and a scar. In fact, my sharpest, earliest memory was the first time I saw Dad after he came home from Somalia.

There were no parades, no yellow ribbons, no rushing across the tarmac to greet him. I don't even remember the drive to the hospital. Someone—oddly, not Grandma Adele—lifted me under the arms and perched me on the hospital bed. Dad sat, propped up by pillows, his shoulder wrapped in gauzy white. He didn't wear a hospital gown, so his other arm, the uninjured one, was bare.

Back then, I didn't know what a tattoo was. The inked barbs on his arm looked so sharp, I thought that they must hurt to touch. But right then, on the hospital bed, I needed to touch a single barb.

If the tattoo was real, then so was my daddy. At three, I knew that much.

The sheets felt cold against my palms, the bed too hard, but his skin was warm. I smiled up at him, feeling both happy and proud that I'd figured it all out on my own—this was my real daddy. Except. He looked sad.

"What's wrong, Daddy?"

"Nothing, princess. Absolutely nothing."

I touched the tattoo again. "What's this?" Now that he was home, now that he was real, I wanted a name to go with the twisted, pointed strands that circled his arm.

"That, princess, is what they call a mistake."

The room erupted with laughter and camera flashes. The picture the newspaper photographer took ran with the caption: *Hometown Hero Returns.*

Dad wasn't originally from Black Earth. He wasn't even from Minnesota. But we stayed after that, with Grandma Adele. So in a sense, I guess it was true.

I didn't know it then, but Dad had already started the paperwork to leave active duty. As a single father, he could request an administrative discharge. I sometimes wondered if that was why he looked so sad. This was a compromise he hadn't counted on. *I* was a compromise he hadn't counted on.

The scars never faded, not the small, almost neat one on the front of his shoulder, or the large, angry one across his back. It was this scar my fingertips worried during the tiny tot swim classes we took together.

"That's where the dragon bit me," he'd say, but he never told me what really happened, although I knew it had happened over there, in Somalia.

Back then, I also believed that if I rubbed the scars hard enough, I could make them disappear.

The FAA
February 1991

Life in the Forward Assembly Area

I sleep in static, my cot
next to the TOC.
In case someone needs me.
In case we need to move.

All night, the radios buzz the air.
Wind throws sand against the rain poncho
I've lashed to my cot, secured tight
with bungee cords and hope.

I work in static, manning three radios
at once, with an ear turned toward
the BBC on shortwave.

Last ditch efforts to stop
The war don't stop us
from swallowing nerve agent pills.

Still, we listen.
Because as long as they talk,
we can hope.

The Kevlar Helmet

It's amazing we can tell
each other apart, one soldier from
the next, the second lieutenant from
the full bird colonel you're better off avoiding.
All of them weighed down

with flak vest and chemical mask,
ammo pouches and, of course,
identical Kevlar helmets.

Until one of them takes the Kevlar off.
Have you ever seen a man do this?
It's one smooth move, from unsnapping
the chinstrap to palming the top.
The liner band leaves an indentation
around the head, reminding you
just how vulnerable the human body—
human heart—is.

Still, I can't take my eyes away
whenever a man does this.
And when that man is Paul?
It steals my breath.

And when it's Paul before me,
helmet in hand, on the eve
of crossing the border,
into Iraq, it feels like fate
has brought us here.

We stand in that diamond-shaped no-man's land
between Saudi Arabia and Iraq,
neither one of us daring to move.

All I can do is stare at Paul's
helmet, and the indentation that circles
his head while I try to forget
just how vulnerable
we both are.

The Slit Trench Latrine Is No Place for a Broken Heart

But it's the only place to go
where no one will see me.

Battered black plastic stretches
between two wooden stakes.
This hides the trench that's deeper
than it is wide. But the black plastic
doesn't really hide
anything at all.

The trench is just wide enough
that you're better off taking your
chances in the desert—drop your pants
and hope for the best—rather than risk
falling in.

Still, everyone says, "Knock, knock," as they
approach, like we can pretend
we're back in the world, like we can pretend
we haven't lost all vestiges
of civilization.

So in that respect, it's the perfect place
to hide when you don't want to be found.
It's maybe exactly the right place to go
when you have a broken heart.

In Which Master Sergeant Collier Gives Me a Cup of Coffee

The metal canteen cup heats
my numb fingers. I let the coffee
burn my throat.

On purpose.

Master Sergeant Collier: Rough day, ma'am?
Me: You have no idea.

He pulls a photo from his wallet.
Strawberry blond with
a sprinkle of freckles across the nose—
as careless as tossed grass seed.
Give her pigtails and she's
a farm girl from Nebraska.

Except for the captain's bars,
and the Airborne badge, the
two rows of ribbons.

Me: Your wife.
Master Sergeant Collier: Yes, ma'am.
Me: She's over here.
Master Sergeant Collier: Yes, ma'am.

I want to laugh,
or cry.
Instead I scald my throat
with more coffee.

Master Sergeant Collier: The only difference between me and
Lieutenant Meyers is I'm older.
Me: And that means?
Master Sergeant Collier: I know when to hang on—and when to
let go.

———

THAT NIGHT, the poems fit my mood—bleak and sad. Everyone had secrets, I thought. Like what happened between my mom and dad somewhere in Saudi Arabia. Something bad and inexplicable—and probably something I'd never know the answer to. Like Nissa's secret and painful crush on Landon.

Like Landon and his scar. Like Dad and his.

My phone buzzed, a text message popping onto the screen.

Landon: You OK?

Me: Yeah.

Landon: You looked kind of sick at practice.

I thought about saying: *You looked kind of scarred*, instead, I replied:

Me: I'm fine.

But I wanted to give him more, so I added:

Me: Reading a journal my mom wrote during the war.

My phone dimmed, then went black. About the time I thought I'd killed the conversation—and maybe our relationship—he responded.

Landon: So that's why you come to school with shadows in your eyes.

For the longest time, I sat there. I was still sitting there when he sent the last text of the evening.

Landon: Goodnight. <3

Chapter 14

ALL WEEK LONG, I obsessed about scars. During lunch, I stared at Landon's chest as if, at any moment, I'd develop x-ray vision. If he noticed my recent obsession, he didn't mention it. At swim practice, he remained totally "cool." If there was any buzz about us going to prom, that—and I suspect Constance—killed it.

It was weird, though, for him to go from the boy who fed me dried mangos at lunch and stole kisses when he could to one who looked at me as if I were just another girl on the synchro team. I thought about that long ago haircut in the Khobar Towers and wondered if pulling on a practice suit was, in some way, like putting on a uniform. I was still me, just the serious swimmer version of myself. And it was something Landon totally got.

But after practice on Saturday, Landon declared Sunday was ours. No swimming. No show talk. No Black Earth anything. We stood in my driveway, Landon presenting—or pestering—Dad with all the reasons we needed to make the trip up to Mall of America. To my surprise, Dad agreed I couldn't get a nice dress in the Black Earth Mall.

"Home before nine thirty," was his only stipulation.

Early Sunday morning, I crept from bed. I had one stealth-girl mission to complete (sending Patti my essay) before leaving on the girly-girl one. Even so, I couldn't resist another peek at the journal. There weren't many pages left and I was hoping for … not a happy ending, but something. A reconciliation. Another haircut. A kiss.

Anything.

———

During

February - March 1991

Riding the Waves

Inside the track, we crunch across the desert,
up a sand dune and down
the other side.
The soles of my boots skid across
slick sandbags packed along the floor.

Up and over,
over and down.
Until I have no choice
but to gain my sea legs.

Inside the track, we breathe
sweat-soaked air. Headphones bite into the flesh
around my ears. Static fills my head.
I can't see the war,
but I can hear it
and smell it.

Up and over,
over and down.

Until we lumber over the berm, and thick oil smothers
the odor of sweat.

Outside the track, we stumble over
unfamiliar terrain like sailors on dry land,
our legs shaky and unsure.
We gulp in the dark Iraqi night. The sand
is damp, the air crisp, but underneath it all
is the inescapable smell of oil.

This Ain't No Disco

The strangest thing about the tank battle
on the horizon is how it makes
the air look warm.
But my cheeks are cold, fingers numb.
I've spent too much time sweating
In my chemical suit for it to be
any use.

Second Brigade is tangoing with the Republican Guards.
It's like a dance with choreography that makes sense
only to the ones executing the moves.
This dance is the kind that consumes the dancer
and will only end when the last turret
stops spinning.

In the middle of the dance floor: Paul.
In a canvas-sided Humvee. I think of tracer rounds
And tank turrets, and shells that rock
the earth beneath my feet
from more than a kilometer away.

The flashing lights and quaking air

Transport my mind back to Germany,
to the clubs, the discos, dancing until dawn.
And I think the same thought now as I did then:

Paul can dance.

There Is No Air

Sweat. Diesel. A half-eaten MRE.
Chicken ala King, I think. Always a poor choice.
Fog. Outside the track. Inside the track.
In my head.
Eating. Sleeping.
These are things other people do.

This four-day war has stolen
all the air over here,
and has left behind
static, stench, and the shells
of things that once were.

———

THE POEMS LEFT ME BATTERED. This was not the end I was looking for. I decided that, if it came to it, I'd blow off sending Patti my essay. Right now, I had to see my mom and dad together. I refused to believe that never happened.

———

After
March 1991

In Which I Exchange a Few Post-combat Words with Master Sergeant

Collier

Master Sergeant Collier: Ma'am, Lieutenant Meyers wanted you to have this, once the war was over. Hope I'm not being premature.
Me: What is it?
Master Sergeant Collier: Suppose there's one way to find out.

Before and After

I slice through layers of plastic
with a knife courtesy of Master Sergeant Collier
until I find a mix tape.
The liner notes are so clean, I'm afraid
to touch them.

I leave sandy fingerprints
across the smooth surface.
But the wind and sand and grime can't steal
the words Paul has written there:

My life was a desert until I met you.
You are my oasis.

Before or after, I wonder. Are these words of hope?
Or words of regret?
I wonder on this so hard, I nearly forget
the tank battle,
nearly forget that all we may ever have
is a before.

Everyday Kuwait

We have no real weather here—no cumulous clouds, no
dew point readings.

The wind brings us sun on one day, smoke
from the oil well fires the next. It's our pretend weather and
the tiny specks from the fires cover everything—like permanent
black rain drops—clothes, canvas, skin.

In this gloom, we gag down irradiated milk
since it makes gagging down malaria pills
that much easier.
We drink our nuclear milk to toast
the nuclear winter around us.
We practice the fine art of holding
our breath.

The Kuwaiti linguists all ran off
to Kuwait City.
We ran after them because they took
their U.S. Army-issued M16s.
I'm not sure anyone minded
this distraction in the land of
boredom, bean-counting, and bureaucracy.
If I have one regret, it's that I never answered
Ahmed's question.

At night, I sit on the berm that surrounds our
compound, one built by the Iraqis.
The oil well fires burn up the horizon, the flame
as cold as those from the second brigade
tank battle.

I know Paul is alive, but this
is all I know.

The feral dogs howl, the oil well fires
silently crackle—I even lean forward,

anticipating a sound to match the glow.
I feel and hear nothing.

The only thing in the air is the echo
of Ahmed's voice:

Where are your men?

And I must admit that even now
I still don't know the answer.

Landmines Have the Right of Way

Sergeant Wilcox and I drive on
makeshift roads, ones carved into
the desert with diesel.
Because if there's something more
plentiful than sand over here
it's oil.

We play *name that piece of enemy equipment*
on the tedious drives to division HQ.
I've taken to shouting out, *T-72!*
no matter what I see.
It's my favorite tank, I tell Sergeant Wilcox,
as if such a thing were possible.

The game is a distraction that really doesn't.
Every day, wind and wear uncover
Something new in the landscape.
Cluster bombs. Landmines.
A diesel covered road is no guarantee.

If danger could be dull, it would be

these drives to division, over the same road that
changes in ways we can't see.
No matter how many times I shout *T-72!*
neither of us can forget that the real enemy
is the one we can't see.

Where Are Your Men, Reprise

Back at battalion, Master Sergeant Collier
and the soldiers greet us—the TOC all crazy-
hyper with activity, all crazy-hyper with talk.

Master Sergeant Collier: He left a message, ma'am. Something
about an oasis, but you know those infantry types—not too
articulate.

I freeze. The soldiers around me grin.
Paul was here. To see me.
If they told us we were flying home
next week, my heart wouldn't beat
this hard.

Master Sergeant Collier: We could chase him down, ma'am.
Me: Or … we could make him wait.
Master Sergeant Collier: Anyone ever tell you you're a femme
fatale, ma'am?
Me: Never. Besides, I have work to do.
Master Sergeant Collier: I stand corrected. La femme de guerre.

Tomorrow is the only other word
Master Sergeant Collier says
before handing me a cup of coffee.
His promise, but it will be
up to me to see if there's a

before,
or after.
Or both.

I study the sand floor, certain I see
Paul's boot prints.
I feel a shift in the wind,
a burst of sun that brings more
hope than heat.

In that wind, I hear the barest echo of a question:

Where are your men?

It's only now that I realize the truth.
They've been here all along.

———

REALLY, Dad? *You are my oasis?* Really? That was right up there with *spun gold*. Just one more thing I couldn't ever imagine him saying. And yet, he had. To my mom. Master Sergeant Collier must have found a way to get them together one last time. I was convinced he could do anything.

They'd been together. They'd kissed. Maybe behind a slit-trench latrine. The knowledge soothed my heart—just a little. No, their love story didn't have a happy ending. But they'd had this one thing, and the thought of it made me feel sad and hopeful at the same time. I tucked the journal under my pillow and headed downstairs to complete my second mission of the day.

———

THE COMPUTER BOOTED, the coffeemaker gurgled, and I was

already way too jumpy without the benefit of caffeine. I went over my essay one last time before pasting the text into an email. Once Patti pulled out her virtual red pen, it would bounce back to me in tatters. Still, I hoped she'd like it. I squeezed my eyes nearly closed, clicked send, then booted down the whole system. What Dad didn't know wouldn't hurt him—or raise his curiosity.

By the time he wandered into the kitchen, I was sipping my second cup of coffee and forcing some toast past my lips without much success. When Landon rang the front bell thirty minutes later, I'd done everything but eat.

On the front porch, Landon and Dad did this thing where they sized each other up—narrow eyes, tense jaws, arms crossed. I was about to tell them to have at it, I was going to the mall—by myself —when Landon cracked.

He held out his hand and said, "Good to see you again, sir."

Apparently, this was all Dad wanted, since he shook Landon's hand, clapped him on the shoulder, and—swear to God—slipped him a twenty.

"What the hell?" Landon said when we were inside the Corvette. He turned the bill over in his hands like he expected it to be counterfeit. "Is this a bribe?"

I shrugged.

Landon peered through the windshield to where Dad stood on the porch, arms folded over his chest. When he noticed us staring, he gave a short wave.

"Or is he messing with my mind?"

I nodded, because honestly, that was exactly something Dad would do. "Can we just leave?" I said.

Landon started the engine. The thing rumbled like it wanted to tear out of the driveway and chew all the asphalt between here and the Mall of America, Instead, he inched his way out of the drive and puttered down the road like the Corvette was a golf cart.

"You're not fooling him," I told Landon.

"Yeah, but it makes me feel better."

He fiddled with the stereo controls and I expected some old school rock and roll, vintage new wave, or punk—Violent Femmes, The Clash, The Sex Pistols—something loud and worthy of the Corvette to blast from the speakers and blast us all the way to Minneapolis.

We hadn't reached the highway onramp when I realized what came from the speakers didn't so much blast as ooze. Sticky, gooey, sentimental—a patented Landon mix, but one I couldn't decipher. When Meatloaf belted out that he'd do anything for love (and seriously, not even Dad listened to Meatloaf—much), I couldn't take it anymore.

I pointed to the stereo. "What the hell is this?"

"Mood music."

"Songs to barf by?" I suggested.

"It's a prom mix," he said, his tone conveying that this should've been obvious. "Because we're going to prom and shopping for a prom dress. It will get us in the mood."

"For barfing?"

I felt him peer at me. "It's a good thing your dad gave me that twenty."

We bumped up the onramp and onto the highway, the same one that passed Scott Industries. Even on a Sunday, a few cars were scattered in the lot. Dad—computer whiz that he was—logged into work from home, which he did more than I thought he should.

Landon rolled down the window. The wind roared inside the car, drowning out the prom mix (a plus) and whipping my braids against my face (a minus). At the exact center of Scott Industries, he stuck his arm out the window, middle finger fully extended. Then, as if nothing had happened, he rolled the window back up until the wind stopped whistling and the prom mix congealed over us again.

"But how do you really feel about it?" I said.

He didn't respond and a pang shot through me. This was serious. This was all about five years ago.

"Do you want to talk about it?" I asked, my voice soft, letting him know he could ignore the question if he wanted.

He shook his head, then nodded. His hand went to the stereo controls. The volume dipped and then the music vanished altogether.

"You know what?" he said. "I do. Besides, I promised to tell you." He cast me a quick look. "Before prom."

I don't know what I expected. Five years. Finally, after all that time. I held my breath, but when Landon didn't speak, let it out with a whoosh. He kept his eyes on the road, but I thought I detected a small smile.

It didn't last though. His hand went from the steering wheel to mine, but he didn't lace our fingers.

"Here," he said. "I want you to feel something."

I jerked. Maybe it was human nature. Or a trust issue. I don't know. Landon kept his grip firm, so my hand went nowhere.

"MacKenna, please."

There it was, that soft, chanting way he said my name. Still. Feeling something—anything—while barreling down the highway at fifty five (okay, sixty five) miles per hour? And what was it, in general, that boys wanted you to feel? I shook my head, my fingers locked in his.

"Five seconds of trust," he said. "That's all I'm asking. Just trust me."

My arm muscles relaxed in increments. I let my fingers go limp. He maneuvered my hand so it was flush against his stomach. I tensed, and again, held my breath, braced to keep my hand above his waistline. But he didn't push my hand down. He eased it up, over his chest until I had to twist and lean forward, until, at last, my fingers rested on the scar above his heart.

"Hang on a sec," he said. "Sometimes it pops out."

"Sometimes it what? Landon ...?" My mind whirled. What popped and how?

He didn't speak, so at last I said, "I saw the scar."

"I figured you'd notice." He released my fingers and I inched my hand back, not wanting to leave his warmth, and sat up.

"Will you tell me about it?" I adjusted my seatbelt and flexed my fingers, trying to memorize the feel of his scar.

"Remember how my family went up to the Cities for that wedding?"

"Back in seventh grade," I added. Yeah, I remembered. He had a huge extended family and was forever being pulled away for this or that event. This particular outrage—Landon snatched from us for the entire long weekend—burned hard.

"It turns out I have something called Long QT syndrome—it had been undiagnosed up until then. But that weekend." He shrugged. "Well, my heart went crazy. My mom did CPR. Luckily, we were at the reception and the restaurant had one of those defib-rillators."

I clamped a hand over my mouth to stop myself from saying something stupid like, "Really?" Of course really. I bit down on my index finger, hoping the pain would clear my head and the tears from my eyes.

"Long story short, they took me to Children's Hospital. I saw a bunch of specialists, ended up going down to the Mayo Clinic to see even more specialists until my parents were convinced that my heart really wouldn't work without a pacemaker."

My chest ached like someone had punched me there. To be twelve and have all that happen to you. "Landon, I'm sorry. I had no idea—"

"No one did. That was the point. My parents—well, my dad—didn't want anyone back in Black Earth to know."

"But why?"

He cast me a look, the Corvette slowing almost imperceptibly. "If I knew the answer to that ..." He let the sentence trail and I felt the speed beneath the wheels again.

For a long while, the only sounds that filled the car were the wheels over asphalt, the steady rhythm of the engine, and my own hitched breathing.

"But ... that summer, when we called. Were you even home?"

"Hardly. I was either at the Mayo Clinic or in the Twin Cities. After my last appointment, my dad convinced my mom I'd be better off at a boarding school, one with a medical staff. Had her terrified my heart would stop during lunch in the caf or something. After Mayo, I came home, packed, and left."

"We called, you know."

"I know. My mom told me. She wanted me to call you guys before I left, but by then." He fell silent again and his fingertips traced patterns on the steering wheel. "By then, I was too ashamed."

"Ashamed?"

"Embarrassed. Whatever. I couldn't explain why I was leaving. So what was the point? It was stupid, I know. After that, I was just angry."

"At us?"

"Everyone, actually, but yeah, you guys too. I thought you didn't try hard enough."

I gave an exasperated sigh. I couldn't help it. "Landon, we tried. Oh, my God, we tried every last thing we could think of. The only thing we didn't do was steal a car and track you down."

"That was one of my fantasies," he said and gave me a little grin.

"Seriously. I don't understand."

"I was mad at the world. It's one of those stages of grief things. I just happened to spend a great deal of time there."

I couldn't blame him. After all, I'd spent a long time building up my own walls of anger, brick by brick, never knowing for sure what had happened, never knowing, for sure, whether it was my fault or not. Landon stared straight ahead, both hands on the wheel now, fingers curled around it.

"I can't go out for sports," he said at last. "Can't play baseball. Fly ball to the chest?" He shook his head. "Too risky."

In my mind, I saw the image of Landon, standing in front of the trophy case, the one that held the awards for baseball. What was that like? The could've-should've-would've beens—the weight of that stole my breath. What would I do if suddenly I couldn't swim?

I thought of the time Mr. Scott had taken all three of us to a Twins game—his expression that day as his gaze traveled from Landon to the ball field, and back again. He tapped Landon lightly on the chest and pointed.

"Out there," Mr. Scott said. "Someday."

"Yeah," Landon said. "I'll be one of the guys in an A's hat."

And Mr. Scott had laughed, knocked Landon's Twins cap from his head and ruffled his hair. What did it mean when your dad stopped ruffling your hair, stopped looking at you with pride? Five years seemed like nothing next to that. If anyone should be ashamed, it should be me.

"I'm sorry," I whispered, my throat thick with tears.

"Don't cry," Landon said, voice sharp. "I mean it. Don't you dare cry. It's not your fault."

I blinked back the dampness in my eyes. "If I'd known, I'd—" Actually, I didn't know what I would've done. I thought for a moment and added, "Well, I wouldn't have been such a bitch this winter."

"Yeah, that kind of threw me. After chatting with Nissa—"

"Wait." My stomach plummeted. Nissa knew? All along? "You told Nissa."

"I told her I was coming back and when I did, I'd explain everything."

"She never said a word."

"It took me a while, but I finally figured that out."

Landon reached over, his thumb catching a wayward tear. "Didn't we promise once never to keep secrets?"

My eyes fluttered shut under the touch of his hand and the weight of that memory. Our clubhouse in Grandma Adele's backyard, curtains drawn over the tiny shed's window, dark, dank, the smell of potting soil rich in the air. The three of us so solemn, so serious. No secrets. No lies. I'd snatched a lighter from Dad and we each took turns holding our hand over the flame to seal the promise.

Landon laced his fingers with mine and squeezed. "No more secrets?"

"None."

———

AFTER THE THIRD STORE, I asked Landon how on earth he knew the Mall of America so well. Because, honestly, the boy was a shopping machine. He tugged me through aisles cluttered with sales tables, knew shortcuts through various departments, and we always landed in the formal wear section with him looking totally accomplished and me completely winded.

"All those specialists," he said. "When we were between appointments, we went shopping." He shrugged. "Retail therapy."

"You and your mom?"

"Yeah." Landon studied the back of his hand, then lifted his gaze to take in the mall. "So, it's almost like a second home."

The dress-buying odyssey took six stores. I was about to give up and get something from Forever 21—just to be contrary—but Landon bullied me into the dress department at Nordstrom's, shoved a bunch of dresses into my arms, and me into a dressing room. Five minutes later a great poof of white floated over the dressing room door and landed on top of me.

"Stop what you're doing," he called. "This is the one."

The dress was heavier than it looked and I struggled to push it off me, then I stood there in my underwear, inspecting Landon's offering.

It was, without question, a wedding dress. I peered out

the door.

"Landon?"

Nothing. It took a few moments, but I worked my way into the faux wedding dress. I found him lounging by the triple mirrors. I whooshed toward him, handfuls of silk taffeta clutched in my fists. If I were totally and completely honest with myself, I'd admit that he found the perfect dress. And if I were totally and completely honest with myself, I'd admit that I wanted to wear it to prom.

"Jesus." Landon exhaled when he saw me. "That's it. That is the most perfect dress, ever. You've got to get it. It totally rocks."

"Landon," I said, my voice careful. "I think this is a wedding dress."

"Can't be." He stretched, his body following his arm. "Those are way over there. They keep them separate so there isn't any cross-contamination."

I snagged the label, looking for proof. What I got was serious sticker shock. Wedding dress or not, no way could I afford it. Even if I used all my savings, it wouldn't make a dent; it wouldn't pay for half. The dress was that expensive. I certainly couldn't charge it to my one and only Dad-inspected credit card either. So I did the only thing I could. I swished toward the lone clearance rack.

"What are you doing?" Landon asked, coming up behind me.

I pawed through last season's rejects. "Finding something I can afford."

He caught me around the waist and hauled me backward. "Whoa. Let me check." He glanced at the price tag. "Oh, that's not bad at all."

I summoned every ounce of willpower not to roll my eyes. It still wasn't enough.

"Let me," Landon said.

"Let you what?"

"Buy the dress for you."

"I'm supposed to buy my own prom dress."

"Says who?"

Dad, probably. In my mind, I heard the refrain.

Dad on rich boyfriends and favors: *It has a way of coming back to bite a girl in the ass.*

"My dad—" I began.

"Will he ask?"

Landon had a point. As long as I covered enough skin, Dad zoned out when it came to fashion. Landon took both my hands and tugged me toward the three way mirror, then spun me slowly. The dress's bodice was modest, with wide shoulder straps that made it look almost sporty—if a formal could look sporty, that is. The full skirt fell to the floor from the cinched waist. As prom—or wedding—dresses went, it was pretty tame. Except for the back which laced up like a corset with large, flat satin ribbons criss-crossing my bare skin.

That was where Landon's fingers were now, crisscrossing my skin. True, the dress came with a modesty panel, and equally true, I'd left it out.

"Please," he said. "I'll buy the dress. You can get the shoes."

I drew in a breath and held it. Dad, if he found out, would go into full-blown, nuclear core meltdown.

"Tell me it's not the most perfect dress," Landon said, "and we can keep looking."

I would. Except. It was the most perfect dress. I loved it, couldn't imagine going to prom in anything else. Who said Dad had to know? I exhaled. "Okay, but I'm paying you back—and I'm buying the shoes."

He didn't freak when I led him to the athletic shoe warehouse. Instead, he cornered the first sales rep who wandered by, and unfurled the dress from its plastic wrap. "We need something that matches this," he declared.

The guy, in his black and white referee shirt, just laughed, and we walked out with a pair of pristine-white Converse All Stars.

By the time we reached the Corvette, the sun was low in the sky. My dress and shoes barely fit in what was optimistically described as the car's trunk. We pulled into the driveway at seven thirty. Mission accomplished with two hours to spare.

I was still stuffed from the waffle cone Landon had bought— using Dad's twenty dollar bill—and my feet ached from the hard mall floors. I sat for a moment before joining Landon at the trunk. Inside, wrapped in plastic, the dress was all poufy skirt.

The front door creaked open. Dad stepped onto the porch, the lamp light casting a circle around him. At first, I thought he might be curious about the dress—stranger things had happened. But he didn't move, didn't smile, didn't even twitch when Landon waved.

Dad's face was all sharp lines and planes—rock solid and unforgiving. The dress slipped through my fingers. My heart thudded a warning.

"Did we miss some sort of secret curfew?" Landon whispered. He checked his watch. "It's not even eight."

Dad still didn't budge, but now he spoke. "You had a phone call."

My thoughts ricocheted. I did a quick review of everything that might prompt a call, and a bad one. My grades were good. I never skipped school and wasn't about to start during swim season. My throat tightened at the thought that Sierra did something, something petty and awful, but couldn't imagine what that might be. I glanced at Landon, but he gave his head a slight shake, his eyes, though, were worried.

"And since you weren't home, she decided to talk to me."

It must be Sierra, although why and how and what she said— well, I guessed Dad would tell me. Still, this seemed low, even for her.

"Your swim coach and I had an interesting chat."

For an instant, relief washed over me. But Dad remained ramrod still, his tone nearly expressionless, his face in pure combat mode.

"Of course, she is also your English teacher, isn't she?"

I nodded, barely, a thin wire of fear tightening around my heart.

"And she wanted to talk about your scholarship application and your wonderful draft essay."

The swim team roster. Patti had everyone's number, including mine. And she'd said something about talking, and on Sunday. But I never imagined she'd call ... or talk to Dad if I wasn't home. But why wouldn't she talk to Dad? Wouldn't most teachers? No one knew how it would set him off—except for me.

I felt the fault lines in my plan as sure as I felt the crumbled asphalt beneath my feet. Even if I'd managed to apply for a scholarship without Dad's knowledge, what did I think would happen when it came through?

"Scholarship," Landon said, his voice soft in my ears. His hand came to rest at the small of my back. I leaned into him gratefully. "Are we talking ROTC?"

I nodded, barely.

"Didn't he lose his shit last time the topic came up?" Landon sounded incredulous.

I nodded again.

"Then why ...?"

Good question. Why risk everything, just for this? Why not wait until I was eighteen and on campus—the Army had scholarships for college students. Why disrupt the delicate balance of life with Dad?

Dad approached, his gait controlled, which meant he was still holding everything in. I wanted to hand him a lighter and tell him to get it over with.

"Care to explain," he said to me.

"What?" I raised my chin. "I have to explain a full-ride scholarship and early acceptance?"

"There are other ways to pay for college," Dad said. "We've talked about this."

"No, you set the kitchen on fire and that's when the conversation ended."

Dad blanched, then stared hard, betrayal in his eyes. I'd broken that unwritten rule, the one that said we never talked about the crazy that was March.

"Sir?" Landon, the most incredible boy on earth did the most incredible thing. He stepped in front of me as if that would block Dad's wrath. "Can I say something?"

"Actually." Dad crossed his arms over his chest. "You should stay out of this."

"There might be good reasons MacKenna wants to join."

"Good reasons? You've got to be f—"

"Have you asked her?"

No, of course he hadn't. I saw the barest flicker of doubt in Dad's eyes, but it didn't last.

"Your mother died in Desert Storm," Dad said to me, the words automatic, as if he'd been rehearsing them. The slightest twitch in his jaw told me they cost him—a lot. "If that doesn't obliterate any and all of your reasons, I have nothing left to say to you."

His words blew away every last one of my reasons, all the things I might say to him, how I planned to explain. Because I realized then they weren't the real reasons. Yes, I wanted to know about my mom—but I had her journal. Yes, being like her meant a lot. But what meant more? Dad actually talking about her. That was why I was pushing ROTC now and not waiting for later. I was pushing Dad, pushing him hard. But maybe I pushed too hard. Maybe he wasn't ready. Maybe he never would be. Which left us ... where?

Dad sidestepped Landon, his glare hot enough to burn. "I thought you understood," he said to me.

Understood what? Those things we never talked about? "I need to make sense of everything," I said, knowing whatever words I chose would be the wrong ones. "I need to know about my mom—"

"You're going about it all wrong."

"What's the right way, then?" At that moment, I really wanted to know, would've given anything to know. "You don't talk about her. You won't tell me anything." Tears pricked my eyes, but I ignored them. "Tell me. What am I supposed to do?"

"I'll tell you what you don't do. You don't go behind my back. You don't hide your plans from me. You don't talk to adults I don't know."

"Patti's my swim coach and teacher, and I can talk to her if I want to. Not only that, I have to talk to her."

"Sir, have you considered that this is something MacKenna needs to do?"

Dad stared uncomprehendingly at Landon. To be honest, so did I. Maybe he understood everything about me, but clearly, everything about Dad escaped him.

"Needs to do? Like she needs more space or needs to find herself?"

"Sir—"

Dad stuck a finger in Landon's face. "Don't 'sir' me. It's getting old. Tell you what, rich boy. What she needs to do is not see you anymore."

Landon and I spoke at once, our protests lost in Dad's next salvo.

"Things were just fine until you came back."

What the hell was he talking about? Things had *never* been just fine. Ever.

"I don't give a damn whose son you are. You." Dad jabbed Landon's chest with a finger, right above his heart. Landon didn't flinch, but I did.

"You are no longer welcomed here. And you." Dad swiveled and caught me in his sights. "You go to school. You come home. That's it."

That couldn't be it. And I was right; it wasn't.

"As far as your English teacher goes, since she's the only

Honors teacher for English 11, you will limit your contact with her to class time only."

The way he said *class time only* set alarms off inside me. "But swimming—"

"She is no longer your swim coach."

For one horrible second, I thought he'd gotten Patti fired somehow. Then it hit me.

"I'm in a duet." Now I regretted pushing Dad so hard. I regretted never telling him about the duet. "You just can't—"

"Don't tell me what I can and can't do." Dad stood there, daring me to move, to speak, to breathe. He pointed to Landon. "You. Go." Then to me. "You. Inside."

Neither one of us moved. Dad took a step forward. I took an automatic step back, but Landon didn't. He did something I'd never seen anyone else do before, other than Grandma Adele. He stared down Dad.

"Sir, please—"

"Listen to me, listen real hard, rich boy. Have you ever been shot at? Know what it's like to take incoming artillery? Put enough firepower down range to destroy an entire village, men, women, and children? Can you even begin to comprehend what it's like to have your wife blown apart by a landmine?"

I wavered, a sudden dizziness washing over me. Land … mine? The word made no sense in relation to my mom. I could still hear Grandma Adele.

It was a Humvee accident.

I stared at Dad until a wash of tears blurred his image. "Landmine?" I said, my voice so weak, no one heard me.

But the word set me off. I bolted, up the concrete stairs. I crashed through the front door and tripped up the steps to my room. I collapsed on my bed and studied the ceiling. My throat felt raw, like I'd swallowed all the tears I couldn't cry. I thought Dad might come up to talk. Or at least check on me before he went to bed. His footfalls never even sounded on the stairs.

Still, I waited for him. When he didn't do the Dad thing—any Dad thing—I reached for the journal. I reread the last entry until my eyes were sore.

———

I TRIED to reconcile what both Grandma Adele and Dad had said with what my mom had written. But all I heard was the question in my head:

Where are your men?

And the answer at the very end:

It's only now that I realize the truth.

They've been here all along.

That had felt so sweet, so right. I didn't want any of that to change, didn't want their story to change. But now, in the silent house, I wondered where all my men were.

Around one in the morning, I couldn't take it anymore and crept from my room. In the kitchen, I opened the refrigerator, then closed it again. What I was after, I couldn't say. I walked to the front door, thought seriously about walking through and not looking back, not showing up for school, not coming home again. Mentally, I ran through how long it would take to pack a bag, what I should bring, and where I could go. I stepped outside.

The cement chilled the soles of my bare feet. Something white and ghostly fluttered by the garage. The sight sent my heart thudding. But curiosity won out. I picked my way across the drive, sharp bits of asphalt jabbing my skin.

Hanging from the rain gutter, still wrapped in plastic, was my prom dress. Beneath it, sat a shoebox. I crouched, lifted the lid, and eased the Chuck Taylors from inside. With a hand, I freed the dress from the gutter. The skirt swished, reminding me of how it looked and how it made me feel. Then I crushed the silk taffeta to my chest and held on tight.

Only then did I cry.

Chapter 15

ON MONDAY, I avoided everyone at school, all those years of stealth finally paying off at last. Even so, I dreaded English. Landon and Patti in the same room? The answer: skating into my seat at the very last second.

Josh gave me an odd look. I imagined, after I was a no-show at today's practice, that tomorrow's look would be even odder. Landon, over by the windows, surrounded by cheerleaders, never had a chance. I ignored him—or pretended to, even with his gaze fixed on my face.

I was mapping out my escape from class when Patti called on me.

"MacKenna? Can you tell us what the symbolism is in this passage?"

Considering I didn't know which passage she meant, never mind what book, that would be kind of difficult. I'd finished the reading on Saturday, but I hadn't reviewed last night. Unless you wanted a world of hurt, you always reviewed for Patti's class.

I shook my head, slunk lower in my seat, my cheeks on fire. Patti gave me a hard look. People shifted in their seats. Josh coughed. Then, predictably, one of Landon's fan-girl cheerleaders giggled.

Class couldn't end soon enough.

When the bell rang, I bolted upright. My books spilled onto the floor. I was grappling with them when Patti said, "MacKenna, a moment please."

Someone let out a long, obnoxious, "Woo, someone's in trouble."

Patti waited for the classroom to clear, thankfully, before skewering me with that same, hard look.

"You never told me your father didn't approve of the scholarship."

If anyone could understand, it would be Patti. She'd understand about my mom, if only I could get the words out, if only Patti would let me.

She didn't. "In all my years of teaching, I can't think of a time when I've been more humiliated. Did you honestly think you could apply for and receive an ROTC scholarship without your father knowing?"

Apparently, I had, or at least believed the scholarship might make all the difference. I shrugged.

"Right." That single word held so much: Sarcasm. Hurt. Dismissal.

I ran blindly for my next class.

———

THE BEST PLACE TO hide in Black Earth High School was the third-floor girls' bathroom in the language wing. If you didn't have a language class, you didn't bother with the hall. At the very end of the corridor was a staircase, one most people forgot about, that led to the side door of the school.

I waited there after last bell, long enough to be certain everyone was at swim practice, including Constance and Landon. After school, I was supposed to march home—literally, on foot—because, oh, by the way, Dad revoked my car keys this morning.

The bonus part? He decided to work remotely, which meant he'd be timing my trek home. He also revoked computer access (a no-brainer), television (it was all crap anyway), and my cell phone (who was going to text me now?).

To make up for the delay, I dashed through the hall, down the staircase, and crashed through the door. The sun struck my face, blinded me for a minute. I took one look behind me, just in case, and broke into a run.

There was only so far you can run with a jacket tied around your waist and a load of books on your back. After a quarter of a mile, I decided it wasn't worth the potential spinal cord injury. I'd walk fast and hope that was fast enough for Dad.

Four blocks later, I made a conscious effort to ignore the car. This was really hard to do since the car was flame yellow. Even harder, it was a Corvette. Hardest of all, Landon rolled down the passenger side window and simultaneously tried to talk to me and drive. If Dad saw the Corvette, he'd freak. It wasn't exactly inconspicuous.

Landon kept the car creeping alongside me. At last, I halted, but I held my ground, standing in the center of the sidewalk. "What are you doing?"

Landon pulled near the curb and let the car idle. "Trying to talk to you."

"You're not supposed to, remember?"

"Fuck that. Talk to me, MacKenna."

"About what?" How my life sucked? How this sucked? How if Dad saw Landon he'd probably get a restraining order? The list was endless.

"You. Let's talk about you." Landon said. "How are you feeling? Shit, I missed you today."

Oh, God. I missed him, so much that the thought of it stole all my breath. I couldn't bear to think about it, not for long. I'd decided the only way to get through this whole ordeal was avoidance mode: avoid thinking about Landon, avoid anything that made me think about Landon, avoid Landon, period.

Of course, Landon was making that difficult.

"So I can't talk to you?" he said.

"I'm not supposed to see you." I waved a hand in front of my eyes. "Here I am, seeing you."

I started down the sidewalk again. Landon put the Corvette in gear and kept pace with me. Up ahead, I saw my house, with its neat lawn, crumbling asphalt, and Dad inside.

"You've got to go," I said to Landon.

"It's not against the law to drive down your road."

"Try telling my dad that."

"Look." Landon leaned so far toward the passenger side window, how he drove was a mystery. "I'm sorry about yesterday. I only meant to help, not make it worse."

"Well, you did." It wasn't nice. It really wasn't fair. But in that moment, Dad and I agreed about something: Things had been just fine until Landon showed up in Black Earth again.

"Next time." His tone went sarcastic, almost nasty. "I won't bother."

"Good." I glanced over my shoulder at the house. Dad's Blazer sat in the driveway. The front door was closed. The Corvette rumbled. The scent of freshly cut grass mixed with its exhaust. I felt wrung out—by all of it—but most of all by Dad.

"You know what it's like to live with him?" I said, louder now, not even talking to Landon—he just happened to be handy. "To always wonder what kind of mood he'll be in? To tiptoe around subjects because mentioning this or that will send him into a two-week funk? I can understand—" I paused, not entirely sure what I understood about Dad. Maybe nothing. "I understand about not wanting to talk about all of it. But nothing about my mom? Ever?"

"MacKenna, honestly, I didn't—"

"Didn't what? Look past your own issues?"

I'd regret these words later; I knew that even as I spoke them. They felt sharp in my mouth, like what I said would cut my tongue, my lips. I couldn't stop—not them, not myself. Everything I'd bottled up for so long came pouring out. Landon was just unlucky enough to be standing underneath it all.

"When I was six, I brought home a CD from a birthday party," I said, on a roll now. "He didn't like a song on it, so he used the album for target practice. Did you totally forget the camping trip from hell? Do you remember no one but you and Nissa talking to me for most of fifth grade?"

Landon looked pale, not healthy, not himself at all. But I wasn't through, not yet. My mind went back to that day in the cafeteria— Sierra leaning forward, offering printouts from the Internet. Maybe it took being a bitch to tell someone the truth. Maybe, of everyone I knew, she was the only one who'd cut through all the bullshit. If I didn't hate her so much, I'd thank her. As it was, it killed me that she was right. And maybe if I said those words, I could finally let them go.

"What part of post-traumatic stress don't you understand?" I didn't expect an answer.

I didn't get one. Landon stared, incomprehension on his face. Then he scooted all the way back into the driver's seat, put the Corvette in gear, and drove away. I tracked the car down the street until the last bit of yellow vanished. Only then did I turn toward the house. And wished like hell I hadn't.

It wasn't incomprehension in Landon's expression, but horror. Because standing on the porch, his face stricken, was Dad.

————

DAD DIDN'T SAY A WORD; he didn't have to. He vanished inside the house, and the screen door rattled. No matter how long I live, I'll never forget the look I put on his face.

Inside, I slipped off my backpack and went searching. No sign of him in the kitchen, or the den. The door to his bedroom was closed. I raised my hand to knock, but let my arm drop. I'd already screwed up enough. I needed help. *We* needed help.

In the kitchen, I picked up the landline phone. Grandma Adele was on speed-dial. On the fourth ring, right before voicemail picked up, she answered.

The words wouldn't come. I sniffled a bit, took a breath, but couldn't manage anything coherent.

"MacKenna, honey?" Grandma Adele said. Thank God for Caller ID. "What is it?"

Her voice opened not a floodgate, but the smallest crack. I felt as though I would splinter. At last, I said, "Grandma, we need you."

———

GRANDMA ADELE BROUGHT FOOD. I hadn't been grocery shopping in a while, which happened during swim season. With this whole grounded for life deal, I might not get to go, ever. That left Dad; we'd end up eating nothing but Hot Pockets and expired MREs from his Army Reserve days. Yum.

"I still can't cook for just one, not even after all these years." Grandma Adele put one pan of macaroni and cheese in the freezer and the other, in a Correlle dish, into the microwave to warm. "And I know you're so busy with swim season."

Well, I *had* been. "Thanks, Grandma."

She shook her head and tutted. "My pleasure."

Grandma Adele rearranged the refrigerator to accommodate the food, and I clattered silverware and plates while loading them into the dishwasher. I told her, in shorthand, what had happened, all about the scholarship, swimming, prom, and Landon. It was easier to talk when my hands were busy. When I finished one task, Grandma Adele gave me another. I was holding the broom when Dad wandered into the kitchen. He didn't glance toward me at all.

"Adele?" Dad sounded—and looked—guarded.

"Paul, how are you?" Grandma Adele said, her voice ringing chipper and false. "I was just telling MacKenna that I went on a cooking spree again and can't possibly eat all this food. I'd hate to see it go to waste."

"Bullshit. What are you really doing here?"

My breath caught. Dad never talked to Grandma Adele that way. Actually, no one did.

Grandma Adele never took it. She turned, hands on hips, and squared off in front of Dad. "Well, excuse me for being concerned."

"It's none of your business," Dad said, "this is between me and MacKenna."

"Oh, yes, of course." Grandma Adele sounded far too reasonable. She was still using her fake chipper voice, but it had a sharp edge to it. "I could remind you that I'm her legal guardian as well as you."

Then Dad did it. I couldn't believe it myself. He rolled his eyes and did it so Grandma Adele could see.

"Mature, Paul."

Dad held up a hand, warding off the lecture. Grandma Adele turned her back on him and focused on me.

"So, MacKenna, honey, when's your swim show again?"

Even though this was a ploy—to draw out Dad—I nearly choked. "It's in three weeks, but I'm not in it."

"I thought you were swimming a duet." Grandma Adele took the broom from me and tucked it into the pantry.

"MacKenna's grounded," Dad said.

"That's a little extreme, don't you think. And it certainly isn't fair to the other girl or the team for that matter."

"MacKenna should've thought about that before she went behind my back."

"Really, Paul." Grandma Adele took a tentative step toward Dad. "Most parents would be thrilled with a child who took the initiative like this."

Dad rounded on Grandma Adele, stuck a finger in her face. "You want her joining the Army?"

She gave his finger a significant look, then pushed his hand aside, gently. "This isn't about that," she said. "It's about MacKenna learning to make decisions on her own—"

I felt the tiniest surge of hope. Grandma Adele was on my side.

"It's exactly about that, about joining the God damn Army." Dad looked like he might point again, but instead crossed his arms over his chest. "Can you really stand there and tell me you want MacKenna in the Army?" Dad kept talking and that bit of hope started to falter. "Do you want her to go off to Afghanistan or Iraq, to fight this war, to die in this war? You want her to be like Beth?"

Without warning, Grandma Adele collapsed in a kitchen chair, like Dad had somehow delivered a physical blow. I wanted to rush to her, but stayed frozen at the sink. She stared at her folded hands, at the table, at everything before lifting her head and meeting Dad's unflinching gaze. "No. I don't."

Those three words tore through me, tore me apart. I always thought Grandma Adele understood, or at least would, if I told her everything. I mean, my mom's ammo crate, the journal, all of it. She gave me those things for a reason.

"Grandma?"

"Oh, honey, come here."

I shuffled to where she sat. She snagged me around the waist as if she were scared I'd slip away from her. "It's complicated, at best."

"No. It's very simple." Dad again. Of course. "MacKenna isn't joining the Army. End of discussion."

A sigh wracked Grandma Adele's body, seemed to flow through her and into me. I felt the exhaustion behind it, the frustration, but really, Dad could do that to anyone when he was in one of these moods.

"What did you expect, Paul," she said. "You only have yourself to blame."

"What the hell are you talking about?"

"You've done everything to encourage MacKenna except give her tacit permission. How many girls her age are marksmen? How many can shoot at all? The camping and field craft. God knows she didn't learn that from me. Actions speak louder than words, and yours were loud and clear. No wonder the poor child is confused." She touched my cheek before nailing Dad with a look. "Honestly, Paul, what did you think your little warrior princess would want to be when she grew up?"

Dad looked dumbfounded. "I never—"

"Good God, give it up. Of course you did," Grandma Adele said. "I'm tired and I'm not going to fight about this tonight."

"There's an easy solution for that," Dad said.

Did he mean Grandma Adele should leave? That was crazy. No way could we navigate this without her.

"I don't want MacKenna joining the Army," was what he said.

"Then tell MacKenna," Grandma Adele said. "Tell her why. You owe her that."

The stricken look washed across Dad's face again. He stood, unmoving, not speaking. The microwave dinged, making us all jump. Grandma Adele scooted me to one side. Oven mitts on, she removed the warmed macaroni and cheese and set it on a stove burner to cool. The warm, gooey smell filled the kitchen. So homey, so comforting, and at the moment, so totally wrong.

Dad looked up, but his gaze went right through me. "I don't want to lose you the way I lost your mom."

"That's a start," Grandma Adele said.

"Butt out, Adele."

Grandma Adele raised an eyebrow, but let Dad talk.

"I don't want you torn to bits by some IED or some suicide bomber. I don't want you in Afghanistan and I don't want you in fucking Iraq. This family has given enough for wars that don't make any sense. I refuse to give you. You're all I have."

I shook my head, but Dad held up a hand. "You're all I have. Go ahead and hate me for the rest of your life. From where I stand, that's a small price to pay."

I stood there, shell-shocked by his words. I felt myself deflate, my will, my anger, the certainty that I was right.

"Paul, I know you feel guilty about Beth." Grandma Adele still wore the oven mitts and she studied them before slipping her hands free. "But her death wasn't your fault. You can't blame yourself for it. And overprotecting MacKenna isn't going to bring Beth back."

Something strange happened then. Dad and Grandma Adele stared at each other, but not in anger, although that wasn't too far under the surface. Grandma Adele seemed startled and Dad like he was trying to work something out, something important. It hit me then. A big part of this battle had nothing to do with me at all. There was something else, something to do with my mom, something about her death that went beyond the bare facts.

It was a Humvee accident.

Landmine.

"Blame myself." Dad sounded like he really did.

Grandma Adele reached for my hand and squeezed it hard. "I'm sorry, honey. I can't support you on this. I can't tell you to go ahead and do what your mother did." She touched my cheek, softly, like she was trying to touch a memory. "Too much of me wants you to live the life your mother never had."

Her words were a blow to my solar plexus, sudden, sharp, stealing all my breath. If I felt it, then Dad must, too. He was pale except for two bright spots of color on his cheeks.

"The life Beth never had," he echoed, the words slow, painful.

"And the worst part of it?" Grandma Adele sighed, an angry sound. "Like any of it was good. After Beth died, the letters kept coming, and she wrote nearly every day." She held me close, stroked my hair. "I'd read the letters out loud to you and show you her picture. Every day. I'd say, 'That's your mama. She's so brave.'"

A lump clogged my throat. The tears weren't anything I could fight. I wanted to remember that. I wanted to remember my mom.

"I know why Beth died," Grandma Adele's voice was soft, but hollow. "It was in her last letter."

Dad gripped the back of a kitchen chair. His knuckles went white.

"She sounded so happy, just like a newlywed." Grandma Adele stared straight at Dad and I wondered how much courage it took to do that. "She loved you, Paul, and I know why she was on the road that day. I know why it was her Humvee that hit the landmine."

Dad was glass, unmoving, fragile. If I touched him then, he'd shatter.

"She was on her way to see you."

It seemed to me Dad must have shattered because I felt my own heart splinter.

Landmines have the right of way.

"I don't blame you," she continued. "It would make more sense to blame President Bush, or the Iraqi Army, or Saddam Hussein." She held me tight, but it was like stone hugging stone. "Honey, no matter what you decide, I'm here. Or rather." She glanced at Dad. "I'll support you, but I think this is something you need to work out with your father."

Then, Grandma Adele did the impossible. She left. Our Rock of Gibraltar, the thing we clung to. Grandma Adele never left. Except. She just did. The door clicked closed behind her, making it official.

Dad still gripped the chair. I had my hands planted on the kitchen table. Even that didn't feel solid enough to hold me upright. On the stove, fragrant steam rose from the macaroni and cheese.

"Are you hungry?" I asked at last. My voice sounded faraway, foreign. I wasn't MacKenna, but a girl playing her in some movie. "I could make a salad—"

"Don't bother." Dad left the kitchen without looking at me. He headed, I knew, for the bedroom and the photograph in its silver frame.

I scooped a plate of macaroni and cheese and forced it down, with no real desire to eat, except I hadn't all day.

Afterward, I went upstairs and tugged the ammo crate out from under my bed and fished the journal from under my pillow. I lined it all up from the teapot to the any-soldier mail and realized Grandma Adele hadn't given me everything when she handed over the ammo crate.

My mom's letters home—not a single one. They were the missing puzzle piece in the picture the journal painted. Without that piece? I'd painted one last, sweet kiss under the desert sun.

With it?

It was a bright day, I decided, the oil well fires spitting streams of smoke into the air. Mom's cheeks glowed pink, from sun and excitement. I smelled the heat, the sand. I wanted to remember Mom like that, in that one last happy moment. I didn't want to think of what happened to a Humvee that hit a landmine. I saw the truth of that in Dad's eyes. He knew and would live with that knowledge for the rest of his life.

I held the journal, Mom's careful script blurring before my eyes. It was all there, the whole time. Maybe it was the word *accident*, but even with all the evidence, there on the page, I didn't see it until now. The mystery behind my mom and how she died. The mystery behind Dad.

I must have fallen asleep that way. At three in the morning, I was still in my clothes, overhead light blazing, my neck aching, journal clutched in my hand.

Deep silence weighed on me, like I was the only one home. I left the light on, tried to keep my eyes open, afraid that if I didn't, I'd wake up and find the house truly empty.

———

BY SEVEN O'CLOCK TUESDAY MORNING, I was nervous about Dad. As far as I knew, he hadn't left his room all night. I thought about the guilt he carried. I wished I'd known. Or been smart enough to figure it out, or at least not have been quite so self-centered. In my mind, the accusation I'd thrown at Landon ricocheted, hitting me full on.

Didn't what? Look past your own issues?

Now, I stood outside Dad's bedroom door. Part of me wanted to call Grandma Adele. But she'd been right. This was our problem. Part of me wanted to call 911. The silence had an eerie feel to it. Instead, I knocked.

"Dad? I'm heading to school now."

Nothing.

"Do you need anything?"

Again, nothing but silence.

"There's coffee."

I strained my ears, going so far as pressing one up against the door. A rustle of covers? Or merely wishful thinking. I grabbed my backpack from where I dropped it the night before and left.

If I'd been in avoidance mode on Monday, today, it was double. Today, everyone knew. At lunch, I didn't bother going near the cafeteria. Eating in the girls' bathroom seemed pathetic—not to mention deeply disgusting. I hid, instead, in the road-less-traveled stairwell, my back to the wall, my Chucks planted on the steps, in case I needed to make a break for it.

I pulled the same stunt with English as I did the day before, sliding into my seat as the bell rang. I didn't dare sneak a look at Landon. If he looked back, I wouldn't be able to take it. And if he didn't look back? I wouldn't be able to take it. It wasn't Landon I needed to worry about. Three seconds after I sat down, a pencil jabbed me between the shoulder blades.

"Hey," Josh said when I didn't turn around. "What gives?" He stabbed me again, but at least used the eraser end this time.

I cast a glance at him. "Nothing."

"I'm talking about swimming. It's totally freaking everyone out. They're going to have to re-choreograph everything."

I couldn't hold in the sigh at that. They would have to re-choreograph the opening and closing numbers, the junior number, the one I swam on as part of Kylie's publicity team.

"And Constance is about ready to kill you, just so you know."

And the duet that was suddenly a solo.

"I wish I could tell—" I began, then broke off, because I really didn't wish I could tell him anything.

"I heard someone say it was drugs."

At this, I spun in my chair to face him. "Someone? Really? Like Sierra?"

His face fell. "Right. Sorry."

"So am I." I turned back to the front of the room in time to catch Patti's glare. "I'm really sorry."

———

THE HALLS WERE quiet by the time I crept from the third floor girls' bathroom and slunk down the stairs to the first floor. I needed to make a quick stop at my locker to swap out books. I was cutting it close again, would probably have to jog part way home, but I took Josh's words as a warning. The longer I avoided Constance, the better, and by now, she'd be at the pool. The risk was worth it.

I was debating the merits of leaving by the school's back door versus the side door when a force barreled into me. I crashed against my locker, slamming the door shut.

"What the fuck is going on?" Constance yanked me by the shoulder and pinned me against the wall. Books flew from my hands and thudded against the floor. "I—I don't even know where to start, I'm so pissed. Patti won't say a damn thing, so you'd better."

I gulped for breath, pulse racing. I pushed against Constance, but she shoved and my shoulder blades met metal.

"What the hell is going on? Is it Landon? He looks like shit and you look worse."

"It's not Landon, not really." Poor Landon. He didn't deserve any of this. "He was in the wrong place at the wrong time."

"Okay, you're making no fucking sense." She let go of me. "Talk to me. If it turns out I have to kill you, I promise it will be quick."

I tried to laugh, but nothing came. "I'm grounded."

"You?" Curiosity and disbelief lit her face. "This I got to hear. What's the sin? Wait." She held up a hand. "You. Landon. And the Corvette. Sure, there isn't a lot of room, but even I'd do it in the Corvette. Your dad catch you two?"

In that moment, all I could think was: it would've been so much better if he had. "I was trying for a scholarship."

"Again, you're making no fucking sense."

"An ROTC scholarship."

Constance raised an eyebrow. "Isn't your dad Mr. GI Joe?"

"He's a combat vet."

She shook her head. "I'm not getting it."

"My mom." I took a long, shuddering breath. "She died during the first Iraq war. And I—"

She held up a hand, her features softening as if she'd been a silent witness to yesterday's fiasco in the kitchen. "It's okay. I get it now. And you don't have to, you know, talk about it, unless you want to."

"Maybe sometime."

Constance nodded and drummed her fingers against the lockers. "So, how grounded are you?"

"I can go to school," I said, "and then I can go back home again."

"Swim practice?"

I shook my head. "No practice, no show. I'm out, at least for the season, if not next." Dad hadn't said, but I wouldn't put it past him, not now, anyway.

"Shit," Constance said, but she was still drumming. A moment later, she said, "You ever been grounded before? Do something equally heinous like give all your lunch money to kids in Africa?"

"No, and yes, it was for UNICEF."

She snorted. "That might give us something to work with."

"Work with what?" I checked my watch, one I'd strapped on this morning since I didn't have my cell phone to tell me the time.

"Am I boring you?" Constance looked like she could shove me all the way inside my locker and leave me there.

"I need to get home." I rubbed my eyes. They felt gritty and raw. "My dad's timing me, and I'm walking."

"He took away your Jeep, too? Are you sure you didn't cause some natural disaster?"

"It just feels like it."

"Listen," she said, and leaned closer. "I don't give a shit about the rest of the show, but you will be swimming the duet if I have to hire people to kidnap you and bring you to the pool."

At least I'd get out of the house. Even as I nodded, I checked my watch again. I couldn't help it.

"Go," Constance said. "But remember, you're swimming. I'll think of something."

I crouched to pick up my books. To my surprise, she knelt and gathered the ones on the far side of the hall. We stayed like that, low to the ground. I sensed she wasn't through, not yet.

"You and Landon?" She handed me my German text. "What's the deal there?"

"I'm not allowed to see him." I held the book tight against my chest like that would stop the hurt. "My dad thinks he's a bad influence."

Constance laughed. "Well, he is. He's also ..." she trailed off and shook her head.

I knew she wasn't going to tell me. And maybe that was just as well.

Chapter 16

BY FRIDAY, I'd spent a record amount of time in the third floor girls' bathroom: about four hours. Dad said a record number of words to me: about four. Grandma Adele called to see how we were. I told her we were "working things out," by which I meant we'd perfected the ability to be where the other one was not.

I don't know if Landon looked my way during English, because I never even glanced at him. Each day, Josh caught my attention with pencil jabs, and on Friday, his update was: "Constance says you'll be back next week."

Then she knew something I didn't, and since I knew Dad, I figured she was wrong. I merely shrugged, grateful that Patti was handing out exams, if it meant not talking. I'd bomb this test, but I didn't really care. The paper landed on my desk with a soft puff of air. Clipped to the top of the page was a note:

See me after school today @ 3:30, my classroom.

My mind went blank, completely. I wrote out responses to the essay questions (Patti never gave multiple choice tests), but the second I finished, I forgot both the questions and the answers. At this rate, I'd go from blowing a single test to needing summer school.

After last bell, I skulked through the halls of Black Earth. Friday meant no swim practice, and I didn't want to meet anyone from the team in the hallway. Friday also meant that Dad might leave work early and was right now waiting on the front porch, gaze trained on his watch. But then, it wasn't like he could ground me any more than he already had.

Patti sat at her desk. I peered in at her, making sure the room was clear of the usual suspects who tended to freak after one of her exams. I hesitated and was still standing in the doorway when she glanced up.

I'm not sure anything would've gotten me into the room at that point, except one thing. Patti smiled. It was rueful and apologetic and very, very real. I took a tentative step forward. She nodded to the chair next to her desk. When I sat, she didn't hesitate at all.

"I owe you an apology," she said.

"Actually—"

"No, please, let me." She let out a long breath and stared out the window. "It's been an odd spring, filled with things I never thought I'd have to confront again." She turned to me. "You know your mom and I were best friends in high school, at least, I like to think we were."

I nodded.

"We kept in touch after graduation, even though we went to different colleges. I understood why she took the ROTC scholarship, although I was surprised when she decided to go on active duty."

Patti paused, as if considering her next words. "Still, I didn't think much of it. Sure, there was Panama and Granada, but you have to understand, back then, no one was going to war unless it was the big one."

She closed her eyes, the furrows along her brow deepening. "I'm not proud of this next part. We lost touch. Or rather, Beth tried very hard to stay in touch and I tried very hard to ignore her. I did fly over to Germany for the wedding. Did you know I was her maid of honor?"

I gave my head a slight shake.

"Well, I was. But ... I didn't like Paul—your father. He was all gung-ho Army. To me, he *was* the Army. I found him ... abrasive."

Who, *Dad?* Abrasive? I nearly laughed at that.

"I'm sorry, he's your father—"

"You're not telling me anything I don't already know." This time, I did laugh.

She gave me a quick smile, but it faded as fast as it lit up her features. "Honestly, MacKenna, it kills me to say this, but I just didn't understand what Beth saw in him."

Oh, but I did. True, I didn't have much to go on, but I squeezed my eyes shut and pictured them together in the Khobar Towers. Dad cutting her hair, uttering the words *spun gold.* Dad, writing his own kind of poetry on mix tape liner notes. There was more, I was sure. I'd probably never know their whole story. But the fact Dad never remarried? Never even had a girlfriend? It was a fairytale devotion that was nearly impossible to find in the real world.

Patti fell silent and I felt something brew between us—not understanding, but something not yet said, something Patti didn't want to say.

"It wasn't too long after you were born that Iraq invaded Kuwait. I heard from Beth that first Paul was being deployed, then she was. I marched in some protests, but in a way, it was an excuse just to be angry, because I was angry at Beth. Then I got scared. Then, I finally got guilty enough to write."

She leaned down and pulled a letter from her tote bag. She slapped the envelope against her thigh. "It spent two weeks in my purse. Then I heard. Beth had died. After all the shooting and all the bombing, after all the danger was over. She ... died."

She swiped the palm of one hand against her eyes. I took slow, measured breaths, but I felt dizzy, like the air didn't hold enough oxygen, or that there wasn't enough air—period—to breathe.

"Someday," she said. "Maybe I'll have the stomach to read this. But until then." She returned the letter to the tote and met my gaze. "I'm sorry, MacKenna. I was angry with myself, not you. And if I'm honest, still a little angry at Beth." She shook her head. "You look so much like her that when you asked for help on an ROTC scholarship, it felt like history repeating itself."

I didn't know what to say to that.

"How can I blame you for keeping a secret, especially that one, when I have plenty of my own?"

"It's okay." My voice hitched and I sucked in another breath.

"Not really, not until we get you back on the team." Patti leaned forward, propping her elbow on her desk. "Any hints on how I might handle your Dad? Let's just say I didn't make the best impression, last Sunday or all those years ago."

I'd been handling Dad for years, but this was different. "He's not even talking to me."

"Oh, honey, I'm so sorry. You don't deserve this."

I wasn't so sure about that, but I nodded anyway. "I should go. I'm—" I glanced at the wall clock and swore under my breath. "I'm really late. I need to get home."

"I'll think of something." Patti stood and walked me to the classroom door. "Maybe have him come down to Saturday's practice, see how much we miss your hard work."

I had my doubts. She gave my shoulder a squeeze and I left, taking the stairs by two and running most of the way home. Because every time I slowed down, I thought about that unsent letter, neatly addressed and stamped, about mix tapes and missed opportunities.

And every time I thought of those things, it hurt to breathe.

A MINIVAN with a dent in the door sat in our driveway, but I hardly noticed it. Dad met me on the porch, a drill sergeant scowl on his face.

"Mind telling me where you were?" he said.

"School work," I said. "I may be flunking English." It wasn't true. At least, I hoped it wasn't, but I said it on the chance it might throw him off kilter.

It did, enough so I could sidestep him and walk into the kitchen. I slipped a frozen lasagna into the oven and set the timer. Then I retreated to my room. The door had barely closed when Dad knocked on it.

"Yeah?" I said, trying to keep the attitude from my voice. Sadly, I had plenty to spare. I braced for the coming assault.

Dad opened the door. "There's a girl here who says you're 'mission critical.'" Here, he drew quotation marks in the air. "To the swim team. I'm afraid if I say no, she'll make me one of the undead."

"That must be Constance," I said.

"The undead have names? Who knew?"

Okay, so Dad still had a major case of the ass. At least he was talking to me in complete sentences. He sat on the edge of my bed, forearms resting on his thighs, hands locked together. "Mission critical?" he asked. "Did you teach … Constance that?"

I shook my head. "Con has a way of figuring things out."

"So, this grounding." Now Dad turned back to contemplating the floor and the colorful rag rug in its center. "Kind of fucks things up for more than just you."

I didn't dare speak, because really, I'd tried to tell him that earlier. Explaining how difficult it was to re-choreograph five numbers, at the last minute, probably wouldn't help. Not coming from me, at least.

"The rest of the punishment still stands," Dad said, at last. "But you can go to practice and swim in the show."

I'm sure the gust of air from my lungs hit the ceiling. "Oh, thank—"

He cut off my gratitude with a curt wave, like it was the last thing he wanted to hear. "Go tell her," he said. "She's waiting."

I hopped up and made a dash for the front door, not trusting that Dad wouldn't suddenly change his mind. Outside, Constance stood on the front steps, hands in black lace, fingerless gloves clasped behind her back. She wore a high-collared blouse and a long black skirt. She'd gone all out, and Dad had no clue how much, either.

Constance turned. She'd even gone light on the kohl around her eyes. "The verdict?"

"I'm back in."

"Sweet." She smiled, not a smirk, nothing snide, but a genuine smile. "I hope you haven't been stuffing your face these past few days."

" Actually, I've barely eaten."

"Make sure you do. We need to play catch up because we are so not going to suck, okay?"

I saluted. "Yes, ma'am."

"Fuck you." But the smile—the genuine one—was still there.

I thought Constance might leave then, but she sat on the cement steps. I plopped down next to her.

"What about you and Landon?" she asked.

"Nothing else has changed."

"Shit."

Constance sounded odd, like she wasn't telling me everything about Landon. I didn't have the strength to look at him for more than a second at a time, and even that hurt like hell. "Is he okay?"

"He told you." Her fingers lighted on her chest, over her heart.

"Yeah," I said. "He did."

We sat, watched shadows cross the lawn, changing the blades of grass from golf course green to something darker, more jungle like.

"Just so you know," Constance said at last, "in case he starts being a real ass. He misses you. If he says anything or does something stupid, it's just—" She waved a hand in the air. "Anyway, I gotta go. I'll call Patti and have her open the pool at seven thirty for us."

I gave her another salute. Constance rolled her eyes before pushing off the porch and heading for the minivan. Behind me, in the house, was lukewarm lasagna and ice-cold Dad. I didn't have the appetite for either. So I stayed outside, thought about the duet, and practiced holding my breath.

CONSTANCE'S VISIT reminded me how lonely I was. For Landon. For Dad. For anyone. Every time I picked up my mom's journal, the ache grew stronger. So sitting in the den with Dad that night, even if he was as comforting as a cement teddy bear, was better than nothing. Plus, he relented, slightly, on the computer restriction. For schoolwork only, he agreed, when I pointed out I needed to access the school's website for my assignments.

Tonight, I pushed it a little. I did complete all my homework—on a Friday because I had nothing better to do—but I also accidently on purpose landed on Google. One search led to another, one click to a new piece of information. I learned a lot that night, like how the pacemaker Landon told me about kept his heart beating, how his previous model had failed in children as young as two.

"It's why I'm back in Black Earth," he had told me over dinner at Mall of America. "The FDA did a recall—"

"A recall—?"

"And I have a brand new one, bleeding edge, you might say."

"Landon—"

"I get to be here because of it." He grinned at me. "My mom didn't want me going back to boarding school. She has this ongoing battle with my dad about it, and this time, she won. So you see? It's lucky."

Scary stuff happened with pacemakers, stuff he didn't bother to tell me about, like the wires that attached the pacemaker to the heart—these were called leads—poking holes in the heart. The leads could get infected, which, in turn, could infect the heart, *his heart*.

I was so absorbed that Dad's approaching footfalls barely registered. My hand hovered on the mouse, but it was too late to hide the screen.

Dad peered at the monitor. "Jesus." He exhaled, then studied me, curious. "Is this for a class you're taking?"

"Sorry, no. I found out … a friend has a pacemaker. I wanted to know more about it." I moved to shut down the browser. "I was just worried, that's all."

Dad nodded. He didn't tell me to stop, but he didn't say good-night, either. All he said was: "It's late, and don't you have practice in the morning?"

We both went to bed without saying another word.

———

ALL WEEK LONG, I swam hard, before school and after practice. Even though I showered twice a day, the stench of chlorine clung to me. I swam too hard to think. When my thoughts did stray, I locked them up tight, like my mom had, only I visualized her ammo crate—in went all the chatter about prom, anything to do with Landon, anything that wasn't swimming or schoolwork. It was hard to forget about any of it with that prom dress taking up half my closet. The dress still had its tag and I had the receipt. The second I was ungrounded, I was driving up to the Mall of America for a refund. Landon would get his money back.

All that week, when I did brave a glance at Landon, I discovered he was no longer staring at me. If he turned in my direction, his gaze slid over me, like I didn't exist. This was far worse than anything he could've done.

That last Saturday in April, I pounded the treadmill in the basement, even though I'd started the day swimming at seven thirty with Constance. Even though we ran through the entire show—minus makeup, Knox in our hair, and costume changes—twice. Even though Constance and I stayed late and ran through the duet again.

A hum of excitement had filled the pool area. The air nearly sparkled with it, and random squeals bounced off the walls. Not even Patti was immune to that electric spark, and she let everyone go early. That way everyone could get their up-dos, professional makeovers, mani/pedis and of course, the obligatory photographs.

Everyone, that is, who was going to prom.

I ran, wondering how many miles it would take before my legs gave out. Ten? Fifteen? And how many miles after that would my heart stop hurting? Dad had no idea what an un-punishment running inside was. I didn't want to be on the streets, didn't want to catch sight of a limo, or God forbid, a stretch Hummer. I didn't want to choke on perfume in the air, or hear the rustle of taffeta. I didn't want to see a single guy in a tux, not the most obnoxious jock, and certainly not Landon.

Because Landon was going to prom.

That morning at practice, he'd been working on his platform stage, his back to the pool, adjusting props, the sound, the lighting with the tech crew. Head set on, he ran through his opening monologue, pausing for an occasional hammer strike.

During lunch, he changed tactics and conducted man-on-the-street, or rather, girl-in-the-pool interviews, asking about dresses and colors, and whether everyone had coordinated with their dates. He sauntered up to Patti, who was looking half amused and half harassed at the sight of him.

"Of course, Black Earth High is lucky to have the loveliest of chaperones. Tell me, Ms. Flynn, what will *you* be wearing tonight?"

"Basic black," Patti said, purposely avoiding the mic. "And I'll be keeping my eye on you."

"Well, it looks like my prom experience will be ... curtailed. Thank you for that, Ms. Flynn."

That was when it happened. Everyone's head jerked toward me, then Landon. I saw the questions in everyone's eyes. Were we still together? Was Landon going stag ... or taking someone else? The team-wide double take sent me underwater, but with the stupid speakers, there was no escape.

I couldn't banish the sound of Landon's voice, of everyone's inane chatter about dresses and tuxes, not underwater, not in the locker room, and not now, pounding the treadmill. Sweat trickled down my legs, gathered behind my knees. I wore a black sports bra and booty shorts with the word SWIM across the butt, the ones Dad never let me wear out of the house.

Speaking of Dad, he eventually wandered down to the basement. He stood, arms crossed over his chest, like he wanted to ban this activity too, but couldn't find a good enough reason.

At last, he said, "Don't run too hard."

"I won't." Never mind I planned on doing just that. Too hard to think, too hard to hear Landon's voice, too hard to stare at the clock all night and wonder what he was doing.

I was still on the treadmill when the doorbell rang at six. The sound jolted me, totally threw me off my stride. I slid off the track and then slapped my palm on the power button. Maybe it was Grandma Adele bearing macaroni and cheese and Key lime pie. We'd all sit at the kitchen table. Maybe we'd even talk. At the very least, I could drown my sorrows in carbohydrates. Hell, at this point, I'd choke down the tuna and pea hot dish.

I took the basement stairs by two, determined to get to the door before Dad. I flung it open, took a second to catch my breath, then froze.

On the porch, in a charcoal gray morning style tuxedo—the sort with a cutaway suit coat—stood Landon.

———

LANDON'S VEST and ascot tie were the exact color of the forget-me-knots scattered in the white rosebud corsage he held. On his feet, the only clue that Landon Scott didn't conform, were matching blue and white checkered Vans.

He looked me up and down, his eyes narrow, without expression. "You know we have dinner reservations at Engelmann's Supper Club at six forty-five, right?"

Wrong. I stood there, pouring sweat, complete with sports bra and booty shorts, and wondered: What part of grounded-for-life didn't he understand?

"Who was that—?" Dad's voice faltered at the sight of Landon. He was still the ice man cometh, and waves of anger rolled off him.

"Jesus Christ," Dad said. "What the fuck now?"

Landon didn't flinch, not at Dad's words, or at his tone. Neither did I, since I was thinking the exact same thing.

"MacKenna is my prom date," Landon said, perfectly calm.

"MacKenna is grounded." Dad was equally calm.

"She's still my prom date," Landon said, as if one had nothing to do with the other.

Dad looked at me, deciding I could shed some light on this fresh version of insanity. "Is he totally unclear on the concept?"

I shrugged and pushed sweat-soaked strands of hair from my forehead.

"Well, if MacKenna can't go, can I get her dress?"

"Her dress," Dad echoed.

"I paid for it," Landon said. "It totally rocks and should be at prom whether she's in it or not."

Oh. My. God. Landon and his big mouth. I couldn't look at Dad, but I felt him turn all his wrath on me.

"I thought we had a talk about rich boys doing you favors."

I hazarded a glance. Anger was one thing, but Dad's expression held disappointment as well. Somehow, that was worse. "We did," I admitted.

"And yet, here we are again," Dad said. "In one ear and out the other."

"I bullied her into it," Landon said. "I wanted her to have it."

Dad planted a glare on Landon. "You know what? That doesn't change a thing."

"Hey, MacKenna?" Landon's voice sounded weird, like an echo of his father's, and I didn't like it. "Can I talk to your dad alone?"

Dad crossed his arms over his chest, clearly unimpressed. "Whatever you have to say, you can say it in front of MacKenna."

Today at practice had been bad enough, but now, after seeing Landon in his tux, the flowers meant for my wrist, I'd have to run another ten miles. Even that might not do the trick.

"Have at it," I told them both. "I'm out of here."

"Go put some clothes on," was Dad's parting shot.

Nice.

Upstairs, I collapsed on my bed. Murmurs came from the front porch, but I had zero desire to eavesdrop. Landon knew I couldn't go to prom, especially not with him. So what was up? Didn't Constance say he might act like an ass? Well, this qualified. Eventually, the voices faded. I peered out the window, the flash of bumble bee yellow all I needed to confirm that Landon was still here.

"MacKenna!" That was Dad, bellowing from the kitchen.

I bolted, nearly tripped down the stairs, and found them at the kitchen table. Dad sipped a Heineken, Landon an A&W Root Beer. It was a regular male bonding fest. Right here. In the middle of our kitchen.

It was weird.

"You'd better hurry," Dad said. "Most people shower before prom."

I looked at Landon—who didn't glance up—then Dad. I shook my head, letting them know I was beyond confused by all this.

244

"A concession," Dad said. "Considering the expense on Landon's part, you may go to prom. Curfew is eleven fifteen."

Here, Landon did glance up. "I'll try, sir, but with prom ending at eleven, there's going to be a lot of traffic. I might not make it out of the parking lot by then."

"Eleven thirty," Dad said. "Not a second later. I'll be waiting up."

Of course he would.

"Well?" Dad didn't smile. In fact, he hadn't smiled for nearly a week. I was pretty certain he wouldn't for a while, maybe never again. "You better get ready."

———

THANKS to three years on the synchro team, I could tame my hair into a passable chignon in about five minutes. I tied it with a white ribbon the Nordstrom's saleslady had added to the bag when she rang up the dress. It wasn't the up-do of my dreams, but it was okay. My makeup was bland. No time for nail polish never mind a manicure. At least my toes were well hidden inside the white Converse. But the dress. The dress made up for a lot. I felt like a princess—something, I realized, Dad hadn't called me for nearly a week now. I pressed my fingertips against my eyelids, sucked in a deep breath, and decided I wouldn't let Dad ruin this, too.

I made my way to the kitchen, the silk of the dress seeming to whisper and sigh. It wasn't exactly a grand entrance, but Landon swiveled in his chair, then nearly fell out of it. That was the reaction I was hoping for.

"Perfect," he said.

White takeout boxes and two pairs of chopsticks sat on the kitchen table. Only then did I catch the heady scent of Pad Thai, the zest of orange chicken.

"Screw Engelmann's," he said. "They're overpriced and most of the entrées suck. Plus, we're running late. I hope you don't mind."

"I like this better."

We ate, serenaded by Dad somewhere out in the yard, using the leaf blower. At one point, the kitchen window rattled. I thought the leaf blower might throw a rock, or possibly that was part of his plan.

"So it has what?" Landon asked, nodding toward the window. "Two settings? Loud and louder?"

"I know. He's not being very subtle." Which was totally Dad.

We didn't talk much over dinner. Uncertainty made me take small, careful bites, like one false move and I'd jeopardize the entire evening. On the way out, though, I hurried down the steps, my goal the Corvette and a few hours of freedom.

Landon, however, lingered and caught Dad's eye. Dad put down the leaf blower (thankfully) and approached.

"Are you going to prom or your wedding?" Dad didn't wait for an answer, which was just as well, since I wasn't going to give him one. Instead, he gripped me by one shoulder and spun me around, no doubt calculating the percentage of skin the satin ribbons didn't cover.

"Doesn't she look great?" Landon asked.

"She looks underdressed." Dad was on the verge of growling, Fury, I thought, welcome back.

I sighed. "I can slip the modesty panel in."

"And we can slip it right back out," Landon muttered.

"Forget it." Dad waved us away. "Just go."

That was all the encouragement I needed.

Apparently, Landon needed more. He stood there, gaze locked on Dad. "Mr. Meyers, sir?" Landon sounded genuinely perplexed. "Don't you want to take any pictures?"

"No." Dad turned from me and headed for the leaf blower. "I don't."

THE POOF of my dress took up most of the front seat. I pulled the silky fabric close enough to hide my face, all on the pretext of freeing up room so Landon could shift gears. My breath came in choppy fits and starts. My stomach ached.

Landon kept a hand on the wheel and pushed the dress away from my face with the other. "MacKenna." The soft chanting way of saying my name was back. "Shit, I'm sorry. I didn't think—"

"Yeah," I said. "Sometimes you don't."

We drove the rest of the way in silence.

In the parking lot, I struggled to get out of the car, the dress blocking my view. Despite the excellent traction of my white Chuck Taylors, I couldn't get a grip on the asphalt. Warm fingers grasped mine. I went flying from the Corvette and into Landon's arms. I tried to push away, but those arms locked around me, holding me tight.

"I've missed you, I've missed you, I've missed you," he said, like a mantra in that soft, chanting way of his.

All at once I melted, my anger vanishing with the breeze that caught my skirt and billowed it around us. "I'm sorry," I said.

"No. I am." Here, he kissed me, his lips hot against my skin, my neck. Tears filled my eyes, and he kissed each drop from my face. "Don't," he said. "Don't cry."

He held onto me with something like panic in his grip, like he was afraid I'd slip away. "If you wanted, we could go play computer games instead."

I laughed, for what felt like the first time in days.

"Or we could go to prom," he added.

"Well, now that we're here."

"All right, then." He kissed me one last time. "Prom it is."

Chapter 17

INSIDE THE HOTEL BALLROOM, the ceiling looked midnight black, strings of tiny light bulbs twinkled like stars you could touch, if you stood on tiptoes. Landon dragged me to the very center of the dance floor and held me close, closer than before, so close, the skirt of my dress flowed around his legs, so close I felt his thigh against mine. His fingertips found the bare skin between the satin ribbons on my back.

At his touch, I lost all ability to think, to breathe. There was nothing but Landon, his fingers, and my skin. He kissed me then, kissed me until we barely swayed to the music, kissed me until the song faded, kissed me until someone nearby faked a cough.

That was Constance. At prom. I glanced at Landon, who looked like he had a dozen things to say, all designed to send her off the deep end.

"I'd hate to think the rest of us will have to watch this all night long," she said. "Please tell me you got a room."

"Constance," Landon said. "My little prom princess. You're looking ... well, nothing like yourself."

"Shove it up your ass."

"You look great," I said, stepping between them. Constance really did look fantastic. She wore a deep red dress overlaid with black lace, and the fabric hugged every curve. An encounter with hot rollers made her hair fall in gentle waves. True, her eyes were still rimmed with kohl, but apparently not even Constance Radley was immune to prom fever.

"So who's the lucky guy?" Landon asked.

"I'm here with Sam Avery."

Swim boy Sam? I couldn't help it. I clamped a hand over my mouth to stifle a laugh.

"What?" Landon looked puzzled. "Swim team, right? So, we've got birds of a feather, or maybe fish of a … fin?"

"Shut up," Constance said, although this was directed at me.

"He's also," I said to Landon, "the president of FCA."

"Of what?" Landon asked.

"Fellowship of Christian Athletes," I elaborated, feeling smug.

Landon snorted, then outright laughed.

"Shut the hell up." Constance grimaced, like she had a Landon-induced migraine.

"So, in other words," Landon mused. "You're in no danger of being felt up tonight."

Constance heaved a sigh. "Unfortunately."

"He's very nice," I said. Although, honestly, Constance Radley and Sam Avery had to be a match made somewhere other than heaven.

Constance rolled her eyes. "What about you? You sprung from prison?"

"For the night." I shrugged and nodded toward Landon. "It was kind of like you said. He just showed up, and things got …" I threw a glance toward Landon, who had drifted over to a group of the tech guys. "Weird."

"Figures." Constance shook out her hair. "You'll excuse me? I need to go spike Sam's Red Bull and introduce him to the sin of tongue kissing."

Without Constance or Landon, I felt unbalanced. I scanned the crowd, Z-pattern style, looking for the one person I should probably avoid. I couldn't help it. When I spotted her, the vice grip on my stomach eased, just slightly.

Prom had always meant so much to Nissa.

She sat with Tim McPherson, Lukas's wingman, he of the pretend homemade beer. Actually, she sat on his lap, an arm draped over his shoulder, his hand protective on her waist. I guess he really *had* been a contender. Her face was bent toward his, her expression half hidden by his shoulder. It didn't matter. I knew her well enough to know: she at least looked happy.

I really hoped she was.

I took another glance around. At the table where Nissa sat, all the other girls were seniors of the cheerleading captain-prom queen variety. I scrutinized the junior tables, but still couldn't find the other two people I should probably avoid. But it didn't look like I'd be running into Jodi or Sierra, at least not at prom.

When Nissa excused herself and headed for the restrooms, I followed.

We nearly collided outside the stalls. She wore a black, form-fitting dress, her hair shiny and smooth. We were opposites—Nissa dark and sleek, with me, light and poufy.

"You look great," I said.

"You, too."

And then nothing but emptiness between us, awkward and heavy. I adjusted my dress, the white high tops peeking out below the hem. Her gaze darted downward, and for one excruciating moment, I thought Nissa might smile.

"I have to get back to Tim," she said.

I stood in the bathroom after she left. A group of girls streamed in, their chatter crashing against the walls. I pushed my way out, a sudden need for Landon stealing my breath. I hiked up my skirt and ran.

The ballroom was too dark; the starlight dazzled my eyes. I spun, frantic, until Landon's arms caught my waist.

"Whoa." He hauled me close, my back against his chest. "You okay?"

"Sort of."

"I saw you both go in there." He nodded toward the bathrooms. "I almost came in after you. Is everything—?"

I shook my head, cutting him off. "It was … nothing." That was worse, somehow, than if Nissa had slapped me or thrown a cup of pink punch at my dress.

"I'm sorry," he said, and gripped my arms tighter. "I wish it didn't have to be this way." When I didn't respond, he added, "Come on. Let's dance."

We danced, the only conversation the play of Landon's fingers along my back. For two songs that was enough. Still, a nagging thought wouldn't let me enjoy prom completely.

"What did you say to my dad?" I asked. "I mean," I added when Landon didn't speak. "To convince him to let me go."

He sighed. "You don't want to know."

Well, now I really, really did. In fact, I needed to know. "Tell me."

"It's incredibly sexist and chauvinistic."

"And yet it worked on my dad," I said. "Go figure. Come on. Tell me."

Landon swallowed back a second sigh. "I hinted that if you had something—or someone—in Black Earth." Here he gave me a significant look. "You might not join the Army."

"Are you talking about—" I couldn't wrap my brain, never mind my mouth, around what he was saying. "So, you what? Convinced him I'd give it all up to be Mrs. Scott Industries." *Oh, come on.* Dad was way smarter than that.

"Pretty much." Landon snorted. "Look, he heard what he wanted to hear. I know he's being a colossal asshole, but he does love you. I've figured that much out." He pulled me close, his arms locked around my waist. "I would never do that to you, never make you give up your dreams."

"What about you?"

"What about me?"

"Your dreams ... you know, after high school."

"After high school." Landon shrugged. "Whatever."

"Come on," I said, "what do you want to be when you grow up?"

"Alive."

He gathered me closer still, so again my dress flared around his legs and our thighs met. I wrapped my arms around his neck, but I knew, I could've flung them out, leaned back, and he'd still hold onto me. And even though I didn't, part of me felt like I was—free falling with Landon there to catch me.

"I love you," he said.

With those words, I continued to fall. It was like all the air had been knocked from me. I never had the chance to land, to catch my breath, never had the chance to respond. Landon kissed me so ardently, so insistently, I wondered if he was scared of what I might —or might not—say. Without thought, without voice, I kissed him back and hoped he'd taste the words I couldn't speak.

I love you too.

———

WE STAYED until the very last moment, stayed until the lights went up and the fluorescent glare erased the dreamy starlight. Chaperones herded couples toward the doors, then looked the other way when a significant number headed for hotel rooms rather than the parking lot.

Landon tucked me into the passenger seat of the Corvette, which considering the dress, wasn't exactly easy. He stood at the driver's side, one arm resting on the open door, the other on the Corvette's roof. I leaned across the gearshift and peered up.

"Landon? You okay?"

"I've got to get you home." He slipped into the car seat. "But really, I wish we had a hotel room."

Heat burst into my cheeks. They burned so hot, I wondered how combustible silk taffeta was.

"I could sleep for days," he added.

Oh. Sure. Because that was what everyone else was doing. He leaned over and met me with a kiss. "Of course, you might be able to persuade me to do a few other things as well."

"A rousing game of Scrabble?" I suggested, my lips a breath away from his.

"Strip Scrabble."

"No fair," I said. "You're wearing more clothes than I am."

"Sounds completely fair to me."

I giggled, but it was only halfhearted. In the yellow lamplight, Landon did look tired, not at all like himself, his skin pale and waxy, a tightness around his eyes.

"I've been stressing you out," I said.

"Your dad? Maybe." He kissed my nose. "You? Never." Landon put the Corvette in gear, pulled from the lot, and drove me home.

———

"LANDON?"

I told myself I had the courage for this. I needed to talk to him before we reached my house. If not now, when? Tonight felt like a fairy tale. On Monday, I'd go back to my dreary existence. I'd be MacKenna Meyers, a little odd, a little on the outside, and a whole lot grounded.

"Landon?" I tried again. He'd been distracted during the drive, probably gearing up to face Dad. He took the turn for my driveway and the Corvette skittered.

He was a better driver than that; the Corvette handled better than that. Landon slumped forward against the wheel as if he'd fainted. The car veered toward the cement porch. A scream filled the space. My throat ached with it, but I swore the sound came from somewhere outside me.

I pushed my hands beneath Landon, grasped the steering wheel. His chest was heavy against my arms and I could barely turn the wheel. Finally, I yanked. The Corvette bounced over some brick edging and plowed straight into the closed garage door. The impact threw me against the seatbelt, then whipped me back. I braced my hands on the dashboard, caught my breath. When I glanced at Landon, a twinge ran through my neck. I ignored it.

"Landon?"

Nothing. The crash had thrown him back. His head lolled, horribly. Everything about him looked wrong. My hand crept over his chest, popped the tuxedo shirt studs, until I felt the soft cotton of his undershirt. Was he breathing? As my hand traveled upward, toward his scar, it hit me.

The pacemaker. His *heart*. I groped his neck, tried to find a pulse, and couldn't.

Don't panic. Think, MacKenna, think.

I flung open the car door and nearly fell to the ground. I grabbed fistfuls of dress and hurried around to the driver's side. Even with the door wide open and seatbelt off, Landon was too heavy to move and I was wasting too many seconds.

I knew from the first aid class I'd taken with Dad, and reading about Landon's pacemaker, he needed the EMTs and the drugs and defibrillator they'd have in the ambulance. I tripped up the porch steps, pushed open the front door, and screamed.

"Dad!"

I screamed again and laid my palm against the doorbell, unrelenting, until inside, the chime rang like church bells. Still no Dad.

Screw it. I couldn't wait. CPR. I'd start CPR. I dashed down the steps, my Chuck Taylors catching the hem of the dress. Back at the car, I tugged at Landon's inert form, inching him from the driver's seat.

Too slow. I was too damn slow.

"What the fuck?"

I jerked, my head smashing against the car roof. I peered through the pain and saw Dad in his usual pose, arms crossed, scowl on.

"Don't tell me," he said. "Alcohol."

I shook my head and sudden spikes shot through it. I winced. How to explain? Then it came to me. "He's my friend with the pacemaker."

Dad's expression shifted. He was fierce, in control, combat mode. "Go call 911," he said.

———

I STAYED on the phone long enough to know for certain the ambulance was on its way, long enough to explain about Landon's pacemaker. Then I tore back outside. Landon was spread-eagle on the asphalt driveway. Dad sliced through the T-shirt with a pocket knife he kept in the Blazer. In the dim light from the porch lamp, the scar above Landon's heart looked pale.

"Remember your CPR?" Dad asked.

I nodded and knelt by Landon's head.

"His airway's clear. I'll do the chest compressions," Dad ordered, "you breathe for him."

With the first chest compression, a crackling reached me, like eggshells being crushed. Cartilage, I reminded myself, just cartilage. I counted the compressions, not that I needed to. On thirty, Dad paused and nodded at me. I brought my mouth to Landon's, watched his chest rise and fall. Counting gave me something to focus on until, in the distance, came the wail of a siren. The sound grew louder, drowned out the thoughts in my head, until all I heard was the siren, and all I felt was the jerk of Landon's body after each chest compression.

The ambulance skidded to a stop in front of the driveway. The

EMTs were out, equipment grabbed, and then, one of them tugged me away from Landon and slipped into my spot.

"He has a pacemaker!" I called out.

The woman nodded and she and her partner went to work. I stepped one way, then the other, my view blocked. I trembled until something soft and warm covered my shoulders. Dad tightened the afghan around me, then wrapped his arms around mine.

"You can go inside," he said. "I'll stay. You don't have to watch."

I shook my head. Dad squeezed my arms in response.

A police car bumped to a halt, half on the sidewalk, half on Dad's lawn. He let go, gave my arm one more quick squeeze, and went to talk with the officers. A few moments later, one of them returned with Dad.

For questioning. Drugs. Alcohol. I gave my head a violent shake, so hard, I regretted it a second later. My neck crackled. Pain throbbed behind my eyes. I cringed, probably looked guilty, because the officer wouldn't stop.

"You sure?" the officer asked. "Maybe when you went to the bathroom, he had a drink."

"Maybe you'd like to give her a breathalyzer," Dad said in his Army command voice. Then he stared at where the EMTs were still working on Landon. "Or him. My daughter doesn't lie." To Dad's credit, he managed that sentence without a single twitch.

After that, the story came out in small pieces, with small words. By the time I was done, the officer's skeptical expression had vanished.

"Smart girl," he said. "You may have saved your friend's life."

May have wasn't good enough. The EMTs readied a stretcher. Dad held me, fierce again.

"He's stabilized," the female technician said. "Let's get him out of here."

They loaded Landon onto the stretcher and into the ambulance. The police sedan pulled around front, lights flashing, siren blaring. I clutched the afghan and waited for the noise and lights to fade.

In the quiet, the Corvette still idled. Dad walked over to the car, reached in, and killed the engine.

———

AT ST. JOSEPH'S HOSPITAL, Dad found someone to show us to a waiting area. He found a drink machine and bought a hot chocolate. He sat me in one of those impossibly narrow chairs and my dress poufed over the sides.

Dad wrapped my fingers around the cup, the hot paper sides heating my icy hands. I shook, all over, and sent ripples across the chocolate's surface. I tried to drink, even brought the cup to my lips, but couldn't swallow.

Dad took the cup, set it on a side table, and pulled me into a hug. "Jesus, princess. I'm sorry. I'm sorry about everything."

Princess. It wasn't that it came too little too late, but that now my nickname sounded unbearably sad. The tremor that had started in my hands flowed through my entire body. The harder I tried to control it, the worse the shaking got. My chest ached, like my heart had broken wide open. First one tear, then another, rolled down my cheeks.

Then I couldn't stop crying. Dad held me tight as if he knew I was trying to banish the images. In the driveway, I'd felt my connection to Landon slip away. Like with my mom, his memory confined to a keepsake box, a collection of things that, when you added them together, never amounted to the entire person. Nothing I could do would bring either one of them back.

Dad pulled a chair from one of the neatly formed rows and sat so our knees touched. He anchored Grandma Adele's afghan tighter around my shoulders. From time to time, he smoothed my hair and whispered, "I know. I know."

The awful thing about it was, he did know. And I wondered how he could stand it.

It was two in the morning when Mrs. Scott found us. She burst into the waiting area and Dad stood. She launched herself at us. Dad looked startled, but he held her hand gingerly, like she was a small child. She bent down and captured me in an embrace then pulled me into a hug, one so ferocious it rivaled the best of Dad's.

"They told me what happened. They told me what the two of you did." She loosened her grip enough to touch my cheek. "This isn't—" Her voice hitched and she glanced at Dad. "This isn't the ideal way to get reacquainted, is it?" She turned back to me. "Oh, honey, you must have been so scared."

Yes. And no. *Now* I was terrified, of the unknown, of what was happening to Landon while I stood here in a beige and blue waiting area, where everything matched and yet nothing was real.

"I'm kind of scared now," I admitted.

"D-don't worry," Mrs. Scott said, but the fresh crop of tears made me do just that. "He's in intensive care as a precaution," she added. "I know it's late, but would you like to see him?"

I glanced at Dad, who nodded, imperceptibly. "Can I?" I asked.

"It's not routine, family only," Mrs. Scott said. "Plus he's sedated. But I'll see what I can do."

"Then he's—"

"Going to be okay." Here, Mrs. Scott did break down, leaning heavily against Dad. "I'm not sure what would've happened without either of you."

"Yes." The strange voice made all of us jump. At the waiting room entrance, Mr. Scott stood, bleary eyed and looking like he'd just arrived.

Landon's mom didn't run to him, didn't collapse into him. Instead, she stood straighter, more composed.

"It seems," Mr. Scott said, "I owe you both a measure of gratitude."

"It was MacKenna." Dad put an arm around my shoulder and I was thankful for the support. "She didn't panic."

Didn't I? Already, the events were fading. I remember flinging open the front door so hard, it smashed against the wall, leaning on the doorbell, fumbling with Landon's seatbelt, all of it laced with panic thick enough to choke on.

"He's going to be fine," Mrs. Scott said, more formally now. "He's scheduled for a new pacemaker tomorrow. He doesn't need new leads, so he'll spend a few days in the hospital, with perhaps a checkup at Mayo, and then—"

"And then," Mr. Scott finished, a strange finality to his words. He led Mrs. Scott from the waiting area, but she tugged against his arm, slowing him down. "I'll let you know," she said to me.

Dad walked to the waiting room entrance and stared down the hall after them. When the bell for the elevator dinged, he turned toward me.

"Well, you know what, princess? It could always be worse."

I choked out something that sounded like a laugh.

Dad glanced around the waiting area, his gaze lighting on me, then the side table, and back to me. "Hot chocolate get cold?"

I touched a finger to the cup. The paper felt clammy. "I think so."

"Want another? They have vanilla lattes, too."

"Hot chocolate's fine."

This time, I drank, gulping the chocolate before it was cool enough, the heat scalding my throat. Dad sat in that chair he'd pulled up to mine.

"You were so beautiful tonight." He pushed a few strands of hair from my cheek. "I'm sorry I didn't take any pictures."

I shook my head as if that would clear prom, pictures, and all the silliness from my mind. "I don't want to remember tonight."

"You never know." Dad stared at something so intently, I almost turned to see what it was. But I knew whatever he saw, it wasn't in this hospital. "You never know."

I took his word for it.

"I've spent the last few days thinking." He turned his own cup in his hands, chemical coffee with extra fake cream. "Adele said some things the other week, things I should've put together before now."

I took another scalding sip and waited.

"Seriously, your old man can be pretty dense." He tapped his head. "I never put it together before now. Camping, swimming, all the things your mom did. I'd be lying if I said it didn't make me happy. And I know it made Adele happy. You know she lost Frank before she came to stay with us."

This was something I did know, although Grandma Adele didn't talk much about Grandpa Frank either. He died a year before I was born. She moved to Germany, where Dad and my mom were stationed at the time, to take care of me when my mom went back to work.

"The guys in the unit used to give me shit, you know, mother-in-law living with us and all." Dad shook his head and I saw the start of a smile—a sad one, but still a smile. "But it was great," he said. "We never worried with Adele around. I think you saved her, once then, and again, when your mom died. I know you saved me."

I didn't think my heart could ache any more than it already did. I didn't think I could stand any more than what I already had tonight. Dad kept talking; I kept listening. Deep down I found the strength because, at last, he was telling me what I'd always wanted to hear.

"So, all those things. It made me happy," Dad continued. "Your grandmother, too. But I have to ask, princess, did it make you happy?"

That question didn't have an answer. It wasn't about being happy.

"I guess it makes sense that you might want to take things a step further." Here, Dad smoothed a strand of my wayward chignon. "Do you want to be like your mom?"

"I want you to—"

"Oh, princess," he said, cutting me off. "If you think you have to do this so I'll love you or respect you—"

I shook my head, unable to explain. Maybe because it was something I'd never explained to myself. This feeling, the idea. It was something that up to now, I'd only touched the edges of.

"I want to be like you." The moment I spoke the words, I felt the truth in them. "I want to be like you," I said again, slowly, because Dad looked like he hadn't understood or even heard me.

"Princess, you don't want to be like me."

But I did. I wanted to be just like Dad, Not shot at, or wounded, or—I stole a look at him—haunted. But I wanted his focus, his strength. "I do."

"No, no, you don't." He leaned forward, arms on his thighs, gaze on the patterned carpet. "You really don't."

How did I explain, when the idea, or at least the words behind it, was so new. "My mom has a Purple Heart," I said, feeling out each word carefully. "And you do."

"Jesus Christ, you don't want a Purple Heart, trust me on that."

"I don't want this gap between us."

Dad looked at me then, his eyes wide, honestly surprised. "There's no gap."

"Really? Between civilian and soldier?" I felt the truth of that, too. It was all there, in my mom's journal. You made the cut—or you didn't. You went into Iraq—or you didn't. And it mattered. It was a one-way road. Dad couldn't travel back, so that left it up to me to travel forward.

"You're my daughter. There's no gap there. You understand me, all of it, better than anyone I know"

"But I'm still a civilian."

Dad let his head rest in his hands. For a long time, he didn't say anything and I thought the gap would remain. But at last, he lifted his head.

"Let's suppose there is one," he said. "This gap you're talking about."

"Okay, I'm supposing."

"There's a term about going to war, about battle. I think it originated around the time of the Civil War. It's called seeing the elephant, because either you have, or you haven't."

"Oh," I said, in a near whisper. "So there really is a gap."

At that, Dad actually chuckled. "Smart ass." He rubbed his temples, ran a hand through his hair. Under the fluorescent lights, he looked older, the lines around his eyes deeper, carved, permanent. He stared at me straight on, making absolutely sure I wouldn't miss a word.

"Tonight," he began, "with Landon. As far as I'm concerned, you've seen the elephant. You've seen it and come out on the other side. Maybe you don't look at it that way, but I do. You saved a life, and that's a hell of a lot better than taking one."

I couldn't answer him. I wanted to. But my eyes were so dry they hurt, and my throat felt clogged—with tears I couldn't spill and words I couldn't say.

He slipped the empty cup from my hands. "More chocolate?"

I nodded, not sure I wanted another drink, except they were hot and that took the edge off the void inside me. Except it gave him an excuse to leave for a few minutes. I needed the time alone, to close my eyes, to find my breath. The tears gathering in my throat now threatened to spill out. I needed a few minutes alone, to cry one more time. Something told me Dad did, too.

Before he cleared the door, I found my voice. "You saved a life."

For the barest second, he hesitated. And I knew: he had heard me.

———

AT FOUR IN THE MORNING, Mrs. Scott returned.

Dad stayed close while we walked down the hall and rode the

elevator to intensive care. My heart pounded furiously, like I'd been swimming hard. I had that breathless feeling that comes from underwater laps. Inside the intensive care unit, everything was hushed and sorrowful.

The nurse on duty let me peek through the observation window at Landon. He looked vulnerable and pale, and so much younger, more like the boy I remembered. But his hands were strong, unchanged, and I remembered how his fingers had felt laced with mine. And I told myself he was going to be okay.

Chapter 18

FIFTEEN MINUTES after we walked through the front door, Dad had breakfast ready. French toast, one of my favorites, and a huge glass of orange juice. I hadn't eaten since the night before, what felt like a lifetime away from where I was now.

I moved slowly, creaked really, like I'd aged eighty years in the last twenty-four hours. What didn't ache, hurt, what didn't hurt, I couldn't actually move. I tried to comb out the mess of my hair, but even that was too much. Every time I turned my head, I discovered a new and interesting twist on pain.

"You know, princess," Dad said. "We spent all that time at the hospital, but never had you checked out."

Yeah. I wasn't fooling Dad.

"I hate to say it," he added, "but I think we should make a trip to urgent care."

I fell asleep in the Blazer on the five minute drive to the medical building. In the urgent care section, he morphed into Avenging Dad and made a big enough fuss that I think the receptionist bumped us up on the priority list. And I think Dad was kind of enjoying himself, being large and in charge, telling anyone who'd listen how I saved a life.

In the waiting room, I fell asleep against his shoulder, and again, waiting for the x-ray results, curled up on the examination table. Back at home, Dad somehow got me from the car and onto the couch. The last thing I remembered was the rainbow afghan being tucked around my shoulders. I slept my Sunday away, while Landon spent his in post-op, a new pacemaker guarding his heart.

On Monday, Grandma Adele brought food, a ton of it, chocolate cake—three layers—and, of course, macaroni and cheese. She hugged me a dozen times, maybe more. But I also saw her speak quietly with Dad. When they embraced, something inside me loosened.

Between pain pills and muscle relaxants, I wasn't quite myself, certainly not up for school. But I was enough of myself to want to see Landon.

"Let me call," Dad said. "No sense going if they won't let you see him."

His grin moments later told me everything I needed to know. "He's in the cardiology wing and can have visitors, but I'm driving."

And I was in no condition to argue.

I left Dad in the same waiting area where we'd spent early Sunday morning. He had Wi-Fi, his laptop, and plenty of chemical coffee. I paused at the threshold and glanced back at him. I wanted to say he looked happy, but maybe it was simply that he didn't look unhappy.

Somehow, that was enough.

———

AT THE ENTRANCE to the cardiology wing, an unpretentious brass plaque declared that this was the *Scott* Cardiology Wing.

Oh. Interesting.

The nurse led me to a private room. Outside the door, she gave me a sharp once over, clearly not impressed. "Try not to overexcite him," she said. "He needs to rest."

"Is he awake?"

"He's been in and out. He wants to see you," the nurse conceded as if revealing this particular fact pained her.

She opened the door and bustled over to Landon. She checked monitors and readouts, then touched his shoulder.

"You have a visitor," she said. "A very pretty one."

Landon turned his head, just slightly. Circles beneath his eyes were so dark, they looked like bruises. He was pale, his hair mussed, but he smiled at me, and those hazel eyes had never held so much light.

"Come here?" he said.

I nodded, but my feet wouldn't move.

The nurse brought a chair to Landon's bedside, one identical to those in the waiting area. I inched forward, finally, and sat.

"You need to rest," the nurse said to Landon, her voice stern.

"Because you know," he said in a stage whisper, "it's real restful getting poked and prodded every half hour."

"I heard that, young man."

"I'm a lousy patient," he added.

The nurse laughed and, on the way out, closed the door behind her.

A weird silence settled around us, not awkward, but unsettling, like we'd done this before only this time we both chose a different path.

"How are you?" I asked.

"Fine, fine," he said as if the question bored him.

"Fine being one of those relative terms?"

"Look, you gotta tell me, because I know no one else will. Okay?"

My stomach clenched, but I nodded.

"Give it to me straight," he said. "How's the Corvette?"

I let out the world's most exasperated sigh. "In better shape than you."

"I'm fine, but seriously—"

"My dad's taking care of the car," I said. "What about you?"

"I just needed a replacement part."

He was so cavalier, that, for an instant, I thought I might scream in frustration. Around us, monitors clicked. I caught the scent of hospital, of antiseptic, but underneath that, something warm, something spicy, something definitely Landon.

"Look," he said, in response to my silence, "I'm hooked up to so much equipment, they know when I blink. My ribs hurt a little, but—"

"Ribs?"

"Your dad." His fingers traced a line over his rib cage. "At least, I figure it was your dad. He did the chest compressions, right?"

In a flash, I saw Dad, hands on Landon's chest, heard the echo of crushed egg shells. "Did he actually break something?"

"No, well, maybe a crack or two, but mostly just bruised."

"We took first aid classes together," I said.

"Can I just say I'm glad you did? What's a few bruised ribs? I mean, it beats the alternative."

I squeezed my eyes shut. How could Landon be so ... so ... non-serious about the whole thing?

"Did you breathe for me?" he asked, the question soft, almost like a caress.

I opened my eyes and stared into those amazing hazel ones. "I did."

"I thought so."

"Then, can you?" I groped for words. "Do you remember any of it?"

"It's ... hard to explain, it's all kind of fuzzy." He closed his eyes, those incredible calf eyelashes brushing his cheekbones. "But I'm glad I don't have to remember a lip lock with your dad."

I clamped my hand over my mouth, but what started as a laugh welled into a sob. I sank into my Dolphins hoodie and hid my face.

"MacKenna, don't. I said it to make you laugh."

"It's not funny."

"Maybe not, but I can't look at it any other way," he said. "For the longest time, I remember nothing but being scared."

I peered through my fingers at him.

"When I was first diagnosed," he added. "Then, later on, I went around acting like the world owed me, because of this." He touched his chest above his heart. "I'm glad you never saw that. I was a total asshole."

Landon grimaced, but after a moment, his expression brightened. "Then, the FDA recalled my pacemaker, and my mom recalled me to Black Earth. And instead of getting angrier, it made me think. Here I was, alive, because of luck, a lot of money, and medical technology. The world didn't owe me shit." He paused, looked up at the ceiling, then back at me. "So, here I am," he said. "With you. And that really beats the hell out of the alternative. Besides," he continued, the words slower now. "This time, I wasn't scared at all."

"Landon—" I began, not sure what to say to all that.

He hushed me, then urged me closer with the barest twitch of his fingers. He touched my cheek, loose strands of my hair, my lips.

"That's better," he said.

Nothing in his face told me how he lived like this. Not knowing whether his pacemaker would work—or not. Not knowing whether his heart would beat—or not. I thought of my question to him at prom: What do you want to be when you grow up?

Alive.

"How do you do it?" I asked, so quietly, that part of me hoped he wouldn't hear.

"How do you?" he countered.

"What?"

"Live with a ghost."

"A … ghost. Do you mean my mom?"

"Yeah, that." Landon blew out a soft breath. "You guys make my family look normal."

I thought of Mr. Scott, of Mrs. Scott's sudden and icy control, of the Scott name plate attached to this hospital wing. "What about all this?" I waved my hand, indicating not just Landon's room, but the entire cardiology wing.

"Ah, you noticed the guilt money. We don't talk about it, because that would be unseemly. Doesn't change anything, though."

"Doesn't change what?" I asked.

"I'm still a disappointment," he said. "Never got the chance not to be."

"But your mom—"

"I'm not talking about her."

"But it isn't even your fault."

"It doesn't have to be," he said. "I told you once that it was possible to break someone's heart with your own."

I couldn't speak, couldn't shake my head, couldn't even think, except for a quick burst of gratitude. Maybe life with Dad wasn't ideal, but to put it in Landon terms: it beat the alternative.

"I didn't tell you why I wasn't scared this time," he said.

"I was," I confessed.

"It was you." He looked at me now. "I knew no matter what, you'd keep me safe."

"How?" My cheeks grew warm under his unrelenting gaze. "I didn't know anything."

"What? Soldier girl not have my back? Impossible."

"Landon, I—" I tried to force the words out, but they lodged in my throat. That thick panic returned, even though he was right here. I could see him, touch him, his skin so warm. "I thought I lost you," I managed at last.

"But you didn't."

"But—"

"You didn't. Still, it's nice to know you want me around." He grinned at me, those bruised, hazel eyes that saw through everything never leaving my face.

"I love you," I blurted.

"Oh. So when are you going to tell me something I don't know?"

Another laughed rolled into a sob, this one quieter, more contained. Landon had me scoot closer. I sat on his right, clear of the IV, the electrodes, and their wires. This near to him, the weight of his exhaustion pressed against me.

"I should probably …" I began. I didn't want to leave.

"No. Don't go. Please?" Landon patted the spot next to his hip. "Put your head down. We'll both rest."

I found an extra pillow in the closet and set it with care at the edge of Landon's bed. I pressed a hand against his thigh, my head by his hip. His fingers slowly undid my braids and tangled in the strands of hair. I wondered if the nurses would let us stay like this. Then I remembered the name of the cardiology wing.

Yeah, I thought and closed my eyes. They probably would.

———

FROM THE SECOND I pulled into my usual spot in the overflow lot on Tuesday morning and didn't see a yellow Corvette parked across two spaces, everything felt wrong. I'd wanted to go to school, to swim practice, pretend everything was normal, or at least as normal as it could be. Sure, I ached all over, but without the fringe benefit of shooting pain. I wanted to swim, almost as much as I wanted to see Landon again.

"You sure?" Dad asked when I walked into the kitchen, all my hair tucked under one of his old BDU caps.

"I want to go to school," I said, "and see Landon after practice."

Dad didn't say a word, but on my way out, I grabbed my backpack and found the keys to my Jeep sitting on top.

Now? I couldn't think of what had brought me to school. I stumbled through the halls, and groups of kids actually parted to let me through. Girls huddled by lockers, whispering when I passed.

Did you hear? Don't you know? Oh, my God, he almost died. I heard some kind of heart thing ... my dad saw the report when he went on shift ... did you know that she ...

My phone buzzed as I walked into English. Josh was at his desk, Patti at the front of the room. I could only think of one person who might send me a text in the middle of the day. I sidestepped the entrance and checked my phone.

Sorry.

That was all the first message said. Before I could decipher it, a second one appeared.

Mom panicking.

I blinked at the words a few times. If Landon's mom was panicking, I should too. I felt a dull ache, somewhere deep inside me and my fingers fumbled on the phone's keyboard.

Me: Everything OK?

Landon: Precaution. Going to Mayo. Poss. Infection. But OK.

None of that sounded okay to me.

Me: Can I call you?

Landon: Mom here. Gotta go. <3

That was it. For several seconds, I held the phone in my hand, willing one last message from it. Only the strange quiet in the room made me glance up. Everyone stared, from Patti to Josh to Landon's little circle of cheerleader fan-girls. The hall behind me was empty. The bell must have rung, but I never heard it.

No one spoke. In their eyes, all I could see reflected back at me was worry and pity. I clutched the phone harder.

"MacKenna," Patti began, her voice soft.

I did the only thing that made sense.

I ran.

———

I BURST through the lobby doors, but when I reached the flight of steps that led down to the main parking lot, I froze. The wind—or my blood—roared in my ears. I couldn't get my legs to move, couldn't reach for the keys to my Jeep. But at the same time, turning around and going back inside?

I couldn't do that either.

I jumped when my phone buzzed in my hand. I stared at it, only now realizing I still held it. My heart thudded and my vision blurred. Landon, I thought. But no, the number on the display was Dad's.

Dad?

"I got a call," Dad said when I answered. "What's happening?"

"It's Landon. They're taking him to the Mayo Clinic. Something about an infection. Dad, I don't know. It was just a couple of stupid text messages."

"Where are you?"

"Standing outside of school."

"I don't want you driving."

How did he know my first thought was to jump into the Jeep and zoom down the highway? Unless he had done the same thing once, had zoomed down some other road, a world and time away from here, a road packed with sand and diesel.

"But—" I began.

"I don't want you driving. Not now. Not like this. It's … dangerous."

"Then what do I do?" I remained rooted on the front steps, my hand sore from clutching the phone.

"Charlie Mike," he said.

Charlie Mike. Military talk. Continue the Mission. Class. Swim practice. It seemed so unimportant, so worthless.

"It's what your mother would do," Dad said, his words so quiet, I barely heard him.

I nodded, although Dad couldn't see me. Mom had run, just like I had, and I could see her on the edge of the battalion, the wind beating the black plastic above the slit-trench latrine. Then she turned back around and went to work again, where Master Sergeant Collier handed her a cup of coffee. Charlie Mike. It's what you did, I thought. You did the stupid, hard thing.

"Okay, I'll go back in."

"And I'll talk to Mr. Scott. By the time you get home, I should know more about Landon, and by the time you reach the office, there will be a pass waiting for you."

He was right. There was. Like a zombie, I took the pass, walked it down the hall, into Patti's room, and placed it into her outstretched hand. Her cell phone was in the middle of her desk and right then, I knew. Of course. Nothing got by Patti. She didn't have a cup of coffee for me. But when I glanced up into her face, I saw she had something just as good.

Understanding.

Chapter 19

I REMAINED a zombie for two days, even though Dad talked to Mr. Scott, and Mrs. Scott, and quite possibly to people who weren't supposed to talk to him at the Mayo Clinic. Landon's prognosis was good, the infection already responding to antibiotics.

But my phone remained stubbornly silent. No texts. No calls. In the evening, Dad stayed with me in the den. I pecked out my homework and tried to think distracting thoughts, tried to put everything I knew and felt about Landon into some kind of box, the way my mom did with me. I filled in the blanks on worksheets without really thinking, but I kept at it. When I faltered, I thought: Charlie Mike.

Thursday night, the desktop went crazy. It pinged and pinged. I'd been so focused on my essay for English, I yelped and Dad came running.

"What's wrong with it?"

Dad frowned. His lower lip jutted out and I was pretty sure he was about to punch the monitor when a smile creased his face.

"I think," he said, pressing a few keys. "Someone wants to talk to you on Skype."

Landon, looking almost as green as his hospital gown, came into view. I stood there like an idiot, mouth hanging open, so the first words he said weren't to me, but Dad.

"Hey, sir."

"Hey, it's good to see you. Feeling better?" Dad asked.

Landon waved away the question as if the whole rush to the Mayo Clinic thing bored him. "Can MacKenna talk?"

Dad gestured toward me.

"No, really. *Can* she talk?" Landon shook his head. "Cuz it doesn't look like she can."

Dad laughed, took me by the shoulders and planted me in the desk chair. "I'll just." He picked up his laptop and pointed to the other part of the house. "Be somewhere else."

"So," Landon said. "Alone at last."

I snorted something between a laugh and a cry.

"I need your help," he said.

"Do you want me to drive down and rescue you?"

He closed his eyes. "If only that would work." He opened them, and despite our lousy monitor and the green of his gown, I swore they looked blue. "I need your help to stay in Black Earth."

"You're leaving?"

"Not if I can help it. My dad wants to hire a private tutor to finish out the school year," Landon said, with that edge that made him sound just like his dad. "And boarding school in the fall." He shook his head. "I'm not going. And finally." Here, he looked toward the ceiling and I got a screen-full of his vulnerable neck. It was all I could do not to kiss the monitor.

"My mom agrees."

"But?"

"I got to pass junior year."

I didn't need much more than that to take on this mission as my own. Landon hadn't missed that much school and might even make it back to class for the last week or two. On Friday, I'd made a circuit of his class schedule, although the barely contained eye rolls told me I wasn't the first girl to ask for Landon's missing work. Only Patti took the situation as seriously as I did, and not only loaded me down with all his regular assignments, but piled on the extra-credit projects as well.

She gave a little shrug at this. "What else is he going to do?"

Other than Skype with me? I shrugged back.

And when she piled the study guides and teacher notes into my outstretched hands, it was just as good as a cup of coffee.

———

HOW THE CONVERSATION STARTED, I never quite knew. Maybe it was the way I raced through the house on Saturday afternoon, braids still damp from swim practice. I didn't even stop at the fridge, but went straight for the computer and Landon on Skype.

I didn't even know how long Landon had been looking at me with that odd expression on his face. For the past few days, I measured time not by the clock, but by the nurses' rounds.

"What?" I said after his afternoon nurse left for the last time.

"You guys are still swimming, right?"

I swallowed hard and nodded. We were swimming, but mostly conditioning laps—water bottles balanced on our stomachs, length after length of ballet legs—all in the strange quiet of water splashing against the pool sides. Josh didn't have the heart to cue up one of Landon's playlists. We didn't have the heart to listen. We swam lengths underwater and at the end of each, I'd grip the pool edge and inhale a long, shuddering breath—the kind you take after a hard cry.

"Okay," Landon said, "but what about the show?"

This time, I only swallowed hard. "Everyone misses you," I said. I couldn't get the actual words from my mouth. At last, I managed, "No one wants to do the show without you."

"That's crazy. What are you going to do instead?"

"Patti was talking about doing an exhibition with some of our strongest numbers, like the senior class routine, and maybe my duet with Constance."

"But no show?"

I shrugged. I couldn't explain how awful it was to swim without him there. It wasn't just me. I saw it every time a girl glanced toward the empty platform stage. Guilt. Misery. Both looked the same when they washed across someone's face.

"Whatever happened to the show must go on?"

I shook my head.

"You guys really aren't doing the show? Come on, that's bull-shit. You've worked too hard not to."

"It just doesn't seem—"

He held up a hand. "Stop. Right there. I'm fixing this now." His gaze was focused on something other than the webcam, his long calf lashes brushing his cheekbones. "I'm emailing Patti, Kayla, Constance, and Brad Stanley."

"Brad?"

"He'll host at the last minute. He's just the kind of upstanding guy who will."

"You have his email?" Oh, what was I saying? No doubt Landon had everyone's email.

Landon waved this away. "And I'm attaching my script. That's all he needs."

A moment later, my email pinged. I sent a questioning look into the webcam on my end.

"Oh, and maybe I bcc'd you as well. In case there's some amusing drama."

"So. We're swimming," I said.

"Are we?" Something in his tone had changed. I leaned forward, closer to the monitor as if that would dissolve the miles between us.

"Can you tell me something?" he asked, his question quiet. "Would you swim without me?"

It hit me that this suddenly wasn't about swimming. It was about something bigger than that, maybe the biggest thing of all.

"I would," I said, my words just as quiet. "If it came to that."

His gaze never left my face. What was it about those hazel eyes? I couldn't deny him anything, especially the truth.

"But it would hurt," I added. "It would hurt a lot."

"But you'd do it, right?" he asked.

I nodded, once.

His smile stole my breath with a full on dimple that I longed to touch. "That's all I needed to hear."

———

BLACK EARTH, Minnesota has two cemeteries, so my chances of picking the right one were fifty-fifty. A foggy memory of rolling hills and huge elms with branches like ancient, gnarled arms helped. Once upon a time, I'd walked a winding path through gravestones, my hand in Grandma Adele's.

I'd been maybe four, old enough to remember, but too young for school. I never told anyone about this trip, not Landon or Nissa. Even back then, I knew enough not to tell Dad. But the hills, the grass just high enough to tickle my ankles, gray head-stones, and flowers that looked too pretty to be sad stayed with me. I don't remember seeing my mom's grave that day, but the words Grandma Adele spoke seared into my mind.

It was a Humvee accident.

And since I was my father's daughter, she didn't need to explain what a Humvee was.

I told Landon all this, later that Saturday night.

"It's almost like a dream," I said after the swing-shift nurse had left. "I mean, I'm pretty sure it happened and I'm pretty sure my mom is here in Black Earth. Is it crazy that I never asked?"

"You probably did." He shifted in the hospital bed, so for a moment, he went off kilter and all I saw were the monitors behind him. "That's why you remember your grandma taking you."

"Do you think I can find her?"

"Without asking anyone?"

I nodded. Asking Grandma Adele, Dad—anyone really, since Patti might know—shot not just fear, but failure through me. It would only bring them more hurt. I needed to do this on my own.

Landon grinned at me. "I know you can."

———

SUNDAY MORNING, I made Dad a full pot of coffee. Next to his cup on the kitchen table, I placed Mom's journal. My eyes were drawn back to the pages. It was, quite possibly, the last time I'd ever see it. Part of me yearned to hold it tight, keep it a secret. But the time for secrets was over. They ambushed you, their attacks large and small, but in the end, they did far more damage than the truth ever could.

Besides, I didn't need the poems to know how much my mom had loved me. But Dad? Maybe her words would help him put things back together.

In the Jeep, I pulled out a map of Black Earth and did a quick terrain analysis. Hills and elms. Simple. I pulled from the driveway and turned toward the older part of town and the bluffs by the river.

At the cemetery, the sun was just peeking over the steepest hill, effectively blinding me. I walked on instinct, tried to think back to those landmarks my four-year-old mind might have registered. And I sent up a prayer to my mom:

Let me find you.

I did, at last, near the crest of another hill, one I only climbed because the old elms looked like they were taking the rest I so desperately needed after an hour of searching. Grandpa Frank's grave caught my eye first. I stumbled past and sank to the earth beneath an elm. Both graves were well tended, so much so, I wondered if Grandma Adele visited on a regular basis. I placed the bouquet I'd bought in a vase on one side of the grave, and stuck a small American flag into the ground on the other. Then I sat and studied the inscription:

ELIZABETH M GREY
1st LT US ARMY
PERSIAN GULF
JUL 19 1965
MAR 26 1991
MOTHER WIFE DAUGHTER
SOLDIER

I stared at the grave, willing something from it, anything at all.

"Can you miss someone you never knew?"

Could you? Did you fill that void with something else or was it permanently empty, a hole for ghosts.

"Because I miss you."

I remembered back in preschool, how moms scanned the room when they first walked in. I watched them, watched their faces light up when they spotted their child. How they held out their arms, and how the little boy or girl running to them would hold out theirs.

Sometimes I'd try that. I'd stand in the middle of the living room, hold out my arms, and wait. Grandma Adele or Dad would walk by, pick me up, hug me. But when they set me down, I'd go back to holding my arms out until my muscles trembled. Then, I'd fold them tight against my chest.

"And then," I said out loud. "It was like I didn't know what to do with them."

I sat, hugging my legs, resting my chin on my knees. For how long, I couldn't say. Maybe fifteen minutes. Maybe an hour. I sat until the sun warmed the back of my neck and the hard ground made my hips ache. I sat until tears blurred my vision and I could no longer see the words on the headstone.

———

DAD WAS SITTING on the porch steps when I got home. He leaned back on the cement, legs crossed. The scent of freshly cut grass hung in the air and our lawn had a checkerboard pattern. But Dad looked cool, like he'd been lounging all morning, not a single grass stain on his shirt or jeans. He scooted when I reached the steps and I sank down next to him, tired from my trek through the cemetery and still a little shell-shocked.

"I was thinking about joining you." He nodded toward the Blazer. "It's been a while since I've been there. I don't know if that's good or bad."

Neither did I.

"That's not how I remember your mom. We were only together a short time, but I still have days when I forget she isn't alive." He stared straight ahead. "That sounds crazy, I know. But the worst part? Even now, I start to tell her about you, then remember that I can't."

"Dad—"

He hushed me, then pulled his wallet from his back pocket. "When you were little, you used to play with this. I guess in the same way other little girls take their mothers' purses." Dad gave a soft laugh. "You'd try to stick it in your pocket, but of course it wouldn't fit."

He shook his head at the memory, laughter relaxing his features. "Then you'd take everything out, inspect it, then put it all back in, or try to."

Dad opened the wallet. The plastic photo insert unfurled. There I was, a photo for every year—even the heinous middle school ones —each tucked carefully in its own panel. At the very back was another picture.

My breath caught. Maybe, at one time, I'd rifled through Dad's wallet, but I had no memory of this. He eased the photo from the holder and held it up by one corner.

"I don't know why I keep this one in here," he said. It was my mom, in uniform, an official portrait without a trace of a smile on her very young face. "Your mom never really liked it, but I did." He considered the photo. "Maybe because the first time I saw her, she was in uniform."

He sighed, the sound heavy, full of regret and longing and an ache that would never go away. "There's a part of the story you don't know."

I clenched my fists and held my breath. I nodded to let him know I was listening, but otherwise, didn't dare move.

"Right before we went forward, into Iraq, I did the unforgivable."

I'd puzzled over what had sent my mom running. What, exactly, did Dad do? What had he done when he saw the ROTC brochure? Did he set the desert on fire?

"I told her she couldn't be a soldier," he said. "Worse, I wanted *her* to ask the battalion commander to assign her to Log Base Echo, in Saudi Arabia."

I thought about the list and my mom's reaction when she thought her name wasn't on it. Even knowing the outcome, I wasn't sure I could deny her that. Being a soldier was part of who she was. She was the original warrior princess.

"For years, I thought if I hadn't said a word, hadn't stormed off like a sixteen-year-old, your mom might still be alive today. She wouldn't have been tempted to come see me, wouldn't have been on that particular road on that particular day."

He slipped the photo back into its home, then pulled something else from one of the leather slots. The aluminum was dull; it didn't catch the sunlight. Dad handed it to me and I felt the raised lettering of my mom's name, her service number, her blood type, all beneath my fingertips.

Her dog tag.

"I finally had to stop wearing the wedding band. People would ask me about my wife." Dad rubbed his left ring finger. "After a while the pity got old. So I took the ring off. And well, you've seen the other photos." He gave me a sidelong glance.

"Yeah." I knew he meant the drawer, with the silver-framed photographs. "I showed Landon a few weeks back."

He took the dog tag and held it in his palm. "I liked having something of hers close, always with me."

As a reminder, or to make sure he never forgave himself? For something so small and light, that dog tag carried tremendous weight. By the time I pulled the words together to ask him, Dad had returned the dog tag and removed one last item, a folded piece of paper.

The paper was creased, well-worn, like it had been folded and unfolded many times, over many years. Dad opened it slowly, with care, to reveal a crayon drawing. Stick people holding hands, one incredibly tall, the other tiny, with a triangle for a dress. Below the drawing was a short note, in Grandma Adele's precise handwriting.

According to MacKenna, this is the two of you. In this picture, you are home and taking her to the park.

"Adele sent this to me when I was in Somalia." Dad shut his eyes and his lips compressed into a hard line. "This is difficult to explain, princess, but there was a time when I thought it might be better if I simply didn't come home from there."

I shifted to stare at him. I'm sure shock registered on my face, because I nearly choked on it. I wanted to ask: *not come home*, or *come home in a flag-draped coffin*? But I didn't dare.

"I thought with the insurance money, you'd be set for life. Without your mom, I thought I was a lousy father. I thought, maybe, this was penance for her death."

"But—"

He put his arm around me and held me tight. "Then, Adele sent me your drawing. To this day, I wonder: did she know? Of course, this is your grandmother we're talking about." Here, Dad managed a curt laugh.

Yeah, Grandma Adele had great timing.

"I realized that back in the world, there was a little girl who loved me," Dad said. "I had one of those flashes, like when I first saw your mom and knew, that someday, I was going to marry her." He gave my shoulder a squeeze. "When I saw your drawing, I knew: I was put on this earth to be your dad."

He folded the paper slowly and tucked it back in his wallet. "I put it in my pocket right before we went out, right before everything went to shit. It brought me home. And every time I switch wallets, it goes in first. And, yeah, I've fucked up the dad part more times than I'm sure we both want to count." He planted a gentle kiss against my hair. "But you're the reason I have a life. You're the reason it's worth living."

My throat closed off. I tried to suck in a breath, but got nothing. My body shook with the effort. I held Dad tight and felt the hot sting of tears against my cheeks.

"Hey," he said. "It's okay, it's okay."

"I love you," I said.

"Oh, princess, I love you."

We didn't speak. I was without words, but not empty, not any longer. That void, the one where ghosts resided, now held a few concrete items: a photograph, a dog tag, a crayon drawing of a little girl and her daddy, and the very real life of a woman I never knew.

The Black Earth High School
Dolphins present

CINEMA SPLASH!

1. Gonna Fly Now (theme from Rocky) ~ all team members
2. Stars and ~~Strips~~ Stripes Forever ~ Sophomores
3. Mulan's Decision (from Mulan) ~ Constance Radley and MacKenna Meyers
4. Kiss The Girl (from The Little Mermaid) ~ Kayla Hanson's group
5. My Favorite Things (from The Sound of Music) ~ Rachel Keller's group
6. Greased Lightnin' (from Grease) ~ Juniors
7. I Could Have Danced All Night (from My Fair Lady) ~ Kylie Hanson's group
8. Footloose ~ Stacey Bell's group
9. Lady Marmalade (from Moulin Rouge) ~ Kayla Hanson solo
10. Surrey with the Fringe on Top (from Oklahoma) ~ Freshmen
11. Bond Girls (James Bond theme) ~ Nissa Jenkins, Sierra Linden, Jodi Swift

12. Fame ~ Kayla and Kylie Hanson
13. Tokyo Drift (from The Fast and the Furious: Tokyo Drift)
    ~ Constance Radley's group
14. Singing in the Rain ~ Seniors
15. Pirates of the Caribbean ~ all team members

SPONSORED BY SCOTT INDUSTRIES

Epilogue

SATURDAY EVENING, the entire Black Earth synchronized swim team crowded into the locker room. A May breeze filtered in through the windows. We could hear people arriving, and with each slam of a car door, my heart jumped.

Costumes hung strategically from open lockers. Girls stood at the mirrors and slathered on waterproof makeup. The smell of CoverGirl mixed with chlorine. Our hair, saturated and slicked back with Knox gelatin, gleamed under the fluorescent lights. We were ready. More or less.

In the end, Brad Stanley agreed to host the show. He worked all week to smooth out his delivery while we swam dress rehearsal after dress rehearsal. If he wasn't funny, at least he was earnest and truly wanted to help. That, I decided, counted for a lot.

Through the miracle of technology and Josh's mad techno skills, even Landon would see the show, via webcam. It wasn't the perfect solution, but considering the alternative, it was enough.

After the opening number, we poured into the locker room, dripping water across the floor. The sophomores struggled into fresh costumes while poolside, Brad delivered the opening mono-logue, his words lost in the clatter of a cart on the tile floor. Patti rolled in with a dozen bouquets, followed by Kayla and Kylie's mom, who carried an armload of flowers. Squeals echoed off the walls, combined with Patti's, "Girls, hush. The audience can hear you."

Constance squirmed into her costume for the duet. There wasn't much to it, mostly strategically placed shiny fabric and a whole lot of fringe.

On the cart behind us, the flower arrangements vanished, one by one. An elegant arrangement of calla lilies for Kayla. Hand-picked daisies for Kylie. A very strange bouquet of black and white roses. For Constance.

"Not a single word," she said to me.

"Sam?" I ventured.

"Not another word." Constance scowled. "Or you end up at the bottom of the pool."

"So, it's what?" I asked, unable to resist. "Yin and yang? Dark-ness and light? No, wait, I got it." I held out my hands, palms up, indicating the flowers. "An artistic representation of his soul and yours—and I'm not saying which is which."

"Shut the hell up," Constance said, but she was bright pink with pleasure.

I laughed.

"I'm not the only one with flowers," she said. "You'd better check that cart."

In the center, two dozen pink roses sat, unclaimed. And they *were* for me. I glanced at the card, not even reading the words, just recognizing the scrawl. Dad. Who else would go totally overboard?

"Oh, how sweet." Sierra crept into view as if she'd been waiting to ambush me. "Those wouldn't be from Landon, would they?" She knew they weren't, so clearly she came armed with a claymore of snark.

"Shut up."

Constance blinked, startled that the words hadn't come from her mouth. She looked toward me, then glanced at the cart where Nissa stood, hands on hips, a glare aimed at Sierra, one so icy we'd end up skating, not swimming.

"No one wants to hear it, okay? So just shut the hell up and swim." Nissa raised her chin like this was some kind of signal. A second later, Sierra slunk away.

I gaped, completely wowed by the transformation. Nissa had gone A-list, and she'd done it with style.

"Your dad always was completely adorable." Nissa touched a rose petal. Then she crouched next to the cart and pulled a single red rose in its own vase from the bottom tier.

"I wanted to tell you," she said, turning the vase in her hands. "That I'm really glad he was with you that night." She studied the rose for a moment, then handed me the vase. "You always knew what to do." She walked to her bank of lockers, ignoring Jodi and Sierra who both looked contrite. Well, *almost* contrite.

I wanted to call after her, but too much had happened. Secrets, like war, had their own casualties. In our case, that was eleven years of friendship. Sometimes facing the truth meant saying good-bye. So I did. Silently. I hoped Nissa knew how much she'd meant to me.

I opened the card that came with the rose and found a computer-printed note.

Soldier Girl,
Tonight, I'll be holding my breath when you do.
Love, Landon

I set the vase in the bottom of my locker, supporting the base with my Chuck Taylor All Stars (the camouflage ones). As I wrestled the pink roses into an out of the way corner, I realized I hadn't read the card from Dad.

There wasn't one. On the outside of the envelope, he'd written:

To: MacKenna, Warrior Princess
Love, Dad

But the envelope felt heavy, the item inside thicker than paper. I opened the flap and shook. There, into my hand, fell my mom's dog tag. I held it in my palm, flipped it over, traced the raised lettering, my breath, all my thoughts, gone.

"We need to head out," Constance said.

The duet came early in the show. The number was so rigorous, we needed to be fresh for it, focused. But I just stood there, my eyes locked on the item in my hand. Constance took the dog tag from me. She inspected it, turning it over, once, twice.

"It was my mom's," I said.

"You want to wear it?"

I never knew what Dad did with the journal. I thought of what he'd told me:

I liked having something of hers close, always with me.

Maybe the journal simply didn't weigh as much as her dog tag. I wondered if he'd given me the last piece of the puzzle or maybe it was simply the first of a larger one. In a few hours, it would be Mother's Day, and I knew this: I wanted to wear my mom's dog tag while I swam. I felt certain she'd like that.

"How?" I asked Constance.

"It's why God made fringe."

She tied the tag to a strand of fringe, then I tucked it up and under my costume. In stealth mode, we crept through the shower area, to the pool door. We were next, after the sophomore number, which was about to begin, the girls on deck, waiting for Brad's introduction. Constance cracked the door a sliver to catch the tail end of his narration.

"I'm afraid there's a typo in tonight's program," he was saying.

In the fancy ones printed up by Scott Industries? Go figure.

"It's not *Stars and Strips Forever*, but *Stars and Stripes Forever*. There will be no stripping during any part of tonight's performance. Believe me, no one is more disappointed than I am."

I felt my eyes go wide. Had Brad really said *that*? But the crowd laughed, the jocks booing, jeering, and pounding their sneakered feet against the damp floor.

Constance groaned under the cover of music. "Oh, God," she said. "It's like he's channeling Landon."

Three minutes and thirty seconds later, the sophomore girls streamed through the locker room door, dripping, ecstatic, muted squeals bouncing off the tile walls. Without a word, Constance slipped out and I followed. We waited in the dark, frozen and silent, for Brad's introduction.

I caught enough words to know I'd never heard this version of the narration before: *Mulan. Father. Decision.* Landon had changed it, but when was a mystery. All I knew was this: He'd gotten it right.

With the last words, I held my breath and dived into the water. I swam on instinct, without thinking. With every note, I was where Constance needed me to be. When she pushed me up and out of the water for the lift, we got so much height, I thought I might arrow through the ceiling.

In the end, we burst through the surface with a final flourish. We kicked furiously, egg-beater style, but above the water, we were absolutely still. We could've stayed like that for an hour, but in the end, I think it was less than a minute.

Josh made the spotlight dance on the water, bits of light like stars. The crowd roared. It took me a moment to realize they were standing, all of them. I caught sight of Dad, Grandma Adele. Sam Avery punched a fist in the air.

Then, at the pool's edge, I saw Landon. I blinked water from my eyes, certain he was a mirage, a case of oxygen deprivation mixed with wishful thinking. But he was right there, a solid oasis surrounded by all this water. He knelt to scoop up a handful of the pool. He tossed it high, and the drops rained over our heads. Handful after handful struck us. Drops clung to my lashes, kissed my cheeks. For the first time in my life, I felt weightless.

For the first time in my life, I felt like I could breathe.

Also by Charity Tahmaseb

YOUNG ADULT FICTION (WITH DARCY VANCE)

The Geek Girl's Guide to Cheerleading

Dating on the Dork Side

YOUNG ADULT FICTION

The Fine Art of Keeping Quiet

The Fine Art of Holding Your Breath

Now and Later: Eight Young Adult Short Stories

FANTASY

Coffee and Ghosts, Season 1: Must Love Ghosts

Coffee and Ghosts, Season 2: The Ghost That Got Away

Coffee and Ghosts, Season 3: Nothing but the Ghosts

Straying from the Path, Stories from the Sour Magic Series of Fairy Tales

About the Author

Charity Tahmaseb has slung corn on the cob for Green Giant and jumped out of airplanes (but not at the same time). She spent twelve years as a Girl Scout and six in the Army; that she wore a green uniform for both may not be a coincidence. These days, she writes fiction (long and short) and works as a technical writer for a software company in St. Paul.

Her novel, The *Geek Girl's Guide to Cheerleading* (written with co-author Darcy Vance), was a YALSA 2012 Popular Paperback pick in the Get Your Geek On category.

Her short speculative fiction has appeared in *Deep Magic, Flash Fiction Online, Escape Pod,* and *Cicada.*